PORTSMOUTH

Spies, U-boats, and Romance on the Outer Banks

Edward P. Norvell

Published by Edward P. Norvell

The paper in this book meets the guidelines for permanence and durability of the Committee on Production Guidelines for Book Longevity of the Council on Library Resources.

Book Design by Angela Harwood

Cover photography by Edward P. Norvell

Printed in North Carolina

Library of Congress Cataloging in Publication Data

Norvell, Edward P.
  Portsmouth : spies, U-boats, and romance on the Outer Banks : a novel / Edward P. Norvell.
    p. cm.
  ISBN-13: 978-0-89587-359-0 (pbk. : alk. paper)
  ISBN-10: 0-89587-359-1 (pbk. : alk. paper) 1. World War, 1939-1945--North Carolina--Outer Banks--Fiction. 2. Outer Banks (N.C.)--Fiction. [1. Hatteras Island (N.C.)--Fiction. 2. Spies--Fiction. 3. Islands--Fiction. 4. North Carolina--Fiction.] I. Title.
  PS3614.O78275P67 2008
  813'.6--dc22
                           2008014609

To Susan, Mary Linn, and Philip. And to the people of Ocracoke—our beloved second home

Acknowledgments

Portsmouth is a fictional story told in a real-life setting during World War II on the North Carolina Outer Banks, mostly taking place on Ocracoke and Portsmouth islands. Because of the realistic setting, it took a lot of research. My sources are listed under "Sources." But I would also like to acknowledge many people who helped me put this book together.

First of all, I want to acknowledge the support of my wife Susan, my son Philip, and my daughter Mary Linn, who supported and inspired this story. I would also like to acknowledge the support of my mother Judy Norvell and her angel Jean Jones, who put up with my many months spent away from home at Ocracoke. In that same vein, I want to thank Rusty Painter, Reid Wilson, Margaret Newbold, Robin Hammond, and Cheryl Johnson, who I work with and who supported my spending my summers at Ocracoke for the past few years.

I would also like to thank my many friends on Ocracoke and the Outer Banks who shared their stories with me and helped engender a true love and respect for these hardy Bankers: Captain Rudy Austin, who first took me on his boat to Portsmouth Island and who survived the hurricane of 1944 on Ocracoke; Philip Howard; Alton Ballance; all the wonderful volunteers at the Ocracoke

Preservation Society Museum; Al, Linda, and Jenny Scarborough; Patti and Hardy Plyler; Ryan, Kathleen, and Ronnie O'Neal; Leonard Meeker; Susan Dodd; Martin Garrish; Martha Garrish; B.J. Oelschlegel; Donald and Merle Davis; Kenny Ballance; Lonnie and Debbie Burrus; Ann Ehringhaus; Fiddler Dave Tweedie, his wife Amy, and the Molasses Creek Band; Pat Garber; Tommy and Julia Hutcherson; Janey and Dick Jacoby; Earl O'Neal; Michael and Paula Schramel; Susie O'Neal; Tony Sylvester; and many others too many to list.

I want to thank the Graveyard of the Atlantic Museum and its staff, board, and supporters who have preserved so much of the history of the shipwrecks off the Atlantic coast of North Carolina, including the original Enigma machine from the *U-85*.

A special thank you goes to the tireless volunteers of the Ocracoke Volunteer Fire Department, who saved the island from being destroyed during a wildfire fed by strong winds on June 8, 2002. I want to thank the employees, rangers, and volunteers at the Cape Hatteras National Seashore Park, who keep the beach at Ocracoke so pristine, and the employees and volunteers at the Cape Lookout National Seashore, who preserve and protect what is left of Portsmouth village. And finally, I am grateful to the Coast Guard sailors, who so beautifully maintain the British Cemetery in Ocracoke that holds the remains of the men who washed ashore from the HMS *Bedfordshire* in 1942.

Chapter 1

Marcia rode her horse on the beach early in the morning Thursday, May 14, 1942. She loved to ride on the beach in the morning before breakfast, to find shells and feel the cool morning air. It was beginning to get warmer as the spring deepened into May. The wind was out of the northeast. Today she searched the beach for debris, not pretty shells. She had heard explosions at sea to the north just before midnight on Monday. With the war and the almost daily loss of shipping to German submarines, she never knew what she would find on the beach. Sometimes diesel fuel or debris would be floating in the distance. Sometimes the beach was littered with black ooze or worse: bodies, blackened, bloated, some with limbs lost, some partially clothed, some naked, always men, mostly young men. Usually the coastal patrol would find them before she did, but sometimes she found them first and called the boys at the Coast Guard Station at Portsmouth.

Marcia was a young widow. Her husband, George Styron, died when his boat went down in high seas while trying to rescue survivors from the tanker *Alan Jackson*, which was sunk off Hatteras in January by a U-boat. Twenty-two sailors from the ship and three Coast Guardsmen died, including her husband, when their boat sank trying to rescue the survivors in the cold, stormy water. His body was never found.

This was their island, their home. Marcia was from Elizabeth City, but she had fallen in love with this place and decided to stay after George died. She had little to return to in Elizabeth City. Her parents and two younger sisters had moved to Hampton Roads, Virginia, where her father had found work in the shipyards. She could have moved there, too, but she received a survivor's benefit check from the government and didn't want to leave. She was doing quite well, thank you, in her quiet place at the end of the world.

Portsmouth Island was the last inhabited island on the North Carolina Outer Banks after Ocracoke. The Outer Banks were a desolate, remote strip of sandy islands between the Atlantic Ocean and Pamlico Sound, and Portsmouth was the most remote of them all. Marcia liked it that way. She had her friends, her routines, and her privacy. Plus she had the gorgeous beach and her horse to share it with. Life was good—as good as it could be without her beloved George Styron.

Thursday, May 14, 1942, was different; she could feel it. She thought the Germans must have torpedoed another ship. German submarines had preyed upon merchant shipping on the Atlantic coast between January and July 1942 virtually unopposed. The unprotected ships were sitting ducks, sunk indiscriminately by German submarines that had the run of the Atlantic. It was even rumored that the submarines would anchor off the coast and the German sailors would ride rubber rafts onto shore to sunbathe and play games on the beaches of North Carolina's completely unprotected coast. It was also rumored that German spies were able to sneak onto land by way of the beach to do reconnaissance and report back to their ships.

As she crested the dune that paralleled the beach, Marcia saw the sand littered with debris and bodies. She could see a debris field in the water not far from shore in the distance. Usually when she came upon a scene like this, she rode to the Coast Guard Station and let the rescue teams take care of it. But this time was different. She saw a dark form struggle in the waves on the beach. She couldn't wait to get help; the man could barely stand—he might drown without her help. She rode her bay horse furiously across the wide white sand and stopped at the water's edge. The young man, who stood about five feet ten inches tall, was slim, athletic, and well built; his face was swollen, sooty, and crusted with the salt water.

He wore the blue ribbed sweater with cloth patches at the shoulders and navy-blue woolen pants of a British sailor. Marcia was familiar with the uniform; she had seen other British sailors at the naval base in Ocracoke.

The wet sweater clung to the man's torso, and his pants were loose and heavy. He would have lost the pants in the battering waves had she not rushed to help him stand. He looked exhausted. She pulled his arm around her shoulder and helped him out of the water and onto the beach. His lips and tongue swollen from the salt water, he was unable to speak. But when he opened his eyes to look at her, they were a beautiful, almost liquid blue. She thought he smiled at her, but he did not seem to be aware of what was going on around him. She quickly checked to see if he had any apparent wounds or broken bones. Finding none, she pulled him up, put his arm around her neck, and hoisted him up on her horse to take him back to the house. She quickly surveyed the other bodies on the beach. There were no other survivors; the Coast Guard could attend to the bodies later. She needed to get her sailor out of the sun and back to her house, cleaned up and under a warm blanket immediately.

When she got to the house, she pulled the sailor off the horse, put her arm around his waist, and walked him to a wide bench on the back porch. She removed his clothes and scrubbed the salt and soot off him as best she could. She gave him some water, then wrapped him in a blanket and walked him into the house, where she put him to bed. He looked up at her with a smile and tried to speak, but she put her finger over her mouth and said, "Shhh. You rest; don't try to speak." He closed his eyes and sank into a deep sleep, exhausted from his ordeal. It had been a long time—too long—since she had seen a man naked, especially a man as well formed as this one. Her husband, George, had been handsome and well built, too, but she did not marry him for his looks; she married him to get away from her family and because he had a good job with the Coast Guard. He was from an old Outer Banks family, the Styrons from Ocracoke and Portsmouth.

Marcia was twenty years old, born January 30, 1922. Tall and slim with long brown hair that she let blow in the ocean breeze, she had flawless skin and gray-green eyes that sparkled when she smiled. She loved the outdoors and was a natural beauty. She did not wear makeup and looked good in whatever she wore, blue jeans and a blouse or a pretty dress.

She couldn't help admiring the beauty of the man sleeping in her home. He could have been a model in a military magazine—square jaw, wide shoulders, narrow waist and hips. The muscles of his abdomen, chest, and arms were strong and well defined. His Adam's apple was prominent, and his close-cropped hair was blond; the tuft of hair in the middle of his chest was very light, as was the hair on his arms and legs. He looked to be in his early twenties and to weigh about 175 pounds. When she had undressed him and sponged his body clean, her eyes had lingered over his uncut sex lying on its nest of curly blond hair. She had never seen one in its natural state and thought it must be a European thing. As a nurse and wife, she had seen her share of naked men and boys. The sailor's skin was pale white except for his face and hands, which were tanned. He also had some pretty bad bruises around his rib cage. But Marcia was in no rush to surrender her charge to the Pennsylvania boys at the Coast Guard Station. As long as he had no serious wounds or broken bones, he could stay with her until he got his strength back. She could take care of him as well as anyone. She wanted him all to herself.

With her charge sleeping, Marcia decided to return to the beach. Some of the bodies were badly burned and mutilated, with limbs lost. Clearly, they had died in an explosion that ripped the ship open. However, two bodies were not burned; one was naked, the other clothed. Their lips and extremities had turned blue; they must have been blown free of the boat and died in the cold water. They both lay on their backs in the sand, their dead eyes staring blankly up at her. The one who was clothed was smaller than the one who was naked. The naked body reminded her of her husband, the same size and body type. She wondered if her husband's body had washed up on some deserted shore. She wanted to cover his nakedness, but there was nothing to cover him with, save the sand. She was glad that it was too cool for the flies. The men would be covered soon enough by Nick and Joe, who would gather up the bodies and bury them in the village. What a waste, she thought, looking at them; it made her sad. The man she had saved could have easily been one of them. Her gaze roamed the beach; so many dead, so much debris from the ship, even a small overturned lifeboat.

She quickly rode her horse to the Coast Guard Station, a structure covered in silvered cedar shakes a mile to the northeast beyond the village, and alerted Nick Galantis and Joe Guidos, two guys from the South Philadelphia National Guard who were assigned to this desolate outpost. They were cutups and liked to joke around with Marcia, flirting, but she was not interested. There weren't many young people on the island; the average age of most of Portsmouth's residents was sixty. With all the young men gone, it was Marcia, Joe, Nick, and a few island girls. Joe and Nick followed Marcia to the beach, where the bodies lay scattered on the sand and in the surf, and thanked her for alerting them. They told her they didn't know what ship had been sunk, but judging by the clothes on the men, it looked like British navy. The British had loaned several ships to the Americans to help with the submarine war. Joe and Nick had heard the explosions the night before and seen the sky lit with fire. They had patrolled the beach earlier and had seen nothing; it takes time for the debris from a wreck to wash ashore.

"There is one more," Marcia said, knowing that eventually they would find out about her sailor. "I found him alive in the waves. I had to get him dry and warm as quickly as possible. He's at my house sleeping. I checked him out, and he doesn't have any broken bones or serious wounds. He was able to walk out of the water with my help. I will let you know when he is better and can report to you guys."

"Sure, Marcia, he's in good hands with you." They knew she had training as a nurse. For the time being, they had their hands full dealing with the dead. They would need to bring the bodies in for processing, call Aycock Brown from the naval station at Ocracoke for possible identification, and then find a place to bury them in a local family cemetery.

Marcia's house was located about a mile southwest of Portsmouth village, several hundred yards from the beach in a grassy area shaded by large cedar trees that had been sculpted by the wind. On one side of the house, a tidal creek flowed toward the sound. The one-story home was square, sheathed with white clapboard and covered with a green tin hip roof. It had two interior chimneys, a porch that ran the length of the front, and a smaller porch on the back. It was built six steps off the ground, supported by brick piers to keep it from flooding during the storm surge of a hurricane or nor'easter. The front and back storm doors were massive. A scuttle hatch was cut into the floor to allow water to rise in the house during a big storm, rather than have it float off its foundation. A wide central hall ran the length of the house with two large rooms on one side and three smaller rooms on the other. The windows had shutters that could be bolted shut during a storm. The home was surrounded by a white picket fence, not to keep anything in but to keep the island's wild ponies and livestock out.

In the side yard were a recently planted garden and several out-buildings. There was an old summer kitchen out back with a big cast-iron wood stove; the kitchen was built to keep the heat and cooking odors out of the house and to protect it in case of fire. Marcia used the smaller kitchen in the house. She didn't have a large family to cook for that would justify using the kitchen in back. The property also included a small barn where she kept two horses, a building that had housed her husband's workshop, a chicken coop, and a curious square screened box set on legs a few feet off the ground that the islanders called a "dairy house" or "cooling house." All four sides of the cooling house were open and covered with screen. A pan of water was placed in the bottom of the house to help with cooling; as ocean breezes blew over the pan of water, the space grew cooler. This was used to store fresh vegetables, milk, eggs, and salted fish, bacon, pork, and ham. Marcia also had a re-frigerator in the kitchen, cooled by block ice brought over from the icehouse on Ocracoke. There was an outhouse, an outside shower, a long board for cleaning fish, and a large whitewashed brick cistern between the house and the summer kitchen, fed by gutters lead-ing from the roof. A pipe led from the cistern to a hand-operated "pitcher pump" at the kitchen sink. The island had no fresh water; residents had to rely on rainwater collected in cisterns.

There also was no electricity. Lighting, heating, and cooking were provided by kerosene brought over from Ocracoke and stored in a metal storage tank beside the house. Marcia and her husband had rented the house from one of his relatives, an old island family. After George died, the family let Marcia continue to stay there.

Established by the legislature in 1753, Portsmouth had been an important commercial port where large oceangoing vessels would download their cargo to smaller, lighter, flat-bottomed boats for transport to the coastal cities of New Bern, Washington, and Bath. Warehouses used to line the harbor for this purpose, and the first residents were either pilots or boatmen associated with the "light-ering" business. When a hurricane reopened the deeper Hatteras Inlet to the north in 1846, the commercial trade in Ocracoke and Portsmouth gradually declined. Then the harbor in Portsmouth was wrecked by a hurricane during the Civil War, and the Union sank several ships in Ocracoke Inlet, effectively closing it. Before the Civil War, the town had more than six hundred residents and a naval hospital. Many residents fled during the war and never returned. Ocracoke, with its natural harbor, continued to thrive as a commercial fishing center. At the turn of the century, a lifesaving station was built on the site of the old naval hospital. It was later taken over by the Coast Guard. But by the 1940s, the population of the island was less than fifty. Ocracoke, across the inlet to the northeast, had eclipsed Portsmouth some time ago. Now with the naval station, an active Coast Guard unit, and its good natural harbor, Ocracoke bustled with activity, while Portsmouth was a backward outpost.

After meeting Nick and Joe on the beach, Marcia returned to her house to check on her charge. She found him quietly snoring on the big double bed with the red-and-green wedding band quilt in her second bedroom. She wiped his brow of sweat and checked his pulse, which was normal, and then she fixed some lunch and went about her chores. She checked on him periodically. He slept through the night, tossing and turning and talking gibberish in his sleep. She couldn't understand what he was saying—it sounded like a foreign language. When she arose Thursday morning at sunrise, she went in to check on him and found his eyes open.

"Good morning," she said with a smile. "It looks like you have been through quite an ordeal. My name is Marcia Styron. You are on Portsmouth Island, North Carolina."

"G-G-Good morning," he said. He smiled at her with perfect white teeth.

"Would you like some tea?" Marcia asked, thinking his British taste buds would prefer tea over coffee.

"Yes, I would very much like some tea. Thank you," he said with a British accent. She brought him a cup of tea and placed it on the bedside table. He pulled himself up in bed with some difficulty, holding his side and grimacing.

"There, there, stay still. It looks like you took a tumble in the waves. You may have bruised or broken a rib or two."

"My side is killing me. The last thing I remember is being in a lifeboat. Then a wave capsized it and threw me into the water."

"What is your name?" she asked.

He hesitated, as if he had to think about it. "My name is Sublieutenant Bruce Hall, from Swansea in Great Britain. What is your name again?" he asked.

"My name is Marcia Styron from Elizabeth City, North Carolina, until I moved out here with my husband, George, who died at sea in January. What was the name of your ship?" she asked as she placed the cup of tea in his hands. She knew the boys at the Coast Guard Station would want to know.

"The HMS *Bedfordshire*," he said, looking into her eyes as if he were drinking in her wild, untamed beauty along with his tea. She could not take her eyes off him either. They stared at each other in silence for a long time.

"What about your shipmates? Did any of them make it?" she asked.

"I believe that everyone died. It happened so quickly, just before midnight on Monday. Two torpedoes were fired and missed us, then a third made a direct hit amidships and blew the ship in two. Most of the men were below deck. I was on the bridge on watch with a handful of others. We were blown free of the boat. Then she sank like a stone. I saw an empty lifeboat in the water. The German submarine was on the surface powering through the debris field, looking to see if there were any survivors. I didn't want them to see me, so I swam underwater and came up on the other side of the lifeboat. I think I am the only one who survived. When they didn't find anyone alive, they motored on and I climbed into the lifeboat. I called out in the dark to see if anyone was alive, but no one called back. I could only see bodies floating in the water. It was terrible. I drifted until I washed up on the beach here when the waves capsized the boat and threw me into the water. I think I was bruised when I was thrown against the overturned lifeboat."

"I found you stumbling ashore in the surf. You are the only one we found alive so far. We found only bodies, though someone could have washed ashore farther up the beach that we don't know about. You need to rest and regain your energy. Keep working on that tea, and I will bring you breakfast if you're up to it."

"Yes, I am very hungry," he said.

Marcia cooked pancakes and bacon and brought breakfast to him on a tray. He quickly devoured the food, then lay down to sleep some more. She sat beside his bed and watched him sleep. She could not keep her eyes off him. She wished he could stay with her forever and never go back to that terrible war, but she knew that was impossible.

She sized him up and decided that George had been about his same build. She washed his clothes and hung them on the line outside. Then she put some of George's clothes on a chair for him to use when he woke up.

Chapter 2

Oberleutnant Zur See Kurt Sanger served as second in command on the *unterseeboot U-558*, one of many submarines from the Ubootwaffe sent to American waters by Admiral Karl Dönitz of the German Kriegsmarine, or navy, as part of Operation Drumbeat. The Kapitänleutnant of the *U-558* was Günther Krech, one of the most successful U-boat commanders of the war. So far he had sunk ten merchant ships with the *U-558*. He was also involved in controversy because he had fired on and severely damaged the USS *Kearny* before the Americans got into the war. At the time, the *Kearny* was protecting a convoy on its way to Great Britain, and U-boats were under orders not to fire on American naval vessels.

Born September 21, 1914, Krech had been awarded the Iron Cross First Class in 1940 and the U-boat War Badge in 1941. He began his naval career in April 1933 and served four years in the German Luftwaffe. In November 1939, Krech joined the Kriegsmarine and began U-boat training. He received his first combat experience under the legendary Joachim Schepke of the *U-100*. He left the *U-100* in November 1940 and in February 1941 commissioned the *U-558*, a new Type VIIIC. The *U-558* was constructed at Blohm und Voss in Hamburg. The captain and his crew went through the

Baubelehrung, where the men got to know the boat during construction, at Bremen.

Based in Brest on the Atlantic coast of occupied France, the *U-558* left harbor on April 12, 1942, for its seventh patrol. In the mid-Atlantic, Krech rendezvoused with one of Dönitz's "Milch Cows," huge new U-boats built to carry oil, diesel fuel, torpedoes, and other supplies to keep the fighting U-boats in the water for as long as possible.

Handsome, brooding, and intense with dark brown hair and steel blue eyes, Krech was known to be aggressive and colorful. Part of his fame came from the sea aquarium he kept in the control room of the *U-558*. In it were tropical fish named for the leaders of countries at war with Germany. After his third cruise, the mean-tempered pirate fish named for Winston Churchill died. He then had the fish preserved in a tube filled with alcohol and hung it from a lamp in his wardroom. When they passed the tube, the crew would touch it for good luck. The submarine was so small and quarters so close that all the men had to pass through the officers' quarters on their way to their general duties. The crew bunks were in the forward compartment filled with torpedoes.

It was a little overcast, but visibility was good. The sky was cloudless and filled with stars, and there was a new moon. The wind was out of the northeast. Sanger could see the light from the lighthouse at Cape Hatteras flashing in the distance as the beam circled in its tall brick tower. You would think the Americans would have ordered a blackout, Sanger thought, but they were new to war, and the Germans were ready to take full advantage.

After a hard-fought submarine war with the British in the North Atlantic, it was a great morale boost to attack the unprotected and unprepared American coast. The first submarines were sent by Dönitz in January 1942 and operated freely—and unopposed—off the Atlantic coast; they sighted their targets against the lights of cars, houses, and cities on the shore. The array of vulnerable merchant shipping was so rich that the Germans could afford to pick and choose their targets, focusing mainly on oil tankers and large merchant vessels. One commander even bragged about sailing freely into New York harbor, where he could see the skyscrapers of the city. The Germans often tuned their radios to local radio stations and listened to American Big Band music and jazz. With the exception of the Coast Guard and a few boats and yachts called "the

Hooligan Fleet," manned by local volunteers armed with rifles, the Americans made virtually no attempt to protect their coast; there was no blackout on shore or on ship, no convoy system or attempt at evasive action, as was done in Britain. There was, however, a news blackout, so no one knew about the attacks except for those who were attacked and the coastal residents who saw the physical evidence. Cruise ships filled with unknowing passengers were targeted, as were merchant ships from all nations, even neutral ones. No one was exempt from the attacks.

More men died at sea during these brutal attacks than died at Pearl Harbor, but the navy refused to act to defend the East Coast. The chief admiral of the United States Navy, Ernest J. King, did not listen to the advice of the British about the need for blackouts, convoys, and destroyer escorts for merchant shipping. Following Pearl Harbor, he focused his attention on the Pacific.

After leaving Brest and refueling in the mid-Atlantic off the Azores, the *U-558* headed for the American coast to pursue merchant shipping, arriving first off Bermuda, then heading toward the North Carolina coast, where it cruised back and forth between Cape Hatteras and Cape Lookout. On May 5, Krech noted in his log that he was off Cape Lookout. The U-boat was on the lookout for destroyers, and Central Command reported that the British had sent submarine hunters to help America defend itself.

Sanger lit a cigarette and looked over the tranquil sea. It was May, but the breeze off the water was cold. He wore his overcoat. Sanger, a native of Dresden, spoke impeccable English learned at the Technische Universität Dresden. A graduate of the university, where his father taught English literature, he grew up hearing English spoken in his home. He was twenty-two years old, born August 9, 1920, and was also a recent graduate of the Marineschule Mürwik in Flensburg, where he underwent one year of basic training to become an officer in the German navy. He was commissioned Oberleutnant on October 1, 1941, and was assigned to the *U-558*.

After they were under way, Krech received orders from Central Command to go ashore on a spy mission to discover the fate of the *U-85*. Central Command had lost contact with the *U-85* off the North Carolina coast after April 14, 1942. The *U-85* was commanded by Oberleutnant Zur See Eberhard Greger, with a crew of forty men. The German command presumed the Americans had sunk the U-boat. They needed to know what happened to the crew and, most importantly, whether the Americans had captured the latest four-rotor version of the Schlüssel M "Enigma" cipher machine on board the submarine. The Germans suspected that the British had begun to break the code of the three-wheel version of the Enigma, so the machines were being updated to contain four rotors. In fact, the British had broken the German code when they captured a three-rotor machine from the *U-33* in late 1939, but when the four-rotor machine was introduced in January 1942, the British could no longer decipher the code. It was a top priority of the Allies to capture a four-rotor machine and break its code. Through a complicated system of rotors and codes, the machines, which resembled typewriters, encrypted messages sent from the submarines and decoded messages from Central Command. The key to successful submarine warfare was good communication. When the submarines hunted in groups, called wolf packs, they were most effective, but this had to be coordinated with good communication. The U-boats were also in constant communication with Central Command in occupied France. It would be catastrophic if the enemy captured a four-rotor Enigma machine and the codes with it.

Sanger looked for the right opportunity to go ashore. He could be dropped off on the beach on one of the islands and try to blend in with the locals, but the Outer Banks were filled with small communities, and a stranger would stand out. He decided a better plan would be to sink a British ship in which no one survived. Then he could take the clothes of one of the dead seamen and wash ashore in a lifeboat with the bodies and debris. He could imitate a good British accent. Although he paid special attention to American radio shows and practiced as best he could, his American accent was not as polished. After he gathered intelligence on shore, he could radio the submarine to pick him up.

A small naval base had been established at Ocracoke, where it would be easy to mingle and learn the fate of the *U-85*. While there, he could also gather information about any plans the United States Navy had to counter the U-boat assault. It would be easy to land on the beach, mingle in Ocracoke, then return to the submarine. There were miles of unprotected beach north of the village and to the south on Portsmouth Island. It would be much more difficult to do this at Hampton Roads or Morehead City, which were more heavily populated. The timetable for the mission was short; he had only two or three weeks before the *U-558* would need to return to Europe in late June.

Kapitän Krech, sporting a scraggly submariner's beard, joined

Sanger on the tower.

"You know, I was in the same class at Marineshule Mürwik with Oberleutnant Eberhard Greger, commander of the *U-85*," he said to Sanger. "I have a personal interest in the fate of the *U-85*. Greger was my friend, and I want to know what happened to him and his crew."

"I will do my best to find the answer for you, sir," Sanger replied.

The Ubootwaffe was a close-knit group; everyone knew everyone else, and there was less formality than in the other branches of the service. Life on a submarine by its very nature was close and informal; strong bonds formed among the men. It was essentially the only effective arm of the German Kriegsmarine, as the British had clear superiority on the surface. Admiral Karl Dönitz and his staff were based in France, as were all of the U-boats operating in the Atlantic. Krech knew the entire Ubootwaffe was depending on him and his crew to safeguard the German code machine.

At 9:20 P.M., Sanger saw a flashing light almost directly astern. At 10:07 P.M., after traveling about thirteen miles at eight to ten knots, Sanger could make out the silhouette of a ship in the distance against the light from shore at a bearing of 305 degrees astern. He pulled out the "Hunting Book," which was the U-boat commanders' guide to the shape and appearance of enemy vessels. It covered the major naval vessels of most of the Allied countries, complete with targeting information. He identified the profile as a British minesweeper that had been built as a fishing trawler, one of the boats the British had sent to the Americans. It was the *Bedfordshire*, a coal burner built in 1935; it was 162 feet long with a 27-foot beam. Earlier that night, the *U-558* had fired on another British trawler, the HMT *St. Loman*, but the *St. Loman* had spotted the torpedoes and managed to avoid them. This was the first confirmation the Germans had that the British had sent armed ships to protect American shipping. That would be another good subject for intelligence. But they must first defend themselves from possible attack. The coast of North Carolina was treacherous because of the shoals that reached out for miles; it would be easy to get caught in shallow water. They had at least 200 feet of depth. The *U-558* was traveling on the surface, following a course of about 230 degrees, and the *Bedfordshire* was 75 degrees off the submarine's starboard bow as the U-boat overtook it. When they were in range at 11:26 P.M., they fired two torpedoes.

"These are for Kapitän Greger and his crew," Kapitän Krech said as he gave the order. It was not unusual for torpedoes to miss their target. After the torpedoes cleared, they counted, but there was no explosion. They had missed their mark. The *Bedfordshire* continued on course and gave no indication that it had seen the submarine.

Krech quickly decided to attack again. At 11:40 P.M., he gave the order to fire tube three. They counted off the seconds, then saw a huge explosion as the torpedo hit amidships on the *Bedfordshire*'s port side. The stern rose high in the water and then quickly disappeared under the waves. The explosion, fueled either by the ignition of coal dust from the *Bedfordshire*'s boiler or by one of the torpedoes hitting a magazine, was spectacular and didn't give anyone a chance to abandon ship.

The submarine surfaced and moved slowly toward the debris field. The German crew found a sailor clinging to a lifeboat in the chilly water and a body floating nearby. They must have been on watch and been blown free of the ship by the explosion. The U-boat ran up beside the sailor and the body and hauled them onto the deck. The Germans tethered the lifeboat to the sub.

"What are you Brits doing off the coast of Carolina?" Sanger asked the sailor in English.

He did not respond.

In February 1942, after weeks of urging Admiral King to use the convoy system, Churchill and his admirals decided to send twenty antisubmarine trawlers to protect shipping on the United States' East Coast. The daily sinking of merchant ships not only affected the United States but also threatened British supply lines. The trawlers were little more than converted fishing trawlers, and when they arrived in New York, they were in such bad shape that they had to be completely overhauled. They averaged 170 feet in length and were very slow, capable of twelve knots at best. They were outfitted with four-inch quick-fire deck guns and .30 caliber Lewis guns. They had depth-charge racks and launchers, but best of all, they had the latest model of British sonar equipment, called ASDIC. They also had battle-hardened crews used to dealing with German submarines in British waters. Though looked upon skeptically at first by the Americans, the British crews and their vessels soon earned the Americans' respect as they did an excellent job of protecting shipping, heretofore aided only by the Hooligan Fleet and a few Coast Guard vessels. The *Bedfordshire* was one of these antisubmarine trawlers sent by Churchill to protect the East Coast.

Krech told Sanger to ask the sailor about the *U-85*.

"Do you know the fate of the *U-85*?" Sanger asked, sizing up the sailor.

The man did not respond; there was almost a knowing silence. In fact, the *Bedfordshire* had just returned from diving the wreck of the *U-85*, but the Germans did not know this. Sanger continued to grill the sailor about the U-boat, but he did not volunteer any information.

At first, he gave only his name, rank, and serial number. He was Ordinary Telegraphist Geoffrey Featherstone. He told them that his commander was Lieutenant R. B. Davis and that the *Bedfordshire* had just left port at Morehead City to patrol off the Outer Banks. It had been sent by the British navy to help protect American shipping.

Sanger sized him up and realized that Featherstone was too small for his needs. He then had the men pick up the body they had pulled out of the water and saw that it was about his size. "Strip the body," Sanger told a crewman, which he did. "Now give me those clothes." He held up the pants and sweater and saw that they were about his size. He found the man's identification papers in the clothes; he was Sublieutenant Bruce Hall. He then handed the clothes to the seaman and told him to take them below and dry them.

"They will think I survived the sinking, and I will be allowed to freely mingle on shore, before they have a chance to check me out. By then I will have discovered what we need to know," Sanger said to Krech.

"Excellent!" Krech answered.

Held at gunpoint wet and shivering in the cold on the deck of the submarine, the British sailor reluctantly answered the Germans' questions. Having interrogated the man to his satisfaction, the captain finally cocked his gun and said, "Back into the water."

"Without the lifeboat?" he asked.

"Without the lifeboat. We have other plans for that," Sanger said.

"I will surely die," Featherstone said.

"Here, take this," Krech said, handing him a life vest. Then he pushed the sailor overboard clutching the vest. He and Sanger knew the sailor would soon die in the frigid water with or without a life vest.

The U-boats were under strict orders from Dönitz not to kill survivors of their attacks. Often the U-boat captains even helped survivors in lifeboats, giving them supplies or telling them which way to head for shore. Dönitz also strictly forbade the U-boats to take any survivors on board; there was simply no room for them. And after all, their business was war, not rescue. But this was a secret mission. Krech and his crew could not risk leaving any survivors. They also did not want to shoot the sailor, first because it was unnecessary and secondly because a bullet-riddled body washed up on shore would raise questions. So the Germans would let the frigid sea do their work. Leaving the man in the water calling out for help in the darkness, the U-boat slowly made its way through the debris field searching for other survivors. The explosion had ripped the *Bedfordshire* in two, and it had sunk in a matter of minutes. It would have been a miracle if anyone else survived. The Germans found no one else alive. For a while, they heard the pleas of the man they had pushed into the water, but after a while there was silence.

Finally it was time for Sanger to board the lifeboat. First he shaved his four-week beard and blackened his face and arms with soot. Then he pulled on Hall's dry clothes and pocketed his identification papers. The clothes fit well; the pants were a little large in the waist, but nothing a belt couldn't fix. Sanger stepped into the lifeboat. His fellow crewmen handed him two oars and enough water and food for a few days. The debris field was drifting southwest toward Ocracoke and Portsmouth islands, blown by a steady breeze from the northeast.

"We will follow, out of sight, and mark the spot where you land. Under cover of darkness, we will hide a radio in the dunes near where you go ashore. It will be marked with a yellow ribbon staked in the sand," Krech told Sanger. "It is too risky to put the radio on the lifeboat with you."

Sanger nodded. "Agreed. I will stay in contact and signal when and where to pick me up as soon as I gather intelligence. If you have not heard from me by the eighteenth, you can presume that I have been killed or captured."

Sanger drifted in the lifeboat with most of the debris field of the *Bedfordshire* until he heard waves crashing on shore early in the morning of May 14. He pulled on the oars to try to cross the waves, but they capsized the boat. He tumbled into the water. Something struck him hard on his side and back, and pain shot through his ribs. He felt sand under his feet. He stumbled through the waves, trying to stand. He thought he saw a woman running across the beach toward him, but it was hard to see, as the sea water stung his swollen eyes. The woman put one arm around his waist and helped him out of the water. She led him to a horse. He hauled himself on its back with her help. That is all he remembered until he awoke in Marcia Styron's house, in a big double bed, naked under crisp white sheets and a patchwork quilt.

Chapter 3

In February 1942, the Coast Guard took over the old lifesaving station in Portsmouth that had been built in 1894 and decommissioned in 1938. Two men from the South Philadelphia National Guard—Nick Galantis and Joe Guidos—were sent initially to begin guard duty on the beach at Portsmouth and take up residence at the old lifesaving station between the village and the beach. On their first reconnaissance trip to the island, the Coast Guard boat could not land at the dock at the lifesaving station because the water was too shallow, so the men had to jump overboard and wade onto shore barefoot, holding their shoes above the water to keep them dry, occasionally cutting their feet on oyster shells in the cold water. They were given only a few sandwiches and told they would be picked up the next day, after which they would return with more provisions. But a storm blew up and they had to stay over a week before being resupplied. They looked for whatever they could find in the old lifesaving station, which wasn't much. At least there were mattresses and old woolen blankets, but no sheets. They found kerosene in the storage shed for the lamps and could get water from the pump leading from the cistern, but it had been awhile since the pump was used. The cistern needed to be cleaned and the water treated with Clorox before they could drink it.

The men became so hungry and thirsty that they wandered into the village and started going from house to house asking for provisions. The residents did not expect the servicemen on their island and at first were too frightened to help them. The men finally stopped at the Babb family home, where sisters Jessie, Marian, and Edna sat on the front porch watching their progress through the village.

"Ma'am, could we have some water? We're staying over at the Coast Guard Station and ran out of supplies."

"Surely," Jessie said. The Babb cistern was at the rear of the house. A pipe ran into the kitchen, ending at a pump in the sink. Jessie did not invite the men in, but she fetched them glasses of water, which they gulped down standing on the front steps. She had not heard a Yankee accent before. It could have been foreign, for all she knew. The men were handsome, in a dark Italian way, and lively, not taciturn and reserved like most of the men she knew from the village. The soldiers were downright forward. They looked to be in their early twenties.

"Tell you the truth, ma'am," Nick Galantis said, "everywhere we go people have given us water, but what we really need is something to eat." He offered a big, toothy grin.

"What is going on out here?" Jessie's mother, Helen Babb, called from inside the house. She walked onto the front porch and stared at the tall, slim, good-looking, dark-haired young men, wearing khaki pants and long-sleeved white shirts with the Coast Guard emblem on them. "Did I hear these boys are looking for something to eat?" Helen Babb was a large woman wearing a bright blue gingham dress. She loved to cook. Having grown up in a family with five boys, she especially loved to cook for men with large appetites. She recognized a good opportunity to fatten up some underfed men with her famous home-cooked meals, meals her finicky, skinny little girls did not appreciate.

"Yes, Momma," Jessie, a cute blond-haired girl of eighteen, replied. The other sisters sat watching, taking it all in from their porch swing. Marian was fourteen, and Edna was twelve. Most of the young men of the island had left in December, signing up for the war. The only men left in the village were either old or ones the service would not take. The Babb women soaked in the exotic manly features of the handsome young Italian strangers.

"Y'all come on in and have some iced tea while I rustle up

some food," Helen said, leading the men into the kitchen, where she briskly and efficiently lit the stove, pumped water into a cast-iron pot, and began to stir in grits. She also called to Jessie to fetch some bacon and eggs out of the cooling house out back. "How about some bacon and eggs with grits for starters, then we can fix some corn bread and start planning dinner? Do you boys like apple cobbler?" Helen Babb made the best apple cobbler on the island—no, the whole Outer Banks, some said.

Nick and Joe had heard of grits from the Southern boys they had met, but they had never tried any. They were hungry enough to eat a horse—so grits, sure, they would eat grits.

"Yes, ma'am, we would love some bacon and eggs, and I'd like to try one of those grits, too," Nick Galantis said innocently.

"Haven't eaten grits before, have you?" Helen asked matter-of-factly.

"No, ma'am. How did you know?"

"Where are you boys from?" Helen asked.

"Philadelphia, ma'am," Nick and Joe said.

"Grits is like porridge or gruel or oatmeal. You don't eat just one; you eat a whole bowlful," she said with a big smile as she stood over the kerosene stove.

"Whatever they is, I'll eat 'em," Joe said. "I'm so hungry I could eat a horse right now. All the Coast Guard gave us was some sandwiches and a bottle of water, and that was yesterday. I've more than used up that sandwich. I need something that will stick to my ribs."

"Grits will stick to your ribs, just wait and see; you might even like 'em," Helen said as Jessie brought in the eggs and a side of bacon. Helen cut the bacon into thick slices and threw them in the iron skillet. "Jessie, set the table. We're going to fix these Yankee boys a fine Portsmouth Island breakfast."

Soon Nick and Joe were seen almost every night at the Babb house, playing gin rummy and 500 rummy with the girls. It was a regular USO house. The other islanders were jealous that the Coast Guard boys with their monthly government checks, charming manner, and good looks hung out at the Babb house, but as Helen told Jessie one night after the boys had left, "They had their chance."

The boys at the old lifesaving station, now operated by the Coast Guard, rode their daily patrol on the beach and looked for the dead or survivors of shipwrecks. At first all they had were horses, which they kept at the stable behind the station. Later they were given a Jeep, the only vehicle on the island. Still, they preferred using the horses, particularly on beach patrol.

Nick and Joe decided to check up on Marcia and her charge. They had already reported the dead bodies on the beach and recovered what ID they could. They buried the men in a small family graveyard in the village until a more permanent site could be found.

"How's Miss Marcia doing?" Nick shouted, tying his horse to a post outside the gate to her fence. Marcia stood on the front porch, her long brown hair pinned in a bun and the skirt of her white dress moving in the breeze. She made a beautiful picture, which was not lost on Nick and Joe.

"Doing just fine. How are you Pennsylvania boys doing this fine morning?" she said with a smile.

Nick and Joe always seemed to wear a smile; they liked to joke around. They were well liked on the island, even if they were Yankees.

"We wanted to see if your English sailor is in any kind of condition to talk to us this morning," Joe said with a smile. "I figured he has had the day to rest. Is he awake? We have some questions we need to ask him."

"Yes, he's awake. He got pretty bruised up in the waves, but he's alert and can talk, though somewhat painfully. I have already fed him some pancakes and bacon, and he seemed to like that well enough," Marcia said, leading Joe and Nick into the house. To the left front was Marcia's room, a corner room with big, sunny windows and a fireplace. Behind it was the second bedroom with one window and a fireplace, the room her visitor was using. To the right in front was the living room, and behind that the dining room, then the kitchen. The house had no indoor bathroom or running water. A two-seater outhouse was in back. The walls were all bead-board painted white. The floors were wide pine boards worn through the years with sand and bare feet. Marcia kept them swept and mopped them with Clorox; there was no finish on them. The rooms were sparsely furnished, with white curtains and hand-loomed rag rugs. Kerosene lamps lit the house by night.

Marcia led Nick and Joe into the second bedroom, where her patient lay in bed under a colorful wedding band patterned quilt. He sat up and smiled.

"Good morning, sir. My name is Nick, and this here is Joe.

We're with the United States Coast Guard and need to ask you some questions," Nick began, pulling out a notepad. "I understand that Miss Marcia found you washed up on the beach with the debris from a shipwreck. What is your name, sir?"

"Sublieutenant Bruce Hall, His Majesty's Navy," Sanger said in his best British accent.

"Can you tell me the name of your ship, sir?"

"Indeed, she was the HMS *Bedfordshire*, out of Swansea. Here on antisubmarine duty. It was about 10:40 P.M. Monday night, May 11. I was on guard duty on the bridge with the captain when I heard the sound of a torpedo heading our way. Before we could sound the alarm, the torpedo hit us. I was blown into the water. I don't know what happened to Lieutenant Davis or the others on deck that night. I don't think anyone else had a chance to escape the sinking boat, it went down so fast.

"After swimming around in the debris for a while in the cold water," he continued, "I found an empty lifeboat. I saw the U-boat slowly making its way through the debris, and I hid in the water behind the lifeboat. I didn't know what they would do if they found me alive. After they saw the lifeboat was empty, they motored on. Then I climbed in."

Nick and Joe asked Hall several more questions, including the name of his commanding officer and the boat's last port. He told them his commanding officer was Lieutenant R. B. Davis, and that the *Bedfordshire* was last in Morehead City, North Carolina.

Satisfied for the moment, Nick and Joe left. They knew they would need to get the sailor to Ocracoke for further questioning, but that could wait a few days until the man had a chance to mend sufficiently. Until then he was under the capable care of Marcia Styron.

Chapter 4

Sanger was still in a lot of pain from his bruised ribs. He wanted to get to the Ocracoke naval base soon to find out what he could about the fate of the *U-85*. He was anxious to gather the intelligence, find the buried radio, and get back to the *U-558*.

"I'm going into town to check the mail and get some provisions. I should be back in about an hour," Marcia told him after Nick and Joe left.

"Do you have any cigarettes?" Sanger asked, smiling, sitting up in bed shirtless. "I may take a walk on the beach and have a smoke."

Marcia retrieved a pack of Lucky Strikes from the kitchen. "These belonged to my husband. I don't smoke. You're welcome to try his clothes, too. You look about his size," she said, admiring his broad shoulders and well-formed chest and arms. "Take it easy with those ribs. I taped them up pretty good, but you need to rest and mend as much as you can before you get up and out much."

"What happened to your husband?" Sanger asked.

"He was with the Coast Guard. He drowned trying to save the men from a sinking ship, like yours. We don't know if his boat was swamped or whether a U-boat sank it. He was never found."

"When did that happen?" he asked, thinking about the *U-558*'s patrols.

"In January, off Cape Hatteras."

"I am sorry," he said. "You must miss him." He was somewhat relieved that his U-boat had not been in the waters off Carolina in January.

"Yes, I do. I miss him very much," she said, quickly walking out of the room. She did not want to talk about her husband; it was still too painful.

She walked out the back door to the barn just outside the fence, untied her horse, hitched up the saddle and saddlebags, and headed for town.

As soon as she left, Sanger got out of bed. He spotted some clothing draped over a chair in the corner—her husband's clothes—and pulled on the white boxer shorts, T-shirt, khaki pants, and canvas shoes. They fit perfectly, except the pants were about an inch too big in the waist. Though the submariners ate better than the men in the other German forces, the food on the submarine was pretty lean, mainly preserved meats, some eggs and bread, and dried potatoes. Sanger had lost most of what little body fat he had while on board.

Once out of the house, he followed the sound of the waves to the beach. It was a beautiful spring day. The sky was cloudless, and the ocean was as calm as a lake. He wondered where his shipmates were. During the day they ran underwater, but by night they ran on the surface. He knew the U-boat had followed him and marked where he had washed up on shore. He hoped to find the radio not far from the path leading to the beach. Dunes stood here and there, but for long stretches the beach was flat with no vegetation as far as he could see—all the way to the rear of the island, where the marshes began. These sand flats were created by overwash during storms.

He had noticed from the deck of the *U-558* that to the northeast, on Hatteras, the dunes seemed larger and more regular, like a wall separating the beach from the island. But this beach was different. He did not know that in the 1930s the Civilian Conservation Corps had built up the dunes along the northern Outer Banks to harden the shore. The engineers had planned to do the same on Portsmouth and Ocracoke, but funds dried up when the war broke out. The beach at Portsmouth was the way nature had made it, with no intervention from man. A clump of dunes with sea grass on top was located a few hundred yards south of the path that led to Marcia's house. He decided to check it out. Sure enough, he found a small yellow ribbon tied to a stake like a surveyor's marker on top of what looked like freshly dug sand. He dug the sand with his hands. A foot below the surface, he found a radio, an expanse of wire for an antenna, a crystal set, a Lugar, some ammo, and other supplies wrapped in oilcloth. He quickly took the supplies to the house. He had already decided that the perfect place for the radio antenna was in the attic of one of the outbuildings.

At the rear of the house was a woodworking shop that had been used by Marcia's husband. The beams of the roof were exposed, there was no ceiling, and the framework of the walls was open, with no siding on the interior. He climbed a ladder and nailed the wire on top of the beams above the shop, spreading them out in a grid that could not be seen from below. He then hid the radio and crystal set in a rain barrel with a lid on it. He stashed his other supplies in an old trunk, covered them with the oilcloth, and walked to the front porch of the house. He lit a Lucky Strike. The Americans got a few things right, he thought—cigarettes and music were two of them. The best tobacco in the world came from the States, unless you liked cigars, in which case the product of choice would be Cuban or Turkish.

"I see you found the clothes I set out for you," Marcia said, tying her horse to the post beside the gate at the front of the house, where Sanger sat, rocking, taking in the salt air, smoking a cigarette.

"Yeah, they fit perfectly," he said, smiling.

"Would you help me with these things?" she asked, lugging a bag of provisions from the variety store. "I figured I needed some groceries, since I've got two mouths to feed now instead of one." He helped her carry the bags back to the kitchen. "Everyone was asking about you at the store and the post office. They've never seen a real British sailor before. I told 'em to hold off coming out to see you until you're feeling better. They were ready to follow me home and give you the once-over. People down here are a curious lot. Not much going on around here, so strangers attract attention, just like when Nick and Joe first showed up. Before they came, only a few people in Portsmouth had ever heard a Yankee accent, much less seen two good-looking Italian guys. People around here make a living by fishing, guiding hunters, or working for the post office, the general store, or the Coast Guard. Everyone else is retired or widowed."

"How did you meet your husband?" Sanger asked.

"He was in the Coast Guard, stationed in Elizabeth City. I saw him downtown in a store one day when I was shopping with Momma, and he smiled at me. We talked a little and ran into each other again, and he asked me out. At first Momma didn't want me to date a sailor, but Pappa said they made good money, so he let me. One thing led to another. We dated, he asked me to marry him, and when the war started, he was assigned to Ocracoke. Housing for married people was hard to come by, with so many navy men moving in, but George had family from here, so we rented this house from a family member, so we'd have a little more privacy. We moved out here the first of the year."

"It is nice out here, very remote, very private," Sanger said, looking around at the sandy yard, wind-twisted cedars, and live oaks.

"I like it that way. Sometimes I get up in the morning and ride Mary Lou, my horse, on the beach for an hour before fixing breakfast." She finished putting away the groceries and turned to him. "Do you feel up to a walk on the beach?"

"Sure," he said with a wide grin and a sparkle in his clear blue eyes. Sanger had left a girlfriend back home in Dresden, but she had written him that she had found someone else, an army officer. She couldn't deal with a man who was gone for months at a time on a submarine, not knowing whether he was alive or dead. She wanted more certainty than that. He had gotten her letter just before they set sail. He thought Marcia was very attractive. It would be a few days before he was sufficiently mended to go to the naval base in Ocracoke. Why not enjoy himself on Portsmouth with Marcia until then? he thought.

They walked down the rutted path in the sand that led to the beach. The wind caught Marcia's hair, pulling tendrils from her bun and sweeping them along the sexy curve of her neck. Silver earrings in the shape of a spiral dangled from her ears. The sky was big and wide as it covered the flat landscape of the beach and water. The calm water looked like a sun-dappled lake as it rose and fell, developing long, lazy lines that formed white-capped waves pushing against the shore with a steady drone. The sun danced on top of the waves and silvered the roughed-up water after they broke. The spider webs of white foam quickly dissipated until the next wave broke. The beach was wide and flat and wet near the water, looking like polished leather where it reflected the sun. The dry sand was bone white and the wet sand gray.

There were lots of birds: lone seagulls standing sentry on the beach, groups of sandpipers just out of the waves, and little sander-lings chasing the waves up and back on the beach. Noisy terns flew overhead, while an occasional black skimmer barely skimmed the surface of the water with its red-and-black beak. In the distance, a graceful line of pelicans glided inches above the water just beyond the waves. A school of dolphins swam in formation a few hundred yards from shore, arching their backs, glistening in the sunlight. Marcia and Sanger took their shoes off, rolled up their pant legs, and walked to the water's edge, splashing through the shallow wa-ter heading southwest. The beach at Portsmouth and Ocracoke ran almost east to west as the islands pointed out to sea running up to Cape Hatteras, which stood farthest east of all the islands. The beach had mostly been cleaned up and the bodies removed, but burned wood and blackened life preservers remained from the wreck. There was no oil because the *Bedfordshire* had been coal fired.

When an oil tanker sank, the beach was covered with oil for days. Sometimes it was weeks before the beach recovered. Marcia found many shorebirds completely covered in oil. It was impos-sible to remove the oil from their feathers, and all she could do was watch as they died. It made her sick. But this day there was no oil on the beach; in fact, there was little to remind them that a war was going on at all.

"Do you have a girlfriend?" Marcia asked. She had noticed that he wore no wedding ring.

"I had a girlfriend; in fact, we were engaged to be married, but just before I set sail she wrote me that the engagement was off, that she had found an army officer at home who asked her to marry him. She said she couldn't stand not knowing for weeks or months while I was at sea whether I was alive or dead."

"People who live on the sea get used to their men being gone for a long time without hearing from them. I am not saying it is any easier, but it is our life. We have to get used to it, if we are to have a man and live by the sea. I wouldn't live anywhere else," Marcia said wistfully.

"I can see why," he said, looking out at the beach and the ocean.

"What is it like where you live—Swansea, did you say?"

"The shore is not like this at all; it is very rocky, but sandy beaches lie between the cliffs and rocks. The water is also a lot colder and bluer—rougher, too. But it is still the sea. I think if you love the sea, you love it whether it is on the coast of the Carolinas, the North Sea," he caught himself, "or southwest Wales."

"I thought you said you were from England."

"Great Britain is made up of several parts: England, Scotland, Wales, and Ireland. They are like states are over here. Wales is one of the states of Great Britain. England is one, too. Wales is on the Atlantic Ocean, the west coast of Britain. Swansea is on the southern coast of Wales. I hope that doesn't confuse you too much. Perhaps we can find a map and I can show you where it is." The coast of the North Sea near Hamburg and at Bremerhaven—a seaport at the mouth of the Weser River that fed the port of Bremen, where he had trained on the U-boat—did not have a dramatic rocky coast like Wales. The beaches were sandy, and there were coastal barrier islands and a tidal estuary, much like the coast of Carolina, but the water was much colder. He was familiar with the west coast of Britain because he had seen it through binoculars from the submarine. He was impressed with the gentle beauty of the Carolina coast, and he especially liked its warm waters.

When they had crossed the Gulf Stream in the U-boat, the water was so hot that the temperature rose several degrees in the submarine, and the men stripped down to their underwear, sweating like pigs. That must be what made the Carolina coast so warm, he thought, but then it *was* the same latitude as Morocco and Tunisia.

"What do you think of our coast?" she asked. "Is it as nice as yours?"

"Oh, yours is much nicer. You can actually swim in the water here, and the sun is so relaxing. The beaches are wide and the wildlife so beautiful. I bet the fishing is good here, too."

"Some of the best in the world. What with the Gulf Stream, we can catch most any kind of ocean fish that you would ever want: tuna, bluefish, mackerel, bull-nosed dolphin, wahoo, red drum, you name it, we got it. Plus there are sea bass, trout, and flounder in the sound, and oysters, shrimp, crabs, clams, and scallops—all you can eat," she said with a certain amount of local pride. "Do you ride horses? We can saddle up my husband's horse. I'm sorry to say I haven't ridden him much lately. It is fun to ride horses on the beach, especially at night."

"Yes, I can ride, and yes, I would like that very much—tonight, after supper?"

When they returned to the house after walking on the beach,

Sanger picked up a photograph of Marcia and a handsome young man; both wore bathing suits and stood on the beach. "Who is this?" Sanger asked.

"That's George, my husband. We loved to walk on the beach, go swimming, and ride horses. He was my best friend. We had so much fun together. We were very much in love. It is so unfair to have had him and now have nothing."

"What do you mean have nothing? You found love. Some people don't find true love in a lifetime. He left you that; even if he is gone, you know what you had, and it can never be taken away from you," he said, looking into her eyes, which were filling with tears as she thought about her husband.

Suddenly he realized that the walk had taken more out of him than he expected. His ribs still hurt. He grimaced and held his side in pain.

Noticing he was tired, Marcia said, "Why don't you lie down and rest before supper? You need to take care of yourself."

Kurt Sanger was not the kind of man who took care of himself. He drove himself. But she was right—he needed to rest, heal, and mend, so he would have his strength when he went to Ocracoke to spy and find out what happened to the *U-85*. He walked into the bedroom, stripped to his underwear, and crawled into bed. He was tired and quickly fell asleep.

He was in the submarine. He heard the familiar sound of explosions; they must have sunk a ship and were on the surface. Then he heard shouts from the bridge and gunfire. There was mayhem as men scrambled to and from battle stations. He heard machine gun fire outside the boat. He found himself in the galley. Hanging from racks and hooks above him were slabs of meat—shoulders, hams, ribs—but they weren't beef or pork. He turned to the cook and asked, "What kind of meat is this?"

"We have been out here for so long that we ran out of supplies and had to start hauling in bodies from the ships we sank. I insist that they be fresh. Meat is meat; we must survive. We eat what we kill. It is the law of the sea. Here, help me with this one," the cook said, hauling a fresh body covered in a blanket onto a long stainless-steel table at the center of the galley. When the cook pulled back the blanket, Sanger recognized the young man from the photos in Marcia's house; it was George Styron.

Sanger woke up in a cold sweat, the image of Marcia's dead husband still fresh in his mind. But sleep would not release him; again it pulled him under, and again he found himself on the submarine. They were diving; fresh meat swung from hooks overhead. Men scrambled to battle stations. He made his way to the control room. The captain stood by coolly as the U-boat dove deeper and deeper. The gauges were far into the red. Bolts began to pop and water pipes burst, but the captain continued to dive. The men knew the submarine couldn't take the pressure, but the captain continued to dive. Soon water began to fill the boat. Men were swimming, yet the boat continued to dive. Sanger saw butchered slabs of meat drift by. The submarine continued to dive, and the metal began to pop and strain, making terrible noises, yet the captain stared ahead emotionless as they dove deeper. The chamber filled with water, and Sanger swam helplessly, trying to find an air pocket. Then he woke up in a sweat.

Marcia stood in the doorway, drying a plate. "Must have had a pretty bad nightmare. I heard you calling out in a language I didn't understand. If I didn't know better, I would say it was German. Are you all right?"

"I am fine. I dreamed I was in the water after our ship was sunk. I can't seem to get the image of the boat sinking out of my mind. It happened so quickly. I saw the Germans on the bridge of their U-boat watching as I struggled in the water. They shined a light on me. I studied German in school. I helped translate messages. I called out to the Germans for help. I didn't have a life vest or a lifeboat. They motored through the debris, not stopping or helping, surveying the damage. Then they were gone, and I was left alone in the water, struggling to fight the cold and to stay afloat in the water. It was terrible." He was genuinely disturbed by his own nightmare, not the false one that he reported. But he was also happy he was able to quickly come up with an explanation for German mutterings. Marcia sat on the bed beside him and put her hand in his.

"I can't help but think of my George as you describe the scene as your ship sank. I wonder if the last thing he saw was Germans holding a machine gun on the deck of a U-boat. I hate this war. It is so unfair. My family is German. My grandfather emigrated from Germany in the 1890s. I remember hearing him speak German with my grandmother. The Germans are not all monsters; the war is doing this to us. I am sure that our people would be just as cruel to the Germans if they survived the sinking of a U-boat. I heard that is what happened to the U-boat sunk off Kitty Hawk. After they sank the U-boat, the German sailors in the water cried out for help. The captain of the destroyer first tried to lower a lifeboat, then he changed his mind. He was concerned that they would be attacked by another U-boat, so he decided to drop depth charges in the water, and the explosions killed all the men swimming. No one survived, but he could have saved them. He must have thought about all the men who died in the water from the ships sunk by the submarines. But they were defenseless. There should be rules even in war."

"Were they all killed?" he asked, thinking this must be the U-85.

"That is what I heard. About thirty bodies were recovered and were buried in a cemetery in Newport News, Virginia."

"Where did you hear about this?" he asked.

"From Nick and Joe at the Coast Guard Station. Everyone is talking about it; it is the first German U-boat sunk by our navy since the war began."

"War is hell," he said. Now that he knew what had happened to the men of the *U-85*, he needed to find out what had happened to its precious technology—the Enigma machines. Did the Americans find them after the U-boat sank? How deep was the water there? Did they dive it or recover anything from it? As cruel and awful as it sounded, at least no one was taken prisoner to give information to the enemy. So Marcia was German. He knew he was drawn to her. He wondered what part of Germany her family came from. Was her family Saxon like his?

Marcia fried some fresh fillets of flounder and hush puppies and fixed coleslaw that night. As it grew dark, she lit a kerosene lamp on the kitchen table. After they washed the dishes and cleaned up, they walked out on the porch. The sun had gone down, and the moon was just a sliver midway in the sky. The sky was alive with stars. They could even see the Milky Way making a giant smudge of stars across the night sky. The first time Sanger had seen the Milky Way was in the Atlantic. He had never seen it at home, nor at the busy port at Brest, with the lights from the city and pollution from the factories.

"Are you up to a ride on the beach?" she asked, the wind catching her hair.

"Yes," he replied with a wide smile.

They walked to the barn, saddled the horses with Western saddles, and rode onto the beach. The water was dark and fairly calm, with a steady breeze from the northeast. They rode to the water's edge and dismounted. Marcia dragged her foot in the sand and watched as little pinpricks of light appeared. "Bioluminescence," she said. "Have you ever seen it before?"

"I haven't seen it in the sand, but I have seen it in the water. When a ship goes through it, it glows with a greenish light, disturbing microorganisms in the water. It must be the same."

"Yes, it must. I love to see the light in the sand; it is magical. When I was a child, I imagined I was a giant walking on the beach, and when I stomped on the ground, all the Lilliputian inhabitants of the sand turned on their lights to see what was going on outside." She laughed. "Is it beautiful in the water?"

"Yes. It leaves a glittering trail of phosphorescent light behind a ship." It was also dangerous, because when the submarine rode on the surface at night, the luminous trail showed where the boat was located.

When Marcia got back on her horse and rode down the beach, he mounted her husband's horse and followed. She galloped ahead, trying to outrun him, but he soon caught up.

"Trying to lose me?" he asked, laughing.

"No, just trying to see if I could beat you," she said with a smile.

They continued to ride down the beach. Then she turned and led him back to the house. Even thought it was dark, she knew the way.

They put the horses in the barn and went inside the house. They would have sat on the porch, but the bugs were bad. When the wind died down, hungry mosquitoes attacked the island.

"Would you like to listen to some music?" she asked.

"Certainly," he responded.

She sorted through her 78 rpm records until she found "Moonlight Serenade" and put it on the phonograph, cranking it by hand.

"Would you like to dance?" he asked. He loved American music, fun, fast, and romantic.

As they danced, he put his lips on the tender skin of the nape of her neck, feeling the gentle touch of her hair and smelling the sweet scent of her skin. It was a long time since he had been this close to a woman, since he had left France, when the men celebrated their departure at a bar in Brest. Then he had danced with a prostitute. Now he danced with a lady, a beautiful American lady, a young widow, alone and in need. He was entranced by the smell of her body, her perfumed clothes (Shalimar by Guerlain, with a hint of vanilla), the softness of her skin, the silkiness of her hair, the touch of her breasts against his chest. Likewise, Marcia inhaled the manly odors of Sanger's body, wrapping herself in the strength of his embrace, the hardness of his body, and the gentleness of his touch. She had not been this close to a man since she kissed her husband good-bye the day before he disappeared.

It was natural; neither could resist. He kissed her, and she kissed him. They were swept up in the beauty of the evening. It was as if they were lost and now were found. They drank in the sweet nectar of each other's bodies, drawn deeper into the influence of the other, both lonely, both young and full of passion, both vulnerable, yet strong. It was inevitable.

At first she was afraid that he would take advantage of her; he was strong and could easily overpower her, and they were far from any neighbor. She was naturally cautious and pulled away, but then she found herself yielding. Her mind said one thing but her body another. He knew not to push too hard, but his body also urged him on, despite what his head told him. Once it began it was impossible to stop. From the first time she laid eyes on him, she knew she wanted him. The first time he saw her, he thought she was an angel and was entranced by her. They could not resist each other. They could not stop.

He kissed her, and she kissed him. She unbuttoned his shirt and he her blouse. They stumbled into her bedroom and began to unclothe each other. He did not force her; he only went as far as she would allow. She thirsted for him as she pulled his shirt off, unbuckled his pants, and pulled down his boxer shorts—her husband's clothes—releasing his urgent sex, turgid, impatient, following its own orders, not waiting for orders from above. He pulled her dress over her head, and she unbuttoned her bra as he pulled her panties down. They made love as if they had been lost in the desert, thirsting for water, their bodies a palm-shaded oasis. They drank each other's bodies up as they made love passionately, sipping the essence of each other, lapping it up hungrily, as if there were no tomorrow.

The record stopped, and the turntable went round and round as they fell into each other's arms. She got up and took the record off and blew out the kerosene lamps. Starlight and the sliver of a moon barely lit the bedroom as she returned. He lay naked on top of the covers. Her eyes adjusted to the light and followed the muscled contours of his body from the flattened dunes of his well-formed chest, across the rippled plane of his abdomen, down to his sex, still wet from their lovemaking and silvered with moonlight. She lay down beside him, drinking in the beauty of his body, the beauty of the night, the beauty of the moment.

He watched her as if she were a dream, walking through the door, lit by dim light, her breasts round and firm; her body was slim and curvaceous, full of promise, full of life and light; her hair, let down, seemed to flow as she walked, the soft light highlighting it with silver. He took in the sweet odor of her body, the muskiness of their two bodies in combination, as she took in the manly odor of his body, its rippled hardness and muscular definition, which contrasted with his tender touch and caresses. They made love into the night until they fell asleep in each other's arms, not waking until the morning sun filled the room with light.

She was the first up, moving his arm from where it lay across her breast and gently slipping out of bed. She took in his nakedness as he lay asleep uncovered on the bed. His sex with its head hidden in its sock end was draped across his thigh, sated, complete. She pulled on her robe and walked into the kitchen, where she lit the kerosene stove, fried fresh link sausage, scrambled four eggs, and brought a pot of grits to a boil. She heard him yawn, looked behind her, and saw him standing in the doorway wearing the same pants and shirt as the night before.

"Smells good," he said, coming up behind her and turning her to face him. He gently lowered his head and kissed her.

They did not talk about the night as they ate in silence at the kitchen table.

"I need to go into town, check my mail, and catch up on the local gossip. I will be back in about an hour," she said after cleaning up.

He put his arm around her waist and pulled her to him. "About last night . . . ," he began.

She pulled away. "I don't know. It happened so fast. I need time to sort things out." Then she quickly left, mounted her horse, and rode into town.

Things had happened fast for him, too, but he did not care. All he knew was that he wanted her and wanted her now. But with her gone, he had another mission—to go to his radio and contact the ship. He did not have much time. He went to the workshop and radioed the boat. All the men from the *U-85* were dead, he reported, killed by the Americans—the barbarians—with some thirty buried in Virginia. He did not know the fate of Oberleutnant Greger. He did not know if the Americans had found the Enigma machines, but he would report as soon as he found out. He needed to infiltrate the naval base in Ocracoke to learn more.

Chapter 5

She returned with fresh flounder caught by a local fisherman.

"Let's have a seafood dinner tonight," Marcia said, storing the flounder in the icebox, which had a block of ice delivered a couple days earlier from the icehouse in Ocracoke.

"That sounds good; I love fish," he said, admiring the fresh catch.

"I mean more than fish. Let's have a real seafood dinner: clams, oysters, shrimp, and fish," she said, smiling.

"That sounds even better, but where do we get the clams, oysters, and shrimp?" he asked.

"Out there," she said, pointing to the tidal creek not far from her house that led to the sound. The creek meandered through a large, grassy wetland that eventually ended in the Pamlico Sound, the second-largest estuary in the United States after the Chesapeake Bay.

"I presume you know how to harvest them," he said, a bit curious.

"I do indeed." She marched into a shed at the rear of the house and got two clam rakes, some pails, and a small hand-held seine net. "This is what we will need," she said. "Oh, yes, and rubber boots to wade through the creek. I suggest you wear a pair of my husband's old pants and a T-shirt."

She went into the house to get dressed. He followed.

"Here. These should do," she said, handing him a pair of old khaki pants and a torn T-shirt. She also gave him a pair of rubber boots that came up to almost his knees.

This was getting interesting, he thought; he had never harvested oysters or clams or netted shrimp.

She came out dressed in loose-fitting long khaki pants, a white T-shirt, and a pale blue blouse halfway buttoned over the T-shirt, the shirttails tied at her belly button. She also wore tall rubber boots. She took a straw hat off a peg in the hall and handed him a worn fishing hat that had belonged to her husband. She handed him a clam rake, two galvanized pails, and the seine net, then took two more galvanized pails and a clam rake for herself. She also picked up two pairs of heavy cotton work gloves in the kitchen.

"It appears you've done this before," he said.

"I think you will enjoy it," she said with a wry grin. She planned to have some fun with him; it was always fun to take someone out in the marsh for the first time.

They walked the short distance to the creek, surrounded on both sides by waist-high marsh grass. It was a tidal creek, and the tide was low, so the black mud along the banks was exposed. She waded out into the cool water with a bucket and reached down into the muck, fishing around for a while with her bare hands until she came up with a clam. She put it in her pail and looked up at him as he stood on the bank watching.

"Come on in. The water is cool but not cold. It's easy."

He cautiously stepped in. His feet sank into the black mud.

"Reach down into the mud until you feel something solid, then bring it up," she instructed, pulling up another healthy-looking clam.

The thought of putting his hands into the black ooze was not very appealing. No telling what he would find—a crab, perhaps, or a piece of glass or a rusted can. "Shouldn't we be wearing gloves?" he asked.

"No, you can't feel anything with gloves; you have to do it with your bare hands."

"What if something else is down there? Other than clams, I mean."

"Oh, there is plenty down there. In fact, they say pirate bones are buried here. You might find one of those, but you can tell the difference; it is easy to tell when you find a clam."

This did not reassure him, but he was not going to be outdone by a girl, particularly an American girl, so he boldly reached his bare hand into the black muck and soon found a good-sized clam. Some shells and a little debris were in the mud, but success bred success. Soon he was pulling up one clam after another. He couldn't believe how easy it was to harvest a meal from this land. Literally, all he had to do was reach out and grab it. What a wonderful thing! He couldn't wait to eat the clams; he loved clams, but he had never eaten them as fresh as these.

They filled two buckets with clams and put them on the creek bank. "This is probably enough clams; we don't need to gather any more than we can eat. They are much fresher if you gather them directly from the creek. No need to save them in buckets for another day."

"How do you prepare them?" he asked.

"I steam them open in a pan of water in the oven, then prepare a garlic-and-butter sauce to sauté them in."

"Sounds delicious," he said, imagining the feast.

"Now let's harvest some oysters," she said. Leaving the clams on the bank in buckets filled with water and grabbing up some more buckets, she walked along the shore of the creek deeper into the salt marsh. The creek wound through the marsh grass, meandering, sometimes deep, sometimes shallow, though there was always a deep channel that a small boat could easily manage. With the tide low, there was a fairly wide shore between the water and the marsh grass. Though it was slow going in some places because the mud was deep, the shore in other places hardened as it became sandier.

"The oyster bed is just around the bend in the creek," she said, working her way slowly through the deep black mud. The sun was directly above them, making it downright hot, but a nice breeze blew from the ocean. The water was cool where it was deep and warm where it was shallow. Their boots made an obscene sucking sound as they pulled them out of the muck, walking slowly through the wet black mud.

Just as she said, the oyster bed was around the corner, its gray clusters visible where the marsh grass met the creek mud. She put on her gloves and began to pull the clumps apart and put them in her pail. He watched how she did it, then put on his gloves and began to gather some clusters of oysters as well.

"The oyster shells will cut you, so be careful. You can tell the ones that are the fattest and juiciest by their size. Try to gather the large ones and leave the small ones to grow bigger," she said, pulling apart a large cluster. After they filled a pail with oysters, they turned back, walking through the deep black mud.

Sanger lost his balance trying to pull his boots out of the mud and fell into the water. She heard him and looked back. She laughed as he lay on his back in the black mud of the creek.

"So you think it is funny, do you?" he fumed, not amused. She put her pail down and walked over to pull him up. When she did, she lost her balance and fell on top of him. He started to laugh.

"Now it is your turn," he grinned, pulling her to him. He kissed her. Unknown to him, she had reached into the water for a handful of mud, which she slowly proceeded to smear all over his face. "What are you doing?" he said in mock dismay.

He could not resist grabbing a handful of mud and smearing it on her. "Just like primitives," he said, wiping it all over her face, making it black.

Her eyes narrowed as they looked through the black mask. She took another handful and smeared it on his face until it was covered in black mud, then proceeded to smear it in his hair as well. He reached into the mud and prepared to smear some in her hair, but she grabbed his hand. "Don't you dare," she said, not amused; it would be much easier for him to clean the mud out of his short hair than for her to get it out of her long hair.

He kissed her and rolled over on top of her. Her head was in the water, and her hair was wet. She began to pound him with her fists. She tried to roll him over, but he was stronger than she. She pulled up one leg and finally rolled him. They kissed for a long time, black mud smeared over their faces. She stood up and began to wash off in the water. He stood beside her. Her wet blouse revealed her nipples, which were erect. His wet pants tented as he stood over her. She grabbed him. "Are you happy to see me?" she asked, squeezing his swelling sex.

He bent down in the water to wash the mud off his face and clothes. He took off his shirt and washed it in the clear water, rubbing it to get the mud out. She removed her blouse, leaving her T-shirt, and rinsed out the mud in the water. She did not wear a bra. He watched her nipples standing erect as her firm breasts moved under the cool, wet T-shirt. Her wet hair was draped across her neck and shoulders in thick, sensual curls. The sunlight danced on her body, accenting the curves of her trim, shapely figure.

They picked up the pails of oysters and put them on the shore.

"Next, we need to catch some shrimp," she said, taking the seine net, folding it carefully, then walking waist deep into the water. She cast the net and let the weights along its edges sink it to the bottom; slowly at first and then more quickly, she pulled the net to her as she walked backward toward the shore. Soon the net came up on the bank, filled with dozens of slippery, jumping little shrimp. She tugged the net together, trapping them inside, and with his help poured the contents into an empty pail. The shrimp seethed and boiled in the deep bucket, trying to escape. She poured some water into it and pulled out the seaweed, grass, and woody debris that had been caught in the net along with the shrimp.

"I think that is about all two people can eat at one sitting, don't you think?" she asked, proud of her catch.

"I agree. What a feast we will have tonight," he said, picking up the pail filled with oysters in one hand and the bucket filled with shrimp in the other. They slowly made their way back through the muck, trying not to lose their balance. Finally they reached the head of the creek and took the buckets of clams, oysters, and shrimp to the back porch of the house, where Marcia proceeded to wash everything down.

"I think I need a shower. Where does one get a shower around here?" Sanger asked.

"Over here," Marcia said, leading him to an open structure with a large wooden bucket on top. "My husband made this just before he died. You pull the string here, and the water comes down through the showerhead. The only problem is that he never enclosed it. He said we didn't need to enclose it out here. No need for privacy, or so he thought, so it is wide open. You can take a shower after I take mine." She headed toward the house for a towel and soap.

"Why don't we save water and shower together?" he asked teasingly, half joking, half serious.

She looked at him, thought for a minute, then said, "Okay."

They walked to the house, got towels and soap, and walked back to the open shower. No one was around. They had already seen each other naked. Why not?

She took her clothes off first. She was a bit shy and held her hands over her breasts and private parts. He then took off his clothes. His body, completely naked in the sunlight, was like a statue of a Greek god. His skin was the color of alabaster, except for his face and hands, which were tanned. The only blemishes on his body were the bruises from his tumble in the sea. His sex began to swell in the sunlight. He modestly covered himself with his hands; though they had already been intimate, it was different under the glaring light of the sun than in the dark secrecy of a bedroom at night. The water was cold as she pulled the chain and let it tumble sensuously over them. His eyes drank in the beauty of her body, so round, so sensuous, so vivid in the sunlight. Her breasts were firm yet plump with their half-dollar-sized nipples, which became erect in the cold water. He kissed her, she pulled his head to her, and they embraced as the cool water ran down their bodies. After they were wet, they soaped up, and then she pulled the chain again to rinse off. They each stole looks at the other, watching the sunlight glisten on each other's body. He touched her breasts and she his chest as they kissed again. They couldn't keep their hands off each other until they left the shower to dry off with the towels.

With fresh clothes on, she washed the seafood again and asked him to help. She put the clams and oysters in a shallow pan in the stove to steam them open. They ate them right out of the shells, sautéed with butter and garlic. Then she dropped the shrimp in a pot of boiling water seasoned with spices and a bottle of beer. When the shrimp turned pink in about three minutes, she took them off the stove, let them drain in a strainer, and ran cold water over them. Then she filleted the flounder and grilled the fillets in a skillet with butter and spices. They ate the flounder with the shrimp and were filled with seafood. After cleaning up the kitchen, she opened two Pabst Blue Ribbon beers in long-necked brown bottles, and they sat on the back porch in rocking chairs, watching the sun set over the marsh.

"What a beautiful day." He sighed and sipped his American beer. "What a beautiful land, so full of plenty. Marcia, you are truly blessed. I hope that you know that," he said, dreamily looking at the big red disc of the sun as it sank into the distant sound behind the marsh.

"It is a beautiful place. Not much to do here, but beautiful nevertheless."

That night they walked out to the beach. The night was clear, the moon was new, and they could see all the stars, including the great Milky Way as it spread across the sky like a blanket of tiny lights thrown to the wind. They walked to the water's edge and saw the bioluminescence in the sand.

"Where will you go?" she asked him.

"When I check in at Ocracoke, I will try to get back to the Royal Navy and will probably be assigned to another ship. I will be in the navy until the end of the war," he said, his arm around her waist.

"Will you write?" she asked.

"When I can. The war makes it difficult."

"Will you ever come back? Or will you go home and never see me again?" she whispered.

"I will return," he promised. One way or another, he wanted to return, if she would have him, once she discovered the truth. No one knew how the war would end, who would win, who would lose. No one knew what the world would look like. But if he could, he would return. He didn't know what it was between them, love or infatuation, but he was completely charmed by Marcia and couldn't get enough of her.

When they returned, they sat on the front porch talking, then went to bed and made love. Afterward, she laid her head on his chest, his arm around her. They were both naked on top of the covers. She ran her fingers through the little clump of hair on his chest, down to his belly button, where she followed the thin line of hair that led to the curly nest above his manhood. She then circled his sex with her fingers; it was soft but plump, still wet from their lovemaking, its flared head hidden inside the foreskin, barely visible.

"I like it this way. Most American men are circumcised."

"It is the European way, the natural way. In Europe the only people who are circumcised are Muslims and Jews." He stopped himself. He didn't want to get political; he may reveal too much about himself.

"I wonder why they do it in America?"

"I don't know. I read it is because of hygiene, but that is a false argument. Maybe the doctors like making the extra money," he said with a cynical laugh. "But this is the way God made man."

"I like it that way," she said, smiling.

He kissed her and touched her breasts; her nipples were erect. Soon they were making love again. Finally they fell asleep in each other's arms, with only a sheet to cover them.

Sound asleep, he opened his eyes and found himself in a submarine control room. It was not his own; it was German, but different. Everyone was pulling on life jackets. The general alarm had been called. He could hear gunfire outside. They must be on the surface. The captain, a handsome young man in his late twenties with dark hair, a beard, a mustache, and beguiling blue eyes, ordered the men to scuttle the ship. He knew this captain; he had met him in France in February. They had been in a bar in Brest, filled with German sailors and French women. He was Oberleutnant Eberhard Greger, the captain of the *U-85*.

There was an explosion just above the control room, at the level of the conning tower; the lights went out, and water began to pour into the boat. The men struggled to get out, falling over each other. He was caught up in the mass of men trying to escape and soon found himself on deck. An American destroyer sat a few hundred yards away firing at the boat; searchlights illuminated the smoke-filled night air. The air was cold; it was mid-April. The sea was calm. The men began to jump into the water as the boat started sinking stern first beneath them. He jumped into the water. It was icy cold. Searchlights scanned the water. The men cried out to be picked up, but nothing happened for a while as the destroyer motored through the sailors in the freezing water. About thirty-five men were in the water. He didn't see Oberleutnant Greger. There would have been about forty-five men on the U-boat, but he could not see the others. Had they escaped in a rubber raft? Were they still on the boat?

The men in the water cried out again for help as the submarine disappeared under the water behind them, and then the destroyer dropped a depth charge where the submarine had gone down. What were they doing? Couldn't they see the submarine had sunk? Why fire depth charges now? The five-hundred-pound depth charge landed near a group of sailors and went off about fifty feet under the water. The men above it died instantly. Then another depth charge was fired, and another and another, each time killing more men. The dead bodies floated face down, wearing life jackets in the water. Then he heard a flash and a charge dropped near him. With the explosion, he woke up.

Marcia lay asleep beside him in the bed as he awoke in a sweat. He must get to Ocracoke and find out what had happened to the code machines. He could not sleep until he discovered the truth. He was beginning to fall in love with Marcia, but they were at war. He had his orders and a job to do. He couldn't let his personal feelings get in the way of his mission. He would sort his feelings out after he had done his job, not before.

Chapter 6

Nick Galantis and Joe Guidos drove up to Marcia's house in a Jeep Monday morning, parking in front near the gate. Marcia was hanging some clothes on the line near the back porch and hailed them. "How are you boys doing? Want some coffee? I just fixed a fresh pot."

"Coffee, now that sounds like a good idea," Nick said, bounding through the gate and up on the porch.

"We are here on official business," Joe said, also stepping onto the porch. "We were sent to bring your British sailor to Ocracoke. He should have had enough time to mend by now."

"I certainly have," Sanger said, walking onto the porch wearing a white T-shirt and tan khakis, holding a cup of hot coffee in his hand.

Marcia finished hanging clothes, walked with Nick and Joe into the kitchen, and poured them each a cup of coffee as they sat at the kitchen table.

"Some more bodies floated onto the beach at Ocracoke Thursday and Friday from the *Bedfordshire*. It looks like Lieutenant Hall is the only survivor. They want to do an investigation and need to talk to him," Joe told Marcia.

"I am happy to tell them what I know, and I would like to find out what happened to the other men. Give me a minute to change clothes," Sanger said.

By the time they finished their coffee, Sanger had changed. Then Sanger, Joe, and Nick piled into the open Jeep and headed to the dock in Portsmouth where the Coast Guard kept its motored flat-bottomed skiffs. It was a thirty-minute trip across Ocracoke Inlet to the mouth of the harbor at Ocracoke. The inlet separated Ocracoke from Portsmouth Island. Ocracoke and Portsmouth were narrow, sandy barrier islands, with the Atlantic Ocean to the east and south and Pamlico Sound to the west. Both Ocracoke and Portsmouth were less than a mile wide. Ocracoke was sixteen miles long and Portsmouth somewhat longer, depending on where Drum Inlet to the south was located at the time, which depended on the last storm.

At the southern end of Ocracoke Island was Ocracoke village, first settled in the early 1700s by pilots who guided ships through Ocracoke Inlet, at that time the only inlet on the Outer Banks open to shipping. One of its most notorious early residents was the pirate Blackbeard, or Edward Teach, who was killed and beheaded on November 22, 1718, after a battle in Ocracoke Inlet with Lieutenant Robert Maynard, sent by Governor Alexander Spotswood of Virginia to put an end to piracy in the region. According to legend, a month before he was killed, Blackbeard convened the largest "pirate festival" ever held on the mainland of North America. Other pirates in attendance were Captain Charles Vane, Israel Hands, Robert Deal, and Calico Jack Rackham, along with their crews. Much rum was consumed and many pigs and sheep barbecued on the beach in what some authors have called "a huge orgy." Reports of this gathering led Spotswood to send Maynard to kill Blackbeard.

Blackbeard left part of his crew off the coast at Beaufort when he scuttled the *Queen Anne's Revenge.* He then took a smaller crew with him aboard the *Adventure* and sailed for Ocracoke, so he did not have a large crew at the festival. After the other pirate crews attending the "orgy" left, Blackbeard was lightly defended. When Maynard arrived at Teach's Hole off Springer's Point, he told the majority of his men to hide below decks and left only a few topside. Blackbeard, seeing a lightly defended ship, boarded Maynard's vessel. When he did, the remainder of Maynard's crew burst from below and engaged the pirates in hand-to-hand combat. After a fierce battle, a British seaman said to be a Scottish Highlander killed

Blackbeard with a single blow to the neck with his long sword, almost severing his head. Maynard examined the body and reported later that Blackbeard had been shot five times and sustained twenty severe knife or sword wounds in various parts of his body. Maynard cut Blackbeard's head off and threw the body overboard, where legend says it swam three times around the boat. His head was taken to Virginia on the bowsprit of Maynard's ship as proof of his death. The head sat on a pole at the entrance to Hampton Roads for many years as a warning to other pirates, and then it disappeared. Later a silver-covered drinking cup made from a human skull showed up at the Raleigh Tavern in Williamsburg; it was reputed to be made from the skull of Blackbeard.

Blackbeard's surviving crewmen were taken to Williamsburg and tried for piracy; most of them were hanged, except his young quartermaster, William Howard, who was saved just before he was to be executed by the king's pardon. In 1759, a William Howard purchased the island of Ocracoke for 105 pounds sterling from Richard Sanderson and made the island his home. Legend in the Howard family has it that this was the same William Howard who was Blackbeard's quartermaster. Blackbeard's fortune, never found, was supposedly buried on Ocracoke.

After those heady days, the village was settled by several families of English and Irish descent: Howards, O'Neals, Garrishes, Styrons, Williamses, Ballances, and others who made their living by the sea and as pilots for the shipping that passed through Ocracoke Inlet, which had been in existence for more than a thousand years. This was quite a feat on the Outer Banks, where inlets open, close, and move on a regular basis.

At the back of the island facing Pamlico Sound was a narrow opening the locals called "the ditch." The ditch opened up into a well-protected small harbor. The locals called the harbor "the creek" because it used to be a tidal creek named Cockle Creek, used as a harbor for fishing boats. In the 1930s and 1940s, local tourism promoters started to call it Silver Lake. Originally the creek was not very deep, but it was dredged in 1933 and again in 1939. When the navy started to build a section base in Ocracoke, it was dredged again in the spring of 1942 to accommodate larger boats. This created a nice full-moon-shaped harbor. The dredge material was used to build up the opposite side of the creek to complete the circle of the small harbor and to fill in some "guts" at the head of the creek, which led almost out to the ocean, dividing the island into two communities, the Creeksiders and the Downpointers. To the immediate left of the ditch were the 1904 former Lifeboat Station and the 1940 Coast Guard Station. Near the Lifeboat Station were the Coast Guard docks and the new docks built for the United States Navy Section Base. During the war, the Coast Guard was put under the control of—and the Coast Guard property at Ocracoke was taken over by—the navy.

In the early months of 1942, sailboats and requisitioned yachts were tied up at the Ocracoke docks. Called "the Hooligan Fleet," this motley assemblage of requisitioned private boats was used to search for submarines. No one knew what they would do if any of these boats actually encountered a submarine, since they were equipped with only rifles and pistols, but they were used anyway. The navy started construction on the new section base in the spring of 1942. It built a big water tower, a two-story wooden administrative building, eighteen one-story wooden barracks designed to hold a total of six hundred men, a large machine shop, and various outbuildings. On the other end of the harbor was Ocracoke village, a traditional North Carolina fishing community of about six hundred souls, and the docks associated with the village, where fishing boats of all sizes were moored. When the navy moved in, the village doubled in size overnight.

Electricity came to Ocracoke in 1936, when Stanley Wahab installed a diesel generator station and ice plant. The island had no telephones; the Coast Guard could radio the mainland in case of emergency.

The roads in the village were not paved. The navy had begun work on a three-mile-long, nine-foot-wide concrete road that led to an ammunition dump behind the village, but it would not be finished until late 1942. An unpaved road led from the village to the beach and the radio and radar tower complex called "the Loop Shack," operated by the navy. At the Loop Shack were radar, listening equipment controlled from shore, and radio high-frequency direction-finding gear connected to a cable that was laid offshore. The locator equipment was supposed to help pinpoint the location of German U-boats, but it was all top secret.

The village was built within an ancient maritime forest filled with live oaks, many of which were one to two hundred years old or more, and ancient cedars, which were twisted by the wind to look like giant bonsai trees. At the center of the town on the north shore of Silver Lake were the Community Store owned by Amasa Fulcher, a few other general stores, the post office, and the dock where the *Aleta* moored. The *Aleta* brought visitors, mail, and supplies daily from the Atlantic on the mainland above Morehead City. Most houses had picket fences to keep the ponies out of their gardens. Many people had cows and chickens. Water was gathered in cisterns that collected rain from the roofs of houses. Ponies wandered the island freely and were only corralled once a year, when the new foals are branded by their owners at a big roundup on the Fourth of July. The Ocracoke ponies were supposed to be the descendants of Spanish horses washed up on shore from shipwrecks.

The large, open sand flat between the village and the beach was filled with the nests of birds. A few large natural dunes stood near the beach, but it was mostly flat and sandy.

Nick and Joe approached the docks at Ocracoke in their seventeen-foot flat-bottomed motored skiff. A sailor met them at the end of the dock and helped them tie up, after which they walked to the Coast Guard Station a few hundred feet from the dock. The new Navy Section Base was being built nearby.

They reported to Aycock Brown, a civilian special agent for the Office of Naval Intelligence. He was in charge of filing reports on the wrecks, identifying the dead, and taking care of their burial. Brown had close-cropped brown hair and wore civilian clothes; he looked something like a private detective.

"What is your name?" Brown asked, once Sanger and Joe and Nick sat in front of him at a metal table.

"Sublieutenant Bruce Hall, sir, I was on watch the night the German submarine sank the *Bedfordshire*, sir. It was Monday night, May 11, at about 11:40 P.M. One torpedo struck us amidships. I was blown free of the ship. Not able to find anyone else alive, I climbed into a lifeboat I found floating in the water. The others died in the water. Their bodies washed up on the beach at Portsmouth with me."

"We buried two men from the *Bedfordshire* on Ocracoke Saturday, Lieutenant Thomas Cunningham and Telegraphist Stanley R. Craig. That is why I came here from Morehead City. The bodies washed up on the beach at Ocracoke Thursday. Anything you want to tell me about the final hours of the *Bedfordshire*, sir?" Brown asked.

"Cunningham and Craig were also on the bridge with us. It was near midnight; the moon was new. It was overcast, but visibility was good. The sea was calm, but the submarine caught us unaware.

After the torpedo hit, the ship sank before anyone had a chance to escape. The submarine cruised through the wreckage. I was afraid they would shoot survivors, so I hid behind a lifeboat that I later was able to climb into. The water was cold. After drifting for two days, the lifeboat washed up on the beach of Portsmouth Island, where the waves capsized it and threw me into the water. I vaguely remember a beautiful woman helping me out of the water. She has taken care of me ever since. Her name is Marcia Styron. She is an angel," he said, looking at Nick and Joe. "Isn't that right, boys?"

"Yes, sir, she is an angel. She also makes some mighty fine chess pie," Nick said with a big smile.

"Marcia tended to me for the past few days until I was sufficiently mended to be able to come to you. I bruised my ribs pretty badly during my tumble in the waves from the lifeboat."

"The *Bedfordshire* was here to help us sink submarines, and a U-boat sunk her," Brown said. "A dangerous business we are in these days. You Brits use convoys to avoid these attacks, but the big brass refuses them. We have lost hundreds of tons of shipping. I hope the brass in Washington soon sees fit to change their ways."

Sanger was well aware of this. The German submarines did not have as much luck in British waters because shipping convoyed very effectively with destroyer escorts, but the Americans acted as if there were no war, shipping as usual. The official German name for it was Operation Drumbeat, but unofficially they called it "the North Atlantic turkey shoot." It was so easy to pick off American shipping.

Brown considered the rescued sailor. "I met Lieutenant Cunningham of the *Bedfordshire* in Morehead City on May 9, two days before you were sunk. After the British tanker *San Delfino* was torpedoed off Cape Hatteras on April 9, 1942, I had the job of identifying four bodies recovered in the surf. Since I knew the *Bedfordshire* was in port in Morehead City, I decided to visit the ship and ask for British flags and a burial party for the men. I flew to Morehead on a navy amphibious plane. When I found the *Bedfordshire* tied up at the navy dock, I noticed men carrying large wicker baskets of coal on board. I asked for the officer on deck and was told it was Lieutenant Thomas Cunningham. Cunningham was a slightly built man with a dark, distinctive beard. After I showed him my identification papers, I explained the need for British flags and a burial party.

"Lieutenant Cunningham told me he didn't have the men to spare for a burial party, but he did give me some British flags and offered me some rum. I accepted, being familiar with the British naval tradition with rum, and then Cunningham brought out a large wicker-covered demijohn and poured two drinks. As you know, each man in the British navy is given a daily ration of rum. We talked, and Cunningham told me that he and his wife, Barbara, were expecting a baby in October, as was the captain of the boat, R. B. Davis, and his wife. After a friendly conversation and a few more drinks, Cunningham noticed the demijohn was empty and offered the empty jug as a souvenir.

"When I was about to leave, Cunningham gave me six British flags—two more than I needed. We then shook hands and parted company. Little did I know that I would be using one of the very flags he gave me to bury him in Ocracoke four days later," Brown said, looking out the window over Pamlico Sound.

"I must not have been on the ship at that time. I do not remember seeing you, sir," Sanger said.

"The *Bedfordshire* was at the wreck of the *U-85*," Brown continued. It was obvious that he liked to talk, that he was a better storyteller than investigator. Sanger was all ears. He nodded in agreement, though he did not know this latest information. "That was an ugly scene, when all those men who survived the sinking were killed in the water. But the *U-85* was the first German U-boat sunk in United States waters. Seems like they could have made better use of those men alive than dead. I know I would have liked a crack at them. We might have found out a lot of good information from those men. But anyway, the navy and the USS *Roper* saw fit to kill them in the water.

"As you know, divers from Washington boarded the *Bedfordshire* twenty-four hours after the *U-85* sank on April 14, at the marker left by the USS *Roper*. The first diver couldn't find anything in the murky water. The next day a diver found the U-boat, though visibility was poor, so no more dives were made during the next five days, due to bad weather. After that, the *Bedfordshire* returned to duty on April 20, leaving the area. But I am not telling you anything that you don't know, isn't that right, Lieutenant Hall?" Brown said, looking for his reaction.

Sanger nodded in agreement. He did not know that the *Bedfordshire* had sent divers to explore the *U-85*. This was useful information. He needed to know more. "What happened after we left, sir? We were at sea and did not hear."

"On April 22, the USS *Kewaydin* resumed diving operations on the boat," Brown continued. "The first diver found an unexploded depth charge and suspended diving until it could be exploded. Seven more dives were made from the *Kewaydin,* then the diving and salvage vessel USS *Falcon* arrived Wednesday, April 29. Submarine veteran Bert Miller made the first dive to the *U-85* at noon on April 30. Using a Mark V deep-sea rig, he saw the wild boar's head with a rose in its mouth painted on the conning tower, which identified it as the *U-85.*"

Sanger knew that symbol well. The *U-85* had left Saint-Nazaire in occupied France on March 21, bound for the United States' Eastern Seaboard, not to return. The boar emblem came from the name of the captain, Eber Greger, *eber* meaning *boar* in German. The rose came from Greger's hometown of Lieberose, which had sponsored the boat, *lieberose* meaning *love rose.* Lothar-Guenther Buchheim, a marine painter in the summer of 1941, painted it on the conning tower. Each submarine commander had an emblem on his boat. The *Sie Wascht, Holzauge* or *Watch Out, Wooden Eye,* after a character in an old German folktale, was painted on the conning tower of the *U-558.* One commander had a red devil painted on his conning tower; each U-boat emblem was different.

"Miller found very little damage," Brown continued. "He entered the conning tower and found the control room hatch closed but not dogged. When he opened the hatch, American occupation money floated up out of the flooded compartment. During the next five days, seventy-eight dives were made to the *U-85.* Gauges, instruments, the 20-millimeter antiaircraft gun on the bridge, and gun sights from the 88-millimeter deck gun were removed. They attempted to remove the aft torpedo storage container and torpedo but were unsuccessful. They tried to blow air into the diving and ballast tanks so they could raise her, but piping was damaged from the depth charges, so it failed. On May 4, the commanding officer aboard the *Falcon* ended the diving operation, marking the site with a red buoy tied to the conning tower."

"What about the German code machines? Did the divers find them?" Sanger asked—the critical question of his mission.

"No, they were not recovered," Brown said.

"Are there plans to raise the boat?"

"Not to my knowledge."

Sanger knew that the *U-85* was outfitted with two updated versions of the Enigma machine with four rotors. If they had gotten into the hands of the Allies, it could be disastrous for the Kriegsmarine and U-boat warfare everywhere. The Americans refused to convoy, and then they stopped diving the *U-85* before finding the

Enigma machines. They were either stupid or thick headed, Sanger thought. Either way, this enemy would be an easy one to defeat.

The Germans had been afraid of the Americans during the Great War—so much so that the generals advised the kaiser that they could not win if the Americans entered, even though the Germans still had one million men in the field. The kaiser signed the armistice, and Germany was humiliated; he gave up too soon. Now they would not make that mistake again. They would fight until they achieved victory or until the last German soldier was standing.

"I doubt that you have heard about the other submarine sinking. It happened just after the *Bedfordshire* left Morehead City. On May 9 at 1714, a Coast Guard cutter, the *Icarus*, sank the *U-352* off Cape Lookout. After a chase and several depth charges, the U-boat surfaced and its men began to abandon ship. Thirty-three men jumped into the water and were picked up by the cutter. Twelve men went down with the boat. The commander of the boat is Kapitän-leutnant Helmut Rathke. The prisoners were taken to Charleston but were later transferred to Fort Bragg at Fayetteville for questioning. I don't think they have been interrogated yet. This is top secret and has not been in the newspapers, but I figured after your experience you would want to know."

"I did not know, sir. Thank you for that intelligence. Are there plans to recover the boat? Were any of the secret codes recovered?"

"There are plans to dive the boat. I don't know if any dives have occurred yet; it was in deeper water than the *U-85* and appeared to be heavily damaged when it was scuttled by its crew. I have not heard whether any codes were recovered."

"Thank you, sir. I am glad we are making some headway against the Germans in American waters."

"We will summon you when we have contacted the British authorities and they tell us where you need to report. Until then you may go back to Portsmouth Island into the care of Mrs. Marcia Styron," Brown said with a smile. "Does that suit you, Lieutenant Hall?"

"Yes, sir, it does," Sanger said, smiling broadly.

As they left the building, Joe turned to Nick and said, "Before we go back to Portsmouth, let's stop for a beer. I know a local joint that has ice-cold beer by the bottle."

Nick, Joe, and Sanger agreed that this would be a good idea. Perhaps Sanger could pick up more information at the bar. Bars were always good sources of information, as enlisted men loosen their lips after a few drinks.

They headed to a local gathering spot and dance hall called the Spanish Casino, owned by Stanley Wahab and located near the Wahab Village Hotel on the other side of Silver Lake on the way to the beach. The island had gotten electricity only when it got an ice plant. Many island homes still did not have power, but any establishment that served the navy did. The Spanish Casino even had refrigerated boxes in which to cool bottled beer. The island was dry, but Wahab knew the needs of navy men and worked it out to get alcohol for his establishment, which even had a Wurlitzer jukebox and a dance floor.

They walked about a half mile from the base to the Spanish Casino, following sandy lanes shaded by live oak trees. Everything in Ocracoke was within walking distance, though you may want to take a Jeep out to the beach. People were generally not allowed on the beach at night during 1942. The navy patrolled it on horses.

The Spanish Casino was filled with cigarette smoke and servicemen. Popular Big Band music wafted from the jukebox. Nick and Joe walked up to the bar and ordered three Pabst Blue Ribbons. They each took one and handed one to Sanger. He took a swig of the beer, which tasted watery compared to the full-bodied German beer he was used to. The Americans may make good cigarettes and good music, but their beer was nothing compared to German beer.

"Where you fellers from?" asked a rather inebriated older man wearing a fisherman's hat. Sanger thought he had a curious accent, almost as if it were an older version of English, from Shakespeare's time.

"My name's Nick, and this is my friend Joe; we are stationed at the Coast Guard Station on Portsmouth Island. We're both from Philadelphia. This here is Bruce Hall. He's a British sailor who survived the sinking of the *Bedfordshire*."

"No shit," the man said in a heavy brogue native to Ocracoke. "Well, I'm from right here on Ocracoke. My family's been here for as long as anyone can remember, some say even back to the time of Blackbeard. My name is Wallie O'Neal. I'm a fisherman."

"Good to meet you, Mr. O'Neal," Nick said, shaking his hand. Nick and Joe had met the local people and were familiar with their unique accent. The Outer Bankers had been isolated for so long from the rest of the world that they still spoke with a brogue similar to that of their ancestors in the eighteenth century.

"The *Bedfordshire*, eh? I was there when they brought the bodies of those poor fellers to the Coast Guard Station Thursday. Arnold

Styron and Oakie, driving a truck on the beach, found the first one in the surf. Thought he was alive, thought they saw the feller waving his hands in the water. But they knew right away it must have been a dead man; the water was too cold for swimming. They dragged the fully clothed body into the back of the truck and covered it with canvas. Then Elwood Austin flagged 'em down on the beach and said he had been fishing at South Point with his wife and saw another body in the surf. Oakie and Styron drove out there, and sure enough they found another body floating face down in the waves. They loaded it up with the other one and took it to the Coast Guard Station. They put the bodies in the old kitchen in back of the station, covered 'em with a tarpaulin, and called navy headquarters. Aycock Brown flew in here in an amphibious aircraft from Morehead City to identify the bodies. They identified the first body as Lieutenant Thomas Cunningham and the other one from his papers as Stanly Craig, one of the ship's telegraph operators. Cunningham had a checkbook on him for an account in Morehead City. They didn't have no coffins, so they had to use two sink boxes used by duck hunters to hunt in the sound. Amasa Fulcher, lay reader from the Methodist church, conducted the service because there wasn't no preacher on the island. The Williams family donated the grave plots. It is the talk of the town." He took a drink of beer. "Lots of ships being sunk—lots of men dying. Some nights the sky is all lit up with fires from the sea. They won't let us fish in the ocean anymore; they mined the waters off Ocracoke, so we fish in the sound. The water in the sound is too shallow for submarines." He took a swig of his beer, then continued.

"The freighter *Caribsea* was sunk off Ocracoke on March 11; its crew were tossed about in life rafts all day until they was rescued by a passing steamship, the *Norlindo*, bound for Baltimore. Twenty-one members of the crew were lost, one of whom was James Baum Gaskill of Ocracoke. Some days later the ship's nameplate washed ashore near the Pamlico Inn, which was run by his parents, Bill and Annie Gaskill. The piece of wood with the nameplate was made into a cross, which is at the Methodist church, put there by his family."

"Did you hear about the German U-boat that was sunk off Nags Head in April?" Sanger asked.

"Yep, I heard they ran the submarine into shallow water, then they blasted it, put a hole in it, and the men started piling out, jumping in the sea with their life vests on. They yelled at the captain to save them, but he killed them all instead." He took a drink of his beer, shaking his head. "That ain't right. You don't kill unarmed men in life vests in the water asking to be rescued, even if they was Germans.

"I heard they marked the boat with a buoy," Wallie O'Neal continued, "but they couldn't raise it, so they left it alone." O'Neal worked again on his beer. "If you want to know what I think, I think it is about time the brass in Washington took this thing seriously. I don't know how many of our merchant marine ships has been sunk, but judging from what I've seen around here, it must be a lot. We need convoys and destroyer escorts like you Brits are using. We've been in the war since December, and we still don't have any protection. Back in 1918 when the German subs patrolled these waters, we had blackouts. They say we are supposed to have blackouts now, but no one enforces it. It's a joke. If I didn't know better, I'd say no one was in charge."

Nick and Joe didn't like the tone the conversation was taking, especially in front of a visitor. Nick turned to speak to two other men at the bar, Ted Mutro from Pennsylvania and his friend Mac Womac.

After introducing himself, Mutro began to tell the story of how he came to Ocracoke. "Me and Mac was sent out here on January 5, 1942, riding on an International Harvester truck on the beach from Hatteras. When we got to the village, I asked where the heart of the town was, and the driver told me, 'You're in it.' We was at the Community Store. I thought we had come to the last stop in civilization, and we was told we were going to be stationed at some sort of resort. I thought after that the only thing we would be fighting would be boredom and mosquitoes. But then the *Empire Gem*, the largest oil tanker in the world, was sunk off Hatteras on January 23. We was sent out to try to save those poor men. Fifty-five in all died. It was a horrible sight, all those men jumping in the fire as the oil burned on the water. Only two survived, the captain and his radio operator. After that I knew we was in for a ride.

"One ship after another was sunk, and we was sent out to try to save the crews," he continued. "We patrol the beach by night, looking for German spies." He took a long swig of his beer. "But let me tell you something. Don't ever take your shoes off in Ocracoke, and don't try the oysters. That is what caught me hook, line, and sinker. I met this girl, Ollie, who started taking me home to her Momma. We'd eat steamed oysters, shrimp, fish just caught, steamed and fried right there in the front yard of her house. I never ate seafood in my life until I come here. She also took me out on the beach and taught me how to surf fish. I was hooked. I tell you, I went from thinking this was the last place on earth I wanted to be to thinking it is an earthly paradise."

Sanger could relate to his story of island life, seafood, and island girls.

"Me and Ollie got hitched by Preacher Dixon. He told Ollie, 'You better catch him while you can,' so we went to the church and he married us, me holding my shoes in my hands and with a tie around my neck."

Joe and Nick looked at their watches; they'd be there all night if they didn't watch it. "Let's drink up so we can get back to Portsmouth before it gets dark," Nick said, taking a big swig of beer.

"Nice talking to you, Mr. O'Neal, Mr. Mutro," Joe said, finishing his beer and beginning to walk toward the door.

"I'm telling you, the top brass is asleep at the switch. No one is looking out after us little guys, or the merchant marine. It's a piece of cake for them Germans; it's too easy to sink our ships. No one's even trying to protect 'em," O'Neal said, ordering another beer at the bar.

Sanger knew what he said was true. The American merchant marine had virtually no protection. They had passed Long Island on one of their cruises and could see people on the beach and hear music wafting across the water from music halls. It was like the Americans didn't realize they were at war. Sanger agreed with Wallie O'Neal—the Americans were asleep at the switch while the Germans sank hundreds of tons of shipping every week.

Admiral Karl Dönitz, head of the German U-boat command, had initiated Operation Drumbeat, or Beat of the Kettle Drums, by sending five U-boats to American waters in January 1942. He wanted to send twelve, but Hitler vetoed it, wanting to focus his efforts on the Mediterranean. Between January 12 and 31, forty ships were sunk. In February, fifty ships were lost; in March, seventy-four ships; in April, sixty-one. While Hitler had his eye on the Mediterranean, Dönitz maintained the American coast was the place to be. The pickings were easy and the resistance nonexistent.

Nick, Joe, and Sanger boarded the boat for Portsmouth late that afternoon.

Chapter 7

That night Marcia prepared a special dinner for Sanger—grilled fresh-caught drum, baked potatoes, and green beans with a salad of greens from her garden. She lit candles on the breakfast room table.

"What is the occasion?" Sanger asked as she busily made preparations for the meal.

"You are the occasion," she said with a coy smile.

He was touched. They sat down and ate quietly. He knew that he did not have much more time on the island. He had found out most of what he came for. It would soon be time for him to leave.

"What do you plan to do after the war?" she asked after they began to eat.

"I don't know. I haven't gotten that far. My father is an English professor at the university. I studied math in school. Perhaps I could teach math in a high school or college. Or with what I know about the sea, I could work on a merchant ship. I love the sea, but I'm not sure I want to make it my life. I want to settle down and have a family, and working at sea would take me away from my family for long stretches of time. I really haven't given it a lot of thought; the war has so totally taken control of my life," he said honestly.

"I would like to find someone to raise a family with. I love the coast and the sea, but I would go inland if I had to, if I found the right man," she said, taking a piece of fish off the tines of her fork.

"I want to raise a family, too. I want to have five boys."

"No girls?" she asked.

"No, I have one sister. Girls are trouble. Never satisfied, always wanting more," he said teasingly, to get a reaction from her.

"I resent that. How do you plan to live with your wife if women are 'too much trouble'?" she asked.

"I will be the man of the house, and my wife will be obedient to my will, of course," he said somewhat tongue in cheek, but also seriously.

"And daughters are different?"

"Oh, yes, daughters must be spoiled and doted on," he said with a smile. "Boys should be sent to the military, where they will learn discipline and become men."

"I am not so sure I like your world. It's much too rigid and authoritarian for me," she replied teasingly, but serious, too.

"You Americans are much too lax and permissive. I have read about you and your child rearing. Not enough discipline."

"It is our way, and we like it. We love to dote on our children, spoil them, and give them what they want, if we can afford it," she said, playing to the stereotype to goad him.

"See, just as I thought. That is why you are soft and we are strong," he said, sounding more like a German officer than a British sailor.

"Are you sure you are not German?" she asked, teasing.

"Oh, no. I am very British. But we have a military tradition in our family that goes way back," Sanger said, catching himself.

"So that explains it," she said. Marcia didn't like what she heard him saying, but she loved watching him say it. He was so sexy and handsome. The more he spoke, the sexier he became. She could have fun bringing him around to her way.

He had similar thoughts; she was sexy as she spoke as well. She was so beautiful in the dim light of the candles. He could have fun taming her, becoming her master and she his mistress.

They made love again that night. Afterward he could not sleep. The wind billowed the curtains as the light from the waxing moon lit the room. He looked at Marcia as she slept. He wished he could stay with this beautiful woman, but he had work to do—he had a war to fight and information to find. Maybe, just maybe, they could come together after the war, but that seemed like a distant dream to him. He touched her forehead and brushed a tendril of hair out of the way, then kissed her on the forehead. He was naked in the bed, so he got up and put on some shorts. He wanted to smoke a cigarette. He settled into a rocker on the front porch and looked at the sky and the moon as he rocked in his boxer shorts. A gentle breeze blew toward the house from the beach. The sky on Portsmouth was almost as beautiful as the sky in the mid-Atlantic on a clear night. You could see all of the stars and the Milky Way. It was a beautifully clear night with only a waxing moon to cloud the view of the stars. There was no electricity on Portsmouth, no streetlights, not even lights from cars to disturb the clear, dark sky.

Service in the Ubootwaffe was dangerous. None of the men knew when they would return; many of his friends had been lost. But it was different from other branches of the service. The men were close; they shared close quarters on the boats, officers and enlisted men alike. It was almost impossible to keep up the formality of command. They dressed, slept, and bathed in front of each other, using large pans of cold salt water. No crew member even had his own bed, as two men shared the same one, sleeping in different shifts. The only thing they had that was private was their locker, and that was tiny. Two heads, or bathrooms, were on the boat, which held about forty men; one of them was packed with supplies. Each man had to sign in to use the head.

They ate better than most other servicemen—sausages, preserved meats, potatoes, canned fruit and vegetables—and they also had a good supply of schnapps, but pickings were lean. For entertainment some of the men would dress up like women, play music, and dance with each other. One time he came upon two men having sex in a bunk. This behavior was strictly forbidden, but it happened a lot more on naval ships and submarines than was commonly acknowledged. Young men, full of sexual vigor and desire, separated from women for months at a time, developed close bonds with the other crewmen, living in close quarters, not knowing what the next day would bring. Sanger did not condone it, but he also could not condemn it. He had told the captain about what he had seen. The captain had told him to forget it.

"What happens on the boat stays on the boat, unless it is insubordination. What the men do in private does not concern me. If they didn't find some sort of relief, they would go stark raving mad."

When in port, one shift stayed on board while two shifts were allowed to go into town. The enlisted men tried to avoid the fancy restaurants and bars where the officers headed because they didn't want to have to salute and feel like their superiors were watching them. They found their share of bars, places to eat, and bawdyhouses with ladies of the night. When on leave in France, they partied like there was no tomorrow, drinking, womanizing, staying up all hours. They didn't know if their next cruise would be their last. Morale had gotten low toward the end of 1941 as more U-boats were sunk by the British, who seemed to know where they were going before they even got there. That is why the Germans suspected the British had broken their code, and why they developed the new four-wheel code machine. But then the Americans entered the war and everyone wanted to go to the East Coast of the United States, where they could sink a huge amount of tonnage and not encounter hard-fought battles like those around Great Britain and in the Mediterranean.

Sanger was proud of his German heritage and thought that Germany and the German people had been humiliated after the Great War and deserved to retake their rightful place among nations and in history. He, like many others, thought the kaiser had capitulated too soon and was too quick to accept the humiliating terms of the Treaty of Versailles. They all cheered when Hitler overran France and made the French surrender in the very railroad car where the Germans had signed the armistice in 1918. Hitler was a great strategist, uniting the German peoples of Europe and defeating France, but Sanger's father did not like Hitler or his advisers. He did not speak of it, but Sanger knew it by the way his father commented on newspaper articles and how he refused to salute the Nazis. He found similar sentiment in the Ubootwaffe. The men fought to defend their beloved Germany, not to defend the Nazis. Neither Sanger nor his close friends had joined the Nazi Party. Admiral Dönitz did everything he could to bring resources and special treatment for his beloved men in the Ubootwaffe, but he, too, did not join the Nazi Party. His command center was in France, not in Berlin, so he was removed somewhat from the goings on within the inner circle around Hitler. It meant he had to work harder to get the ear and support of Central Command, but it also meant he was closer to his men, the boats, and their commanders and knew their needs intimately.

Everyone in the service was devoted to Dönitz because they knew how devoted he was to them. There was no German navy beyond the U-boats, as far as Dönitz was concerned. Hitler wanted a big surface navy, but it never materialized, not with British superiority at sea. What the U-boats could do was destroy the merchant shipping upon which Britain depended for supplies. If Dönitz could get enough U-boats in the water, he could strangle Britain, and if Britain capitulated, it wouldn't matter if the Americans were in the war or not. They would have no place to go and would leave Hitler alone; that would leave only the Russians to be dealt with.

"Penny for your thoughts?" Marcia said, coming up behind Sanger as he rocked on the front porch. "Can't sleep? Is something bothering you? Did I get too personal tonight, asking what you would do after the war?" She sat beside him on a rocking chair.

"No, I am thinking about the war and about how I need to get back to it. It has been wonderful being here with you, Marcia, very safe and comfortable, but my friends and compatriots are being killed and wounded. I need to get back to them and see this war through to its conclusion. It is not right for me to have so much peace and freedom with you when I have a job to do."

"I don't think I will ever be able to understand the mind of a man. Why can't you just stay here with me and forget the war? But you can't do that, can you? I want to have you for as long as I possibly can. When you leave, I don't know if I will ever see you again, and that is unbearable."

"A man has to do what a man has to do, and when there is a war on and a job to do, we must do it. When it is over, I can come back, go home, start a family. Then it will be time for peace, but not now." He looked at her and reached over to touch her hair. "You are very beautiful, Marcia. If I don't return, you will make someone very happy someday."

"Don't talk like that. You will return; I feel it in my bones. Someday you will return, and we will live together. It has to be. There can be no other way."

"I hope you're right, Marcia."

The next morning Sanger got up early and decided to run on the beach. On the boat he was able to lift dumbbells and do push-ups, chin-ups, and isometric exercises. The crewmen also were allowed to sunbathe on deck for short periods and to swim when possible. But he never got the chance to run or really work out when he was on the boat; it was simply too small and crowded. He loved to run. He was very athletic and was an excellent soccer player, helping win the pennant for his school when at the university.

The morning was bright and sunny with clouds on the horizon. The water was calm; the waves rolled in, making perfect curls. The water was so clear he could see through it like green glass. He wore a pair of George's shorts and one of his white T-shirts. There wasn't a soul on the beach. He ran for a mile, then stopped and sat on the sand alone. He looked at the waves; they were so tempting, the water so clear. He stripped off his clothes and ran into the water naked, feeling the cool, refreshing water wash over him. He dove in the waves and swam for a while, then came out and let himself dry in the wind on the beach. He ran naked on the beach to dry off, just because he could. Then he put the T-shirt and shorts on and ran back to Marcia's house. What a glorious day, what a glorious place this Portsmouth was. He hated to return to the dark, close quarters of the submarine with its foul odors, canned food, and preserved meats.

Back at the house, he found Marcia fixing breakfast in the kitchen.

"I couldn't resist. I wanted to run on the beach. I so rarely get to do that, being on a boat," he said, taking a cup of coffee that she offered.

"I like to walk and run on the beach, too. I also like to take an early-morning swim. I don't swim at night. They say that is when the sharks feed," Marcia said. She fried some eggs and bacon, which Sanger ate heartily. "I need to go into town for some provisions and to hear the local gossip. Do you want to come with me?"

"No, if you don't mind, I think I will stay here and take a shower. I need one after that run."

When Marcia left, Sanger dug out his radio and reported to the submarine. "The Americans dove the *U-85*, but they did not recover the Enigma machines. They tried to raise the U-boat, but it was too heavily damaged. They have no plans to return to the boat and dive it, as far as I can determine. They are too dense to see how important it is. They also told me about the sinking of the *U-352*. The boat surfaced, and thirty-three men escaped; twelve were lost. All thirty-three were taken prisoner. It sank within minutes of surfacing. I don't know the condition of the boat; it sounded like it was damaged when it was scuttled. They have not tried to dive it or raise it yet."

The U-boat radioed back to him. "Stay until you find out more about the crew of the *U-352* and whether the Americans are going to dive it or not. We believe it went down in shallow water."

He hated that another U-boat had been lost, but it would give him more time with Marcia, a comfortable bed, good food, sunshine, and clean air. He decided he liked this spy business.

Marcia returned in an hour, and Sanger helped her unload the horse and her provisions.

Chapter 8

"People in town have heard about you now and want to meet you. I don't think I can keep them away any longer," she said. She wanted to keep him all to herself. She didn't want him to leave. She wanted him to stay for as long as he could, forever, for that matter. But she knew better. She hoped the boys from the Coast Guard Station would at least keep their hands off him for a while. He was her gift from the sea. She needed to enjoy him for as long as she could. That was the best she could do; the rest was in the hands of God.

She brought back some fresh flounder and cornmeal in which to fry it, new potatoes, and cabbage to make slaw.

"Let's take the horses on the beach," he said after they ate a light lunch of sandwiches.

They rode out on the beach in the full sunlight. Marcia generally tried to avoid the midday sun, but you know what they say about Englishmen and mad dogs. He wanted to be in the sun, and it was the worst time of day, but he was very active. Maybe they wouldn't get too burned. They rode down the beach for about a mile, and then he got off the horse.

"Let's go for a swim," he said. The water was so clear they could see through the waves. The ocean was calm, the waves rolling in in perfect formation, just as they had that morning. The sun was bright, and there wasn't a cloud in the sky.

"I didn't bring my bathing suit," she said coyly, knowing what he had in mind.

"Who needs a bathing suit?" he said, stepping out of his shorts and pulling his T-shirt off. He stood in his boxers, which clung to his body with the stiff breeze. She could clearly see the outline of his manhood. She watched it quicken under her gaze.

She slowly got off her horse and said teasingly, "What's it worth to you?"

"This," he said, walking up to her and kissing her long and hard. Not a soul was anywhere to be seen on the beach. He reached behind her neck and pulled her head to him and held her close. His manhood began to rise, and she felt it press against her. He then began to unbutton her blouse.

"What do you think you are doing? We are on the beach in broad daylight. What if someone sees us?" she sputtered.

"There's not a soul for miles around." He grabbed her and kissed her. "Silly."

"I know," she said with a sexy smile.

He continued to kiss her while unbuttoning her blouse. She then stepped out of her short shorts and unbuttoned her bra. "Let's see what the lieutenant has to offer," she said, pulling his boxer shorts out and looking at his stiffening member. She then grabbed it and squeezed it hard with her hand.

"Ooh, that feels good." He enjoyed the way she handled him.

"Catch me if you can," she sang, stepping out of her underwear and letting her bra drop to the sand. Then she ran toward the surf. She ran through the swallow water and dove into a clear green wave as it curled in front of her.

He stripped off his boxers and ran after her, diving into a wave. She was a strong swimmer and tried to swim away from him, but he soon caught up with her.

"Trying to get away from me, are you?" he asked, swimming up beside her.

She turned and jumped on his head, dunking him.

"Are you trying to drown me now?" he asked, bouncing off the bottom and rocketing to the surface, slinging water as he flung his head in her direction.

"No, just seeing how strong a swimmer you are." She swam away again, toward the shore. Soon she was out of the water, and he was in hot pursuit. He tackled her in the sand and started to kiss her. "Get off me; I can't stand to wallow around in the sand. That's why I brought some towels." She pulled two towels from her saddlebag and handed one to him. "Here, one for you and one for me."

She walked back to the water and swam some more, washing the sand off. He sat on the beach and watched, then jumped in and washed the sand off as well. She walked out of the water, picked up her towel, dried off, and spread it out in front of her. Then he picked up his towel, spread it out on the sand beside hers, and lay on his back. The sunlight silhouetted her body against the bright reflection from the water. She looked down at his body fully lit by the sun, pale but beautiful, arms behind him and legs spread wide. He patted the towel beside him. "Have a seat; enjoy the sun," he said. "It is so rare that I get to enjoy this much sun."

She lay down beside him, snuggling close. "I love the sun, too. I don't get out much this time of day, but it does feel good, as long as we don't stay out too long."

"Don't worry. That won't happen, I assure you." He closed his eyes and tilted his head back, taking in the direct rays of the sun. She turned and ran her tongue over the triceps of his left arm. He quickly turned to her. "What are you doing?"

"I'm licking the salt off your arm. You taste good," she said in a sexy voice.

"Oh, really." He licked her arm. His member began to spring to life.

"Does the little man want to play?" she asked teasingly.

"I think I'm going to let him speak for himself," Sanger said, and began to kiss her deeply. He rolled on top of her, and she dug her fingernails into his back, teasing his face and neck with her tongue. He began to kiss her breasts, and his fingers ran down her arms and sides, making their way to her privacy. They kissed deeply, and then he began to pleasure her. She guided his erection toward her wetness. He then took it from her and began to tease the entrance to her tunnel with its glistening head, now completely hatless. She took his hand, loosened his grip, and directed his erection into the depth of her mysteries, wet and waiting. He plunged deeper and deeper. She cried out until he, too, finally cried out and surrendered to her.

Afterwards, they lay in each other's arms on the towels, naked in the full sunlight. He dozed off first, then she did.

When they woke in each other's arms, they had a surprise waiting for them. She noticed it first, standing and looking down on his once-pale body. He had fallen asleep on his back, and she had lain face down with one of her arms draped across his middle. His body was bright pink except for a pale white band that had been covered by her arm. Her backside had received the sun's worst, but since she had a tan on her back and legs, only her bottom was now bright pink.

"Get up; you're as red as a lobster," she said with concern.

"You're not exactly pale yourself," he said, looking up at her bottom, which glowed pink from the sun.

He got up and ran into the water; she followed. They splashed each other as they waded waist-deep into the water.

"I want to get the other side done now," he said.

"I don't think so. I think you're going to suffer tonight. Look what else is red!" she said, pointing at his sunburned body. Even his privates were burned by the sun.

"It does burn," he said, touching his arm and watching the white spot disappear.

They put their clothes on, he with some degree of pain. Then they gathered the horses, which had wandered off in the dunes, and rode back up the beach toward Marcia's house.

Once inside, she got some lotion. "This should help," she said, slipping his shirt off and rubbing the lotion where he was sunburned. They both then lay down on the bed and took a nap.

When he opened his eyes, he was standing on the conning tower of the submarine with the commander and another man. It was nighttime. They were in the middle of the Atlantic. He looked up at the black sky filled with stars. The stars were so clear that he felt he could almost reach out and touch them. Low on the horizon was the bright swath of stars that made up the Milky Way. He felt he could step off the boat and walk the bright path into the depths of the universe.

His commandant brought him quickly back to reality. He scanned the horizon with binoculars. "A ship—I think I see the outline of a ship in the distance. We must make full speed ahead."

Sure enough, there was a ship, an ocean liner lit up festively, lights strung from one end to the other. They could see passengers dressed for the evening on the deck taking in the air. He thought he could hear the music of a band playing on board.

"Load the torpedoes; prepare to fire," the commandant called down to the control room.

"It is an ocean liner!" Sanger cried.

"This is war. In war nothing is safe and nothing is sacred," the commandant said.

Sanger woke with a start. Marcia was still asleep beside him. He wanted her to be safe. He wanted a safe harbor for himself, but he knew it could not last; he had a job to do. It wasn't safe to check the radio now; she might wake up. He would check it when she was gone. He lay down and was soon asleep again.

When he opened his eyes, he was back on the deck of the submarine, and the night sky was lit by burning fuel and debris on the water. He could hear the sounds of people wailing and crying out for help. The submarine slowly motored through the debris field. He could see faces in the water, looking up at him, imploring him to help. He knew that the crew could take no one on board. They found a life raft full of frightened women and children. The captain motored close to it and gave them some water, food, and supplies.

"Can you tell us which direction is the land?" asked a gentleman dressed in a tuxedo, pulling an oar. The captain turned to Sanger to translate.

"Follow that star; that will take you west," Sanger replied with the permission of the captain, pointing to a star in the western sky.

"How far?" the gentleman asked.

"About fifty kilometers," Sanger replied.

They continued to motor through the debris. The boat slid past several bodies. Many people were in the water. It was very cold. Sanger knew they would not last long.

When he woke again, Marcia was not there. Then he heard her in the kitchen, preparing dinner. She fixed a meal of drum encrusted with breadcrumbs and Parmesan cheese and baked in the oven, fresh green beans, and potatoes.

"Does your sunburn hurt?" she asked, touching his arm across the table.

"Yes. But it is much better thanks to the lotion that you put on it," he replied, taking her hand across the table.

After supper, they rode out to the beach on the horses. The sky was dark and full of stars; only a few clouds were on the horizon in the distance. Then a surprising thing happened. The sky gradually lightened at the horizon, and suddenly the moon began to rise out of the ocean. Though not quite full, it was beautiful, first bright red, then orange, until it turned whiter as it rose in the sky. Sanger had seen the moon bright near the horizon before, but he had rarely seen it rise out of the water like that.

They rode down the beach. A stiff breeze from the water blew Marcia's hair. When they rode close to the water, the hooves of the horses stirred up the bioluminescence in the sand. The waves made a loud roar as they rolled onto the shore; the sea was rougher than the day before. A storm must be brewing out at sea. He wondered if his comrades were in it. The U-boats had to dive during a storm. They preferred to ride on the surface at night, since it did not burn as much fuel and the air was better.

When Sanger and Marcia returned from the ride, they were both tired and went to bed. The wind rose and blew the curtains in the room. More clouds formed. They were both sunburned from the day, but they were young and full of passion and decided to make love again. The sunburn hurt a little, but that did not keep them apart. They both slept soundly that night.

The next morning he got up just before sunrise again and decided to run on the beach. It was cloudy, and in the distance over the ocean he could see rain coming from the clouds. The sun began to rise where the ocean met the beach to the east, coloring the bottoms of the clouds with a magnificent rose and purplish blue. As it emerged from the ocean, it was big and red, and he could look directly into it. Then, as it rose higher in the sky, it became more yellow, then white, and he could no longer look at it. The sun created a golden pink path along the water that reached from the horizon to the waves breaking just in front of him. At a distance, the wind blew the tops of the waves toward the sea in a white mist and spray. Magnificent storm clouds were on the horizon, drifting in the distance over the ocean. He could admire it from the beach. He knew his comrades did not have the same luxury; they were probably dealing with the seas created by the storm. Though he had seen many a magnificent sunrise in the middle of the Atlantic, he was happy he was on the beach and not the boat. A small rain squall headed his way. He had already run about a mile down the beach, so he just kept running. The cool rain was refreshing as it drenched him. His T-shirt and shorts clung to his body, but it felt wonderful. Soon the rain stopped, and he saw a rainbow over the beach to the south. He quickly dried out in the sun and breeze from the ocean.

The feel of first the hot sun and then the rain and then the water as it evaporated off of his skin was wonderful. He felt like he could run forever.

After about two miles, he stopped, stripped off his T-shirt and shorts, and ran into the water. The whitecaps were fairly big, and there was an undertow. He did not stay long in the water. He decided to run naked, so he carried the shorts and T-shirt in his hands. Before he got back to Marcia's house, he pulled on his clothes. The clouds were lower and darker, covering the sky now, bringing not just squalls but a steady rain. He walked onto the back porch soaking wet.

Marcia could see his chest and abdomen through the white T-shirt. His white shorts also clung to his body, revealing all.

"You aren't even decent," she said, staring at him. "Here, take this towel and dry off." She handed him a towel and gave him a hot cup of coffee. He changed clothes, and she cooked scrambled eggs and sausage for breakfast. They settled into a rainy day at home. He had wanted to get back to Ocracoke but settled for staying in while it rained. Sheets of rain poured down, pounding the tin roof of the house. There was lightning, too, and thunder. They drank their coffee and sat on the rockers on the front porch watching the storm.

"I love the sound of the rain on the tin roof and the cool breeze from the storm. It is so soothing and calming," Marcia said, sipping her coffee, not minding that it had gone cold. She did not have a dog, but several cats came up every once in a while to be fed. A big red tabby came up on the porch, soaking wet, followed by a black cat and then a tiger cat. They purred and rubbed against the rockers. "Hungry?" Marcia asked the tabby. She went inside, returned with a towel, and wiped the cats dry. Then she poured some milk in a bowl and mixed in some scraps of fish from the night before to feed them.

They listened to the birds and the sound of the rain. The tabby cat curled up on Sanger's lap after it had eaten.

"I have a cat at home. My family has always had cats. We have dogs, too, but I like them both," he said, rubbing the cat.

"I hate to keep saying this, but I wish you could stay. Do you need to report in, or could you just stay out here with me? It has been so wonderful having you around. I don't think I have ever been as happy and relaxed as I am right now." Marcia picked up the black cat and settled it in her lap, rubbing it as it purred.

"I want to stay. But I could be arrested for desertion. They know that I survived the sinking; they will be looking for me sometime. Aycock Brown said he would send for me as soon as he figured out who I am supposed to report to," he said, gently rocking, drinking the rest of his cold coffee, and rubbing the purring cat. He was relaxed and truly wished he could stay—maybe in another world, another time. He knew he must gather more intelligence and get back to the boat, but it could wait until another day, couldn't it?

The rain finally stopped, and the sun came out. A beautiful rainbow formed toward the beach over the water. Sanger and Marcia watched as it slowly dissipated into the morning air. After they ate some lunch, they heard the sound of an engine coming down the path from Portsmouth. The only people with a vehicle on the island were Nick and Joe.

"We got orders from Aycock Brown in Ocracoke to bring you over there. He has some information he needs to share with you," Nick said to Sanger after he bounded up the back porch.

"And how are you doing?" Marcia asked Nick, who had not even said hello to her.

"Oh, I'm sorry, good morning, Marcia. How are you?"

"Fine, thank you," she said, smiling. She didn't want anyone to take her man.

"I need to get dressed," Sanger said, and disappeared into the house to don his British uniform. He didn't know what Brown wanted, but he needed to gather more information, and Ocracoke was the place to do that. Brown also seemed forthcoming; perhaps Sanger could find out more about the U-352. But he had a bad feeling, though he couldn't put his finger on it. What if Brown told him he needed to report to Morehead City or Norfolk? He would need to get back to Portsmouth and contact his boat to pick him up. It was a dangerous business. He felt his relaxed time with Marcia was quickly coming to an end.

"You-all will bring him back to me, won't you?" Marcia asked Nick and Joe. She also had an ominous feeling about this trip.

"If that's what they tell us to do, we will. We do what we're told," Nick said with what looked to Marcia like a dumb smile. She didn't like this trip to Ocracoke; in fact, she had a terrible feeling about it.

When Sanger dressed and came out to meet Nick and Joe, she took his hand and said, "You will come back, won't you?"

"Yes, I will come back. I have to," he reassured her before he realized what he had said. He meant that he had to get back to the radio and the submarine, but none of them knew that. He could see that Marcia was agitated and concerned. He turned her face so he could look her straight in the eyes and said with all sincerity, "I promise that I will return, Marcia." He meant that no matter what happened, eventually he would return. It surprised him as he said it, but when it came out he knew he meant it. Even though it was crazy and impossible, he knew that he must return to this beautiful woman. He knew in that instant that he loved her.

She felt his sincerity. She took his words in and knew that he meant them. It was crazy; it could mean he would return that day with Nick and Joe, or it could mean he would return after the war ended. Any way she took it, she could feel the love that accompanied those words.

He bent to kiss her good-bye and whispered to her, "I love you, Marcia."

"I don't want you to go. I'm not ready for you to go," she pleaded with Sanger. Then she looked at Nick and Joe with dark eyes. "Don't take him from me."

"Ma'am, we're just taking him to Ocracoke. We'll be back this afternoon," Joe said innocently. Even he knew that this could be the last time the two saw each other. He was moved by how upset she was; Marcia and Sanger had known each other for only a few days, but that was an eternity to them. "We'll take care of him, I promise you," Joe said, trying to think of something to say to calm her down.

She reached for Sanger and kissed him, then whispered in his ear, "I love you, too. I will wait for you to return."

"I don't mean to rush you two, but we need to get on. Mr. Brown is waiting," Nick said, walking to the Jeep and starting the engine.

Sanger walked slowly to the Jeep with Nick and Joe. He looked back. There were tears in Marcia's eyes. She ran to him one more time and hugged him. He kissed her.

"Don't worry. Not even a war can keep us apart. I promise that I will do everything I can to come back to you." He held her head in his hands; her eyes were swollen with tears as she looked up at him.

"I love you," she said, and kissed him. That is all she could say as she choked back tears. Sanger got into the Jeep, and they drove off. Would she ever see him again? she wondered. She had just lost her husband; she could not bear to lose another man so soon. She knew her heart would break and then close. There was not enough of it to lose two loves and find another. She had to believe he would return to her. It was her only hope.

Chapter 9

As Nick, Joe, and Sanger drove through the village, several people stared at the Jeep and the handsome blond young man riding in the backseat dressed in a British sailor's uniform. They had all heard about him but not met him. Even though the Coast Guard boys whisked him by, some of the villagers got a good enough look to see why Marcia Styron was so interested in him.

At the docks the three boarded the Coast Guard skiff and motored toward Ocracoke. The storm had passed, and the skies were clear, but the water was still choppy, with whitecaps in the sound and the inlet. Sanger noticed things this time that he had not taken in before: the fishermen hauling in their nets, the numerous stakes in the water marking crab pots and fish traps, the shrimp boats with long arms on either side holding the nets. He noted the pelicans, seagulls, skimmers, plovers, and the occasional ibis, heron, and larger birds. He spotted the islands in the sound and the inlet, as well as the sandy spits, some filled with birds, others bare. He saw the duck blinds sitting like black boxes on top of the water and noticed how shallow the water was. Charts showed it to be no more than twenty feet deep throughout the sound, one of the largest inland water bodies on the Atlantic seaboard. Most of it was less than ten feet deep. There was a lot of activity in the sound and the inlet, mainly fishermen and shrimp boats. Fishing in the ocean had been restricted because of the U-boats. He could see the south point of Ocracoke Island, a huge, sandy tongue of land. Farther inland he could make out the radio tower at the Loop Shack hill.

Looking back toward Portsmouth, he could see the radio tower at the Coast Guard Station and the station itself, a turn-of-the-century shingled structure. He saw the steeple of the Methodist church at Portsmouth and the neat white houses, some one story, some two, scattered among the cedars and live oaks. He saw the general store and post office in the village.

A beautiful promontory was located on Ocracoke Island just above the village. Covered with wind-shaped live oaks, it was called Springer's Point. This was where Blackbeard the pirate had spent his last days before being killed at Teach's Hole, a channel in the sound just off the point. Sanger saw the Ocracoke Lighthouse, a whitewashed and stuccoed brick structure built in 1823. As they entered "the ditch," the entrance to Silver Lake, the Coast Guard Stations were on the left. A big water tower and the buildings of the naval station were still under construction.

After tying up at the docks, the three men walked in the heat of the midday sun to the new Coast Guard Station. As they waited outside Aycock Brown's office, a secretary offered them water, which they happily took.

Aycock Brown strode into the hallway where the men waited and invited them into his office. He was beaming.

"Well, gentleman," he said after they sat down in front of his big oak desk, "I have some good news and some bad news. The bad news is that we found two more bodies from the *Bedfordshire*. Arnold Styron was aboard a Coast Guard patrol boat five miles northeast of Ocracoke Inlet and found them floating in the water. The bodies were badly decomposed, but they wore the blue turtleneck sweaters of the crew of the *Bedfordshire*. We do not know their identities, but we buried them yesterday with the others." He then rose, headed toward a door leading out of his office, and knocked. "The good news is that when the boat was in Morehead City, apparently two men—Sam Nutt, a stoker, and Richard Salmon, lead cook—went out drinking the night before the *Bedfordshire* left on May 10 and were arrested for drunk and disorderly conduct. They were not aboard the *Bedfordshire* when she went down. Mr. Nutt, meet Sublieutenant Bruce Hall." And with that Brown opened the door and out walked a short, clean-shaven, wiry young man with a wide grin on his face. He was about five foot seven with dark hair.

When he looked at Sanger wearing the blue turtleneck of a *Bedfordshire* crewman, his smile turned into a scowl. "This is not Sublieutenant Bruce Hall. I do not know this man."

Brown turned bright red. He truly thought that he was going to give Hall a great surprise, and he did indeed. Sanger, of course, had no idea that he was going to encounter a surviving crewman of the *Bedfordshire*. Instinctively he turned and ran out the door and down the hall toward the exit. Brown called for guards, and Nick and Joe chased after Sanger, tackling him in the hall before he could make it to the door. Guards soon arrived on the scene and handcuffed Sanger. They then brought him into the interrogation room near Brown's office. Joe and Nick stood outside. Although they were not allowed to take part in the interrogation, they wanted to know who this man was—this man who had taken advantage of Marcia Styron and made fools of everyone—and where he had come from.

The ruse was up. Sanger knew he could either be tried for espionage or treated as a POW—it was Brown's call. His days on the submarine were over. At least he could conduct himself with honor. He had already given some thought to what he would say if he were captured. So when Brown entered the room and sat down at the end of the table facing him, Sanger was ready. Two armed guards stood in the room.

Brown was a civilian, dressed in civilian clothes, but he was trained in interrogation. "Well, mister, what exactly is your name?"

"Oberleutnant Zur See Kurt Sanger of the *U-358*, sir."

"A German officer come ashore from a U-boat! You know, we thought that you guys were sending spies on shore, but none have been caught yet. Lots of rumors, but you are the first. You speak impeccable English."

"I studied at the Technical University of Dresden, sir. I was first in my class in English. My father is also a professor of English literature at the university," he said with some pride.

"Why are you here? Why did you impersonate an officer of the *Bedfordshire*?"

"The reason I came on shore was to find out about the men of the *U-85*. We lost contact with the boat and knew nothing of the fate of her crew."

Brown was not proud of the way the crew of the *U-85* were killed in the water, defenseless, begging for help. The men could have been much more useful if they had been captured alive and interrogated.

"Then the *U-352* was sunk," Sanger continued, "and I was ordered to stay until I found out what happened to her crew. The Ubootwaffe is a very close-knit group. We all know each other. Our captain went to school with Eberhard Greger, the commandant of the *U-85*. They were good friends. We do not like to leave our comrades behind. I hope you can understand that." Sanger had decided to appeal to Brown's humanity, since the American had the power to try him on espionage charges, and espionage could carry a penalty of death. He did not, however, say a word about the Enigma machine.

"What about the *Bedfordshire* and your uniform?"

"It was just before midnight. We were riding on the surface when the *Bedfordshire* spotted us and opened fire. Then we loaded two torpedoes, but they missed, so we loaded a third. It hit amidships, sinking her. We were able to pull a body on board, and I took the man's clothes and papers. It was the body of Bruce Hall, sir." He omitted telling Brown about Seaman Featherstone.

"What about Marcia Styron? Did she know about this?" There were rumors about American collaborators helping the Germans. Brown had no reason to suspect Marcia, but he knew it was his duty to explore every avenue of investigation.

"Marcia Styron knows nothing about this. She thinks that I am a British sailor. She had absolutely no knowledge that I am German." Sanger looked directly into Brown's eyes and spoke with absolute sincerity. Brown believed him. "I do not want to do anything that would hurt Marcia Styron. She is a widow and was all alone. She was kind to me, and I am grateful to her for that. I hope she will not suffer because of me. She is completely innocent."

"I hear she has some German heritage. I am sure you are aware of the German American Bund, German Americans sympathetic to the Nazis. We will have to question her. There are rumors of American sympathizers aiding the U-boats and giving them information about our military activities."

"To my knowledge these rumors are not true. We do not need help from sympathizers. Marcia Styron does not know that I am German or that I came from a U-boat. Please do not mistreat her because of me."

"It is admirable of you to defend her, but we will need to make our own determination of her guilt or innocence. In the meantime,

I will place you in the brig until I can decide what to do with you. You will be treated well, according to the Geneva Convention, and with the respect due an officer in the German navy. Good day, Oberleutnant Sanger." Brown then watched as Sanger was led from the room handcuffed.

Sanger was locked in the base brig, where he was segregated from the other prisoners, mainly base men in for offenses like drunk and disorderly. There was no jail on the island, and the navy policed its own.

Sanger was distraught. He was not so much concerned with his own fate. However, he was worried about Marcia Styron. He truly cared for her—no, loved her. He wondered if she would ever forgive him for his deception. He did not want her to have to pay for his association with her.

Rumors had circulated about German spies on the island. Brown did not want to confirm these rumors and send the populace into fear; he wanted to keep this affair quiet. All Brown would tell Nick and Joe was that Sanger was an imposter and a German. He needed to interview Marcia Styron immediately. He decided the best way to deal with her was to go to Portsmouth with Nick and Joe and confront her at her house that very day. He needed to search the house. Sanger must have had a radio and other supplies, perhaps a weapon or, worse, explosives for sabotage. They needed to find them. He truly did not think that Marcia knew about Sanger—she was a Coast Guard widow who had lost her husband—but he had to make sure. He could see that Sanger cared for her.

Nick and Joe took Brown back to Portsmouth. It was late afternoon. It took about half an hour to cross the inlet, and then they drove to Marcia's house, where they found her rocking alone on the back porch.

She stood up as the Jeep approached, then ran to meet Nick and Joe when she saw that Sanger was not with them. "Where is Bruce Hall?" she asked, visibly upset. "Who is this man?" She stared at Brown.

Brown stepped forward. "Calm down, ma'am. My name is Aycock Brown, special investigator for the Office of Naval Intelligence at the naval station at Ocracoke."

"Where is Lieutenant Hall?" she asked, in tears. "Why are you here?"

"We have come here to talk to you about Lieutenant Hall,"

Brown said. "May we go inside out of the sun?"

"Yes," she said. Marcia had a terrible feeling about Hall's trip to Ocracoke. She had felt a sense of dread all day. She also wanted to get out of the sun. She felt faint and slightly nauseous and needed to sit down. This Brown man seemed nice enough, but he looked to have come about serious business, and the news he was going to give her did not look to be good news. She led him into her kitchen, and he sat at the kitchen table. Nick and Joe were worried about her. They liked her and knew that she cared for Hall/Sanger. They did not know how she would take the information. She had just lost her husband. Could she survive losing someone else? They followed Brown into the kitchen. At first Brown objected, but he saw that their presence helped calm Marcia, so he allowed them to stay.

"Mrs. Styron, the man who has been staying with you for the past several days is not Sublieutenant Bruce Hall. He is a German named Kurt Sanger, an officer on a German U-boat."

This was more than Marcia could take. The color drained from her face. She felt faint. "This cannot be. I rescued him from the sea. He was wearing the clothes of a British sailor. I saw his identification papers. . . ." She trailed off; she had heard him speak German as he slept. But it was impossible. He was so wonderful, so gentle, so kind to her. He told her that he loved her and that he would return to her. Was this a lie, too?

"I am afraid he is an imposter. He took advantage of the sinking of the *Bedfordshire* to come ashore and spy. You must tell me everything that you know about him. Did he do anything that was at all suspicious or that could have led you to believe he was not who he said he was?"

She thought. "No, not that I can think of. He seemed to act the part of a British naval officer well. One time while he slept, he cried out in German, but he had a good explanation for it. He told me that he spoke German and had a nightmare about struggling in the water after the *Bedfordshire* sank, crying out for help to the German U-boat as it motored through the debris field. Did his U-boat sink the *Bedfordshire*?"

"I am afraid so, ma'am." Brown turned to Nick. "When I came to inspect the bodies, one of them was naked, wasn't it?"

"Yes," Nick answered. "But it did not appear to have been shot or to have died other than by drowning. Another body was fully clothed and could have survived the blast but died in the water. Others had lost limbs and were blackened by an explosion."

"Was one of them about Sanger's size?"

"Yes, the naked body was, sir, " Nick said.

Marcia covered her face with her hands and started to cry, then looked up with teary eyes.

"We may need to check the bodies," Brown said. Then he looked at Marcia, who was distraught and confused. "We also need to search your house and the outbuildings. Sanger must have had a radio and perhaps a weapon."

"Certainly, search all you want. I just can't believe this." Though she did not say it, she thought, I shared my bed with this man. I shared my thoughts and feelings. I opened my heart to him. I told him I loved him, and he is likely a killer and a spy.

They searched the house, then the outbuildings. They found the radio in the workshop with its antenna in the rafters. They also found the Lugar, wrapped in oilcloth. They showed it all to Marcia as if to prove to her that the man she had fallen in love with was really a spy. Brown asked her more questions but soon realized that she knew nothing and was innocent. Nick and Joe vouched for her, too, and he had checked into her background before leaving Ocracoke. He had no reason to suspect her. Her grandfather was German, but her father worked in the shipyards in Norfolk, and her husband had worked for the Coast Guard. The family had a good reputation in Elizabeth City. She seemed genuinely distraught.

"We must keep this absolutely quiet. No one can tell what happened here today, or that we had a German U-boat man among us. Do you understand, Marcia, Nick, and Joe? You are the only ones who know. I will know where it came from if it gets out. Tell no one. If the people in the village ask what happened to Sanger, simply say he was sent back to another British ship, and that's all," Brown instructed. "No one needs to know that he is a German prisoner. For all anyone in Ocracoke knows, he could be a sailor from the brig being taken to detention."

In England, when U-boats were sunk, there was much publicity, but not in America. So far the United States Navy had engineered a total news blackout about the U-boat action offshore and about the American shipping being sunk. Only those living on the coast and actually seeing the shipwrecks and damage knew about the German assault. There had been little, if any, publicity about the sinking of the *U-85* and the *U-352*. The top brass didn't want people to know that German U-boats were operating freely off the American coast, or that U-boats had been sunk or their crews captured. And they certainly did not want to fuel fears about German spies operating on American soil.

Naval intelligence dug up the bodies of the British sailors who had washed up on the beach and were buried in Portsmouth. Sam Nutt from the *Bedfordshire* identified the naked body as Hall's. It showed no sign of foul play; Hall had apparently died by drowning. The bodies were then taken to Ocracoke and buried with the men who had washed up there. The site became known as the "British Cemetery." Despite more intense interrogation, naval intelligence got nothing more out of Sanger. Brown had to decide whether to bring in the FBI or send Sanger to Fort Bragg, where he could join the men of the *U-352* as a prisoner of war. He did not like the FBI. He saw no reason to bring them in. Sanger was a U-boat officer trying to find the whereabouts of his comrades. There was no evidence that he was a saboteur or that he had any business other than finding out their fate. Indications were that he would have been picked up by his U-boat as soon as he found what he needed. There was no need to make this any messier than it already was, Brown decided. He ordered an amphibious aircraft sent to Ocracoke from Morehead City.

Brown flew Sanger to Morehead City in handcuffs. In Morehead City they boarded the train heading west. On the train Sanger asked Brown about Marcia. "Have you seen her? Have you questioned her? Is she all right?"

"I did question her, and I am convinced she did not know that you were a German spy. I think she genuinely believed you were a British sailor. As far as I am concerned, there is no case against her." He looked at Sanger and saw the relief in his face. "We found your radio, gun, and other items in the work shed. Once we showed them to her, she knew that you were an imposter. She was upset and very mad, but I am sure Nick and Joe will check in on her and she will be fine. It shouldn't take long for her to get over you, so don't worry about her. She will be fine." Brown was not a cruel man and saw Sanger had a genuine concern for the woman. He had no reason not to be honest with Sanger.

"Thank you for telling me that, sir," Sanger said. "I will sleep better knowing that she is all right. She was truly kind to me. I do not want my status to put her into harm's way."

At the Selma station, they changed trains and went south to Fayetteville. Before he left Ocracoke, Sanger had asked his guard how he might write someone in Portsmouth. The guard had told him simply to write the person's name, General Delivery, Portsmouth, North Carolina.

Chapter 10

Marcia had refused to believe that Bruce Hall was a spy until Aycock Brown showed her the radio equipment and the gun in the shed. Then she knew it was true. She was devastated. She had opened her heart to this man and let him in. Now her heart was closed, and she didn't know if it would ever open again. After Brown left with Nick and Joe, she saddled her horse and rode out onto the beach. There were dark clouds in the distance, and the sea was high and choppy with whitecaps. She felt betrayed, deceived, hurt, but most of all angry. He had lied to her, used her, tricked her into believing him so that he could use her home as a base for spying. It made her sick to her stomach, she was so angry. She had opened her bed to him; they had made love. He had been so convincing, and she had fallen for it. He knew that she had just lost her husband, that she was vulnerable.

She wanted a man in her life, but this man, a sailor from a German U-boat? She could not get the image out of her mind of him standing in the midday sun with the water from the outdoor shower spilling over his naked body. She could not stop thinking of his eyes, the color of the sky, that melted her every time he looked at her, or their lovemaking, so rich, so full, so gentle, yet so exciting.

Could all of that be a lie? She did not know what to think, and she could do nothing. She wanted to hate the man who had declared his love to her that morning. How could she survive? Even if Brown had let her see Hall/Sanger, she did not want to see him; she would have killed him. She wanted to forget him if she could.

At least she would not have to endure questions from her neighbors. Once she explained that he had gone to another British ship, that would be the end of it. Maybe after a respectable time she could even say he had died at sea. She needed him to die at sea, then she could go on with her life. The fact that he was a German spy would be a secret that only she, Joe, and Nick would share with Aycock Brown.

It started to rain as she and Mary Lou rode down the beach. It was a light mist at first, but she knew by the dark clouds gathering that it would get worse. Still she did not turn back; there was no lightning—she would be fine. The rain fell harder, and soon she was soaked. She rode and rode, the hard rain stinging her face. She did not want to stop until she and the horse collapsed. Thank goodness it was raining, or the heat would have affected Mary Lou. When Marcia heard thunder, she knew she must turn around. The waves were churning. The clouds hung low over the beach. Finally she made it over the dunes to her house and put up the horse. Again the thunder rumbled in the distance, but she saw no lightning. She sat on a rocker on the porch, soaking wet, sobbing out loud as tears rolled down her cheeks.

In the morning Marcia did not feel well. She tried to cook some breakfast, but the smell of eggs made her nauseous. She heard the sound of an engine outside. It must be Nick and Joe. She did not want to see them.

"Hello," Nick said, tapping on the screen door. She did not want to open it. "Hello, Marcia, are you in there? It's Nick and Joe. Let us in; we have some fresh cantaloupe from Miss Dixon's garden."

"Go away. I don't want to see you or talk to you," Marcia said, standing at the kitchen sink, not turning to look at the two through the screen door.

"It's not our fault, Marcia. Don't shoot the messengers. We only did what we were told to do," Joe said, pleading.

"Oh, all right. I'll let you in. But I don't feel well. You can't stay long."

She unlatched the door, and the men walked in, wearing khaki pants, white shirts, and Coast Guard caps. She wore a robe, and her hair was disheveled. She had not slept well. When she awoke and still felt sick, she had turned over and gone back to sleep. So she had slept late. She had little reason to get up, and no reason to get dressed or comb her hair. She felt like sleeping all day—all week, for that matter.

"You-all have a lot of nerve, coming out here after what happened yesterday."

"It's not our fault that he is a German spy," Nick said. "We came out to see how you're doing."

"Yeah, we want to cheer you up," Joe said.

"The best way to cheer me up is to leave me alone," she said, bags under her eyes. She did not offer them a cup of coffee, which she would have done normally. She was truly mad at them; she knew that they had only been following orders, but what havoc they had wreaked upon her life. She knew it wasn't fair to blame them, but she was mad, and right now part of her anger was directed at them.

"Since we are the only ones to know about this, I have been thinking," she said. "The best way to explain it to the village is to say he went back to the British navy and then, in a few weeks, we need to kill him off. I want him—no, I *need* him—to be dead. Do you understand?"

"Sure, I understand," Nick said. "In a few weeks, we will let it be known that we heard he was killed on a British navy ship, fighting the Germans. Will that make it easier for you, Marcia? That will be the end of it. No more questions after that, right?"

"Right," she said. Then she stood up, ran out the back door, and threw up off the porch.

Nick and Joe looked at each other with knowing eyes. They had seen the way Marcia and Sanger looked at each other—a lonely widow, her husband just dead, a handsome young sailor who had drifted in from the sea. It wasn't hard to figure out what had been going on.

Although Marcia was not ready to verbalize it, she knew instinctively what was going on with her body. She came back in, her face blanched; she looked terrible.

"We need to go, Marcia. Listen, take the day off and get plenty of rest. We'll check on you tomorrow. Do you need anything?" Joe asked, standing.

"No, just go," she said, walking toward the sink, where she splashed water on her face.

She stayed in bed most of the day, drifting in and out of sleep.

She had several dreams. In the first, she and Sanger were in her bed sleeping under the light of a full moon. She woke him up, and they made love. After they made love, he started talking to her in German. He had a swastika tattooed on his shoulder. She got out of bed and ran from the house. In the second dream, she was walking on the beach, and she came upon several bodies that had washed up with the tide. One was the naked body she had seen on the beach the day she found Sanger. It was the real Lieutenant Bruce Hall. Then she saw Sanger struggling in the waves. She walked to him. He looked up at her, eyes and lips swollen from the salt water. She took the gun she was holding in one hand and shot him between the eyes. He had a startled look, then fell back into the waves, where the ocean washed his body away into the darkness of the early morning.

Nick and Joe checked in on Marcia the next morning and each day thereafter, bringing her food and supplies. She felt sick in the mornings, and her nipples were sensitive. She knew that she was pregnant. She gradually began to feel better, but something was different, something lost. Nick and Joe saw it in her eyes. A certain sparkle and light had been doused. They could only guess what it was.

Several weeks passed. Marcia was usually very regular, but she missed her period. She continued to be sick in the morning and found herself taking frequent naps. After a while she noticed that she was gaining weight and that she had strange cravings, such as ice cream, which was impossible to find on the island. So she made milk shakes with chocolate syrup.

One morning Marcia rode into the village to the variety store to get groceries and visit the post office, which was in the same building. Her mail usually was comprised of the occasional letter from her mother and father in Norfolk, her monthly check from the Coast Guard, *Life* magazine, and *Colliers* magazine, but that was about it. This time there was a letter from Fort Bragg, North Carolina. It had been opened and looked as if it had been read and resealed; it was from Kurt Sanger. Annie Salter, the postmistress, looked at Marcia kind of funny when she handed her the letter. "It must be from my cousin Kurt, who is stationed at Fort Bragg," Marcia explained before Annie could ask. "They open the mail from the military—you know, censorship."

She wanted to throw the letter away. Certainly she would not read it. But for some reason she could not bring herself to throw it away. She was going to have a child, his child. As angry as she was, she decided to keep the letter. She put it in a box on the mantel in her living room, unopened.

She could have been angry about the child, but she was not. She actually felt good about it. She would have a companion, someone to take her mind off the war and its horrors. Something good had come of the pain of their relationship. It was almost time to kill off Hall/Sanger, to tell everyone that he had died. Surely people would talk, but they would also feel sorry for her. She had gotten pregnant, and the man had died. It was wartime. People did things they didn't ordinarily do during peacetime. She wanted to have this baby, and she didn't care what people thought.

She rode Mary Lou on the beach. It was a beautiful day, cloudy and cool. It had been so hot that summer. Clouds drifted out to sea, looking like huge mountain ranges floating over the ocean. It rained that afternoon, a refreshing rain that cooled things off and filled the cistern. She sat on the porch and rocked by herself. A child, she thought. If only Sanger knew. It would be her secret. He did not deserve to know. She was still angry with him, but she knew that someday she would probably tell him.

That night she walked on the beach and kicked up the bioluminescence in the sand at the water's edge. The clouds had cleared up, and the night was crisp and cool. The stars were bright; she could see the Milky Way just above the horizon. It was a beautiful place— this, her island home. She loved it here. Now she would be able to share it with someone, a child who was her gift from the sea.

Chapter 11

Aycock Brown delivered Sanger to the military authorities at Fort Bragg for processing. He was told to strip, and he was sprayed with delousing chemicals. From delousing he went in his underwear to the base doctor for a medical exam. Then he was asked to fill out a three-page form that requested his personal medical history, fingerprints, serial number, an inventory of personal effects, and information about his capture. This became his personal record. Copies of these forms were forwarded to the International Red Cross so that the prisoners' families could be informed of their fates. Then Sanger was given a prison serial number, which he was to use for the remainder of his captivity. Later serial numbers would reflect the theater where prisoners were captured, the country they were from, and an individual number. But this was the first group of POWs, so they were given a basic number representing the service they were in, the military district in the United States where they were held, the first letter of the country they were from, and an individual number. The prisoners were allowed to keep most of their personal effects but not their money—if they escaped, it could be used. Even the money they made as day laborers was given to them in the form of credits to be used in the camp PX.

Sanger was issued prison clothes. He also was given the option of keeping the clothes that he wore in addition to his prison clothes, but since they were those of a British sailor, he declined. He was first given dark blue work clothes that had a large white *PW* stenciled on the back of each shirt to identify him as a prisoner of war and, if necessary, to provide a target for guards to shoot at in the event of escape. In addition to the work clothes, each prisoner was given one belt, two pairs of cotton trousers, two pairs of wool trousers, one pair of gloves, one wool coat, one overcoat, one pair of shoes, four pairs of socks, four pairs of drawers, four undershirts, one raincoat, one wool shirt, and two pairs of shorts. After prisoners were issued their clothes, a base officer explained the rules of the camp regarding damage to property, precautions against fires, maintenance of sanitary conditions, medical and dental inspections, the length and legibility of letters to their families, and the punishment for escape. They were allowed to send one letter a week, and the letters were read by censors before they were mailed.

When Sanger stripped down for the delousing, the American soldier in charge stared at his full-body sunburn, which was turning into tan. The other Germans from U-boats were pale as ghosts. The soldier could not help noticing the tan and the white band across Sanger's abdomen.

"Lying out in the sun, I see. Only what is that white band?" the soldier asked.

"None of your business, soldier," Sanger said, looking down at himself, remembering his last day on the beach with Marcia. The white band was where her arm had been draped across his stomach.

When the processing was finished, the guard took Sanger into the barracks with the survivors of the *U-352*. They were the first German POWs on United States soil, so temporary accommodations had to be made for them at Fort Bragg. A high metal storm fence topped with barbed wire was thrown up around an old plywood army barracks. The enclosure had enough room for a parade ground and an area where prisoners could exercise and play sports. An infirmary and a mess hall were also constructed.

Eleven men died when the *U-352* went down, and one died shortly thereafter from loss of blood when he lost his leg in the mayhem. The thirty-three survivors were commanded by Helmut Rathke, a thirty-two-year-old graduate of the naval class of 1930. He came on active duty in 1935 and had served on various types of surface vessels. He had twice been around the world. Born in eastern

Prussia, he was a resident of Flensburg, where his wife and small daughter lived. Rathke had been in a skiing accident before taking over the *U-352*. He was in a wheelchair during the final stages of the submarine's construction. The *U-352* had been on its second cruise when it was sunk. It had sunk no enemy ships. It was in Saint-Nazaire when the British commandos raided the town and did much damage to the German facilities.

The Americans allowed the Germans to keep their command system in place. It promoted discipline and order in the camp and worked to their advantage. One drawback, however, was that the Nazis in the group were firmly in charge, and infractions against their will were punished.

Every morning the men drilled. The Americans encouraged them to exercise, and Rathke wanted to keep his men in good shape. One day they would try to escape, and they would need to be in good shape for that. But escape in America was problematic. It was such a vast country. To the north was Canada, which because of its close ties with Britain was more hostile to Germany than the United States was. To the south was Mexico, but it was hundreds of miles away and, again, hostile territory. To the east was the Atlantic Ocean, and to the west was the Pacific. If they escaped, where would they go, what would they do, how would they blend in? But it was nevertheless the duty of every POW to try to escape.

The average age of the group was twenty-two. Thirteen of the men were under twenty-one. They were young, inexperienced, and homesick. The busier they stayed, the better off they would be. Rathke and the Americans encouraged the men to participate in sports. They organized teams and played soccer. Sanger, a former soccer star in school, became the coach of one of the teams, and he worked the men out using a vigorous routine, getting them up every morning at five o'clock to exercise before the others arose at five-thirty for reveille.

The camp housed an assortment of men with an assortment of political ideas. Rathke gave unqualified praise to the National Socialist Party and Hitler when he was interrogated by the Americans, calling Hitler a military genius who had united the German peoples of Europe. Rathke was considered courteous but arrogant by the Americans; however, he commanded great respect from his men. Midshipman Ernst Kammerer, son of a Berlin engineer, was a product of the Hitler Youth movement. He was born in Canton, China, and had been in the navy since 1940. After serving on a destroyer, he volunteered for the U-boat arm. He was an outspoken Nazi. Leutnant Sur Zee Oskar Bernhard, twenty-five years old, had served the *U-352* as a navigator pending his commission as an officer; he was a quartermaster. A native of Nuremburg, he made his home in Hamburg-Altona, where he taught navigation at the nautical school. He joined the navy in 1940 and also served in the engineer corps of the German army and participated in the Polish campaign. A Catholic, he was a loyal and conscientious German but was not an unflagging supporter of the National Socialist Party. He had received the Minesweeper Badge, the U-boat Badge, and the Iron Cross, Second Class.

Rathke told his men to reveal nothing to the Americans when they were interrogated. All of them were interrogated one by one within three months after they were captured. The only topics they were allowed to discuss were personal matters about their families and where they were from, the bars and prostitutes in eastern France, but nothing of strategic importance. Rathke was worried that his men, being young and impressionable, would talk if he didn't keep them tightly reined.

Sanger wrote his first letter to Marcia a few weeks after he got to Fort Bragg. He knew the censors would read his mail, so he was careful not to say anything that would bring her under suspicion or make trouble for her. He kept his letter short:

Marcia,

Please forgive me. I hope I have not brought you pain. I did not reveal my true identity to you for a reason. It is wartime. I hope that you will eventually understand that and forgive me. I arrived at a prison camp located at Fort Bragg in Fayetteville, North Carolina, three weeks ago and have joined other German prisoners of war. I am a soccer coach to the younger men. They appear to like me. I am getting lots of good exercise and like being outdoors, just as I enjoyed being outdoors and on the beach on Portsmouth Island. It is much better than being shut up on a boat. They feed us well and have treated us with dignity and respect. Our quarters are respectable and clean. German officers are in charge of the day-to-day functions of the men in the camp, and there are good relations between our captors and us. I hope that you are well and things are as lovely in Portsmouth as I remember them.

Always,
Lt. Kurt Sanger

He wanted to say he loved her, but he knew she was not ready to hear that, and if he professed his love for her, it could cause trouble for her with the authorities. He did not expect her to write back. He knew she must still be angry, but perhaps with the passage of time and with luck she would mellow. Her silence would not keep him from writing her. He kept the vision of their brief time together in Portsmouth as a sort of beacon of hope and happiness while he endured imprisonment. He knew every word he wrote was read and censored. He also wrote his family in Dresden. Finally he heard from his father. His father had been ill, and his mother was sick to hear that Sanger had been captured, but they were happy that he was safe in America for the duration of the war.

One night he had a dream about being back on Portsmouth. He found himself running on the beach just after it had rained. The air was clear and fresh. He wore a T-shirt and some athletic shorts. Dark clouds were over the ocean from the rain, but the sun shone between them. The ocean was calm; the bottle-green water of the waves rolled in so clear he could almost see through them. He decided to take off his shorts and T-shirt and dive into the waves. He swam naked, diving underwater. Then he saw the bodies of two young men floating with their arms outstretched, one naked and one clothed. The bodies looked familiar; they were those of Bruce Hall and Geoffrey Featherstone from the *Bedfordshire*. He tried to get away from them, but they seemed to follow him. Soon he was tangled up in their legs and arms. They clung to him; he could not get away. Hall's eyes were hollow and blank, like the birds had eaten them. Sanger felt like he was drowning as the bodies pushed him down under the water, then he woke up.

Chapter 12

Aunt Charlotte O'Neal was an experienced midwife who lived on Ocracoke but served both islands. She had birthed more than five hundred babies on Ocracoke and Portsmouth, often staying with the young mothers for days or weeks after the births to make sure they and the babies were fine. Marcia called on her early in her pregnancy for advice about what to eat and what to do and not do. Aunt Charlotte was kind and gentle and not judgmental. She knew that the father of the child was the British sailor who never returned, she knew that the child was conceived in May, and she knew Marcia's husband had died in January. But she also knew women and the hard times they were having and what people do in hard times. She helped Marcia in every way she could, including heading off the town gossip.

"'Judge not, lest ye be judged,'" Aunt Charlotte told Miss Annie Salter, the postmistress. "She met this handsome British sailor, and he went off to sea and died. They probably would have been married if he had lived. It is wartime; people don't play by the same rules that we do during times of peace."

"But she was not married to the sailor, and her husband had just died," said Miss Annie, who was something of a busybody.

"All the more reason to understand what she did; she was grieving, she knew her husband was gone, and here was this good-looking man paying her attention. Maybe it was not the smartest thing to do, but I can understand it. Can't you?"

"Maybe," said Miss Annie. Annie Salter had never married. If a handsome young sailor had entered her life, who knows what she would have done? She decided not to say anything else about it and to not speak ill of Marcia. With the men in the village gone, so few people were left. Those who remained needed to stick together and support each other. Marcia was one of her people, a resident of Portsmouth Island. Marcia could have left, but she didn't because she clearly loved the island. She had an infectious smile and was always pleasant and kind.

Nine months passed quickly. It was the middle of February 1943 and very cold. A nor'easter had just passed through, blowing some cedars down, tearing into the dunes on the beach, and causing minor flooding in the village. Nick and Joe checked on Marcia every day. One morning when they came to see her, she told them her water had broken. They rushed into the village to get Aunt Charlotte, passing through puddles of high water in their Jeep along the way.

Marcia's labor lasted for several hours. Nick and Joe waited outside the bedroom like anxious fathers, asking what they could do to help.

"Stay out of my way," Aunt Charlotte scolded. "That is what you can do. Oh, and by the way, you can boil some water and bring me some towels." She would need the towels to clean up after the baby came.

Finally the men heard the sharp cries of a baby. After a few minutes, Aunt Charlotte brought the baby out wrapped in a big white towel. She was a beautiful little girl with curly blond hair and blue eyes that looked all around, taking everything in.

"How is Marcia?" Joe asked.

"She's sleeping. She had a pretty rough time of it, but she'll be fine. No hemorrhaging. She's just tired. Do you want to hold the baby?" she said, handing the tiny bundle to Joe.

Joe took the baby and held her awkwardly. It was like balancing a dozen eggs in his hands, the baby was so limp and helpless. She looked up at Joe with big blue eyes, and Joe melted. He had not seen a newborn up close like this. The baby smiled at him.

"Don't you worry, sweetie pie, Uncle Joe will protect you and won't let anything bad happen to you as long as he is alive."

"I want to hold her," Nick said, reaching for the baby. "I'm her uncle, too, you know."

Nick took the baby and held her. "Now don't you listen to a thing that Joe tells you; I am your uncle, and I will take care of you. You remember that."

"Here, let me have the baby," Aunt Charlotte said, taking her from Nick. "You two goofballs, if you don't stop arguing over her, you are liable to drop her." She then took the baby to her mother. Nick and Joe could see Marcia through the open door. Her hair stuck to her forehead in wet tendrils. She looked very tired, but her eyes lit up when Aunt Charlotte brought the baby to her so she could start feeding her.

Marcia named her daughter Stella for the stars—the stars she saw at night and the stars she saw in the sand, the bioluminescence. Stella was her gift from the sea. Marcia felt Stella would be a special child, a shining light, a child of Portsmouth, a child of the sea, a child of the moon and the stars. Perhaps someday she would know her father, but for now she belonged to her mother. Marcia decided not to let Stella's father know that he had a child; she was still too angry with him.

Nick and Joe fell in love with Stella and came to visit her every day, playing with her, bringing her toys and treats. They called themselves Uncle Nick and Uncle Joe, and they acted like proud fathers, spoiling her and doting on her. They were the only ones on the island who knew Marcia's secret, so they felt a special bond with Marcia and her beautiful daughter.

Sanger continued to write, at first every two weeks, then settling for once a month after Marcia did not respond. The letters came from Fort Bragg, then from Mississippi; later they came from Fort Papago, Arizona. By her first birthday, Stella was walking, then she was all over the house, and Marcia really worked to keep up with her. She was a ball of fire, full of energy. It was a cold winter on the Outer Banks, so when spring and summer finally came, Marcia welcomed them. She enjoyed taking Stella to the beach to play in the sand and the tidal pools and to chase the birds.

The German assault on commercial shipping had ended by August 1942. After the oil companies and other commercial interests put pressure on President Roosevelt, Admiral King finally was forced to do something to stop the carnage; he ordered commercial ships to convoy. The navy gave the convoys destroyer escorts and sent airplanes out to search for U-boats. When he saw that the Americans had finally developed a backbone, Admiral Dönitz decided in August 1942 to abandon Operation Drumbeat and seek more fruitful hunting grounds elsewhere. More than 259 Allied and neutral ships were sunk in American coastal waters during the first few months of 1942. Although more men were killed during Operation Drumbeat than had died at Pearl Harbor, because of the news blackout virtually no one knew about it except the coastal people who dealt with the debris and the human loss.

In the summer of 1943, the East Coast was relatively calm and peaceful. The Ocracoke station remained operational, but things were quieter on the Outer Banks than in the months of Operation Drumbeat. Marcia no longer dreaded going to the beach for fear of finding burnt and mangled bodies and flotsam and jetsam from merchant ships that had met a horrible fate at the hand of the Germans. The beach was generally peaceful now and bore few signs of the horrors of 1942. However, the United States marine aviators from Cherry Point used the beach several miles below the village for strafing targets. Her part of the beach was not used for target practice, but just to be on the safe side Marcia used it only on the weekends, when the planes did not practice. That is when she took Stella on the beach to play.

Still other terrors lurked off the Outer Banks that were not caused by the hand of man. Storms were something that the Outer Bankers had to deal with on a regular basis. The worst to hit Ocracoke and Portsmouth in recent memory were the storms of 1899 and 1933. After the 1933 storm, several families left Portsmouth for the mainland. Those storms did a lot of damage, but the people always managed to pick up the pieces, rebuild their homes, and get on with their lives, hoping it would be many years before another storm hit. The nor'easters were almost as bad as the hurricanes. They came in the winter and caused much flooding and wind damage.

Chapter 13

On August 1, 1944, a strong hurricane came ashore at South-port and damaged Carolina Beach and the beaches in the Wilming-ton area but did little harm to the Outer Banks. Quickly on its heels, however, came the storm of September 14, 1944. While it never touched land in North Carolina, the eye of the storm passed just off Hatteras on its way north, where it slammed into Long Island and did much damage to New England. Forty-five people died on land and 344 at sea, as five ships sank during the hurricane, including the Coast Guard cutters *Jackson* and *Bedloe*, which went under off the North Carolina coast.

On the morning of September 14, the weather station at Hat-teras recorded barometric pressure of 27.97 inches, the lowest read-ing to date for that location. Winds were clocked at 110 miles per hour at Hatteras before the anemometer was blown away. At Cape Henry, Virginia, winds were clocked at 138 miles per hour. As the storm approached, the strong southeast winds filled the shallow sounds with ocean water, which backed up into the marshes, rivers, and creeks of the Pamlico Sound estuary. But as the eye passed, the winds turned around and the waters of the Pamlico and Albemarle sounds rushed back toward the Outer Banks. During the 1930s, the

Civilian Conservation Corps had built up the dunes at Avon using hurricane fencing. The high dunes acted as a dam for the waters, and the town flooded like a bowl. People had to escape the high waters on the second floors and roofs of homes. Ninety-six of the town's 115 houses were severely damaged or washed off their foundations.

At Ocracoke at 7:00 A.M., winds were clocked at 75 miles per hour until the anemometer flew off the water tower at the naval base. Later winds were estimated at 100 miles per hour. The barometer was at 28.40 inches. By 7:30 A.M., the winds shifted to the northwest, driving water into the village from the sound. Tides were estimated at fourteen feet, and the island was completely underwater. Water rose two to four feet in many homes. Most of the boats in Silver Lake Harbor were blown onto land, including the mailboat *Aleta*, which washed up in front of the Island Inn, causing considerable damage. Six houses were completely destroyed, and the Pamlico Inn, which faced Teach's Hole and looked across Ocracoke Inlet toward Portsmouth, was damaged beyond repair. Many people opened their front doors and hatches in the floor to keep the houses from floating off their foundations. People sought shelter in second floors and attics. By 9:25 A.M., the wind velocity dropped, and by 12:30 P.M., there was complete calm. This was by far the worst storm to hit Ocracoke in recent memory. Electricity and all communications with the outside world were knocked out.

Soon after noon on September 13, Nick and Joe got a radio report from Ocracoke about the coming storm and were told to close and shutter the windows of the Coast Guard Station and warn the residents of Portsmouth. They could see a huge bank of dark clouds coming in from the south, moving in a circular pattern. They quickly got to work warning the residents of the village, who were mostly women and a few old men. The residents took the warning seriously, boarding up homes and making plans to move in with neighbors who had two-story houses. There were only about sixty residents in Portsmouth at that time, including those working off island and in the service. The school had closed in 1943 because the island did not have enough children to support it. When the hurricane hit, no more than forty people were on the island, including the men at the Coast Guard Station. Nick and Joe offered the station for shelter, but most people stayed in their homes. When they drove out to Marcia's house, they did not ask her to come to the Coast Guard

Station—they insisted she come. "You do not need to be out here away from the village with an eighteen-month-old baby. You need to come with us to the station." The station was a moderately sized two-story shingled structure with a third story lookout built by the Lifesaving Service in 1894. It was well built and had survived the 1899 and 1933 storms. Four men were at the station in Portsmouth at that time: Nick, Joe, Sam Gentile, and Victor Gugeletta. The large barracks room on the second floor had several beds and mattresses, so there was plenty of room for Marcia and Stella and anyone else who wanted to stay at the station during the storm. They would put Marcia and Stella in one of the private rooms on the second floor.

"I'm fine right here," said Marcia, who was very independent.

"You don't understand. This looks like a bad one. If you don't want to do it for yourself, at least do it for Stella. She needs to be safe. Besides, your house has only one floor. What if the water gets into the first floor, then what will you do?"

"Go to the attic, I suppose."

"Not with the baby." Nick looked at Marcia sincerely. "Come on, let us help you board up and gather your things and the baby's things. Come with us to the station. Besides, if something happens to you out here, we won't be able to check on you during the storm. If nothing else, it will be an adventure."

Finally she relented.

They closed the storm shutters on the windows and slid boards into the metal brackets that held the shutters shut. She stored the clothes and personal items that she did not take with her in the attic. She didn't try to empty the kitchen cabinets. She simply moved everything on the floor and in the lower cabinets to the counter-tops and rolled up the rugs and put them on the beds, which she propped up with cinder blocks. Then she opened the hatch in the floor. The house sat thirty-six inches from the ground on brick piers, but like the other homes on Portsmouth it was not anchored to the ground or the piers. It merely rested on the piers, so if the water rose above them, the house could float off its foundation. The hatches let the water into the house so that it would not float; a wet house was better than one that had floated away. The walls were wooden, so if water got into the house, it wouldn't destroy plaster or wallboard; the wood just had to dry out. She also latched the doors to keep the wind out, though some people opened them during storms so if the water rose too high it would wash through the house.

Marcia decided to take the horses with her. The station had

a good stable that was on higher ground than hers. She took in the porch furniture and everything lying in the yard that could be blown about. She untied the cow and let her wander; she would find high ground. That was all Marcia could do. As for the chickens, they would have to fend for themselves. Marcia gathered the eggs and left the chickens in their chicken house. Then she packed her bags, and she and Stella left with Nick and Joe, the two horses tied to the back of the Jeep.

They got settled in at the station, and Nick, Joe, and Sam went around getting everything in and shuttering the windows and doors. They rode through the village one more time to make sure everyone had prepared for the storm. They helped Miss Annie Salter seal up the post office and the variety store. Henry Pigott and his sister Lizzie were the only black family on the island; they lived in a bright pink house with a white picket fence overlooking Ocracoke Inlet. Henry, who received a modest stipend for picking up the mail from the mailboat, helped the many older women board up their houses and get things in. Most people took shelter in one of the handful of two-story houses, so they could go upstairs to get away from the high water if need be. Most houses sat on piers like Marcia's, which kept them dry from the majority of storms.

When Nick, Joe, and Sam got in about seven that evening, Marcia had a big dinner fixed for them. They all sat down to country ham, mashed potatoes, green beans, corn on the cob, and her specialty, lemon chess pie, in the station kitchen on the first floor.

"This is the best eating we have had in a long time," Sam said, elbows on the table, carving up his country ham.

Nick buttered and salted his corn and started to eat. "Yep, the best we have had in weeks, I can tell you that." He smiled through the butter gleaming on his cheeks and face.

After they finished eating, they lit the kerosene lamps and waited. Sam pulled out a deck of cards. "Gin, anyone?" he asked. Nick and Joe soon joined him.

"I don't know how to play," Marcia said.

"It's easy; we'll show you," Joe said, dealing four hands. Victor was on watch that night.

"After I put Stella down," she said, taking Stella to their room. After a while, she returned and joined the men to play cards.

It started to rain about ten that night, and the wind began to rise. By midnight the wind was close to gale force. Marcia could not sleep. She looked in on Stella as she slept. Nick, Joe, Sam, and Victor were all over the place, dressed in yellow rain suits, checking the stables and the dinghy at the boat dock, making sure all the windows and doors were secured. They also went up to the third-floor lookout to see what they could see. They climbed the stairs to the second floor, then climbed a heavy ladder with brass rails to the third floor, where they opened a hatch to the tower. Surrounded by windows, the tower provided a 360-degree view of the island, the village, the beach, and the inlet over to Ocracoke. They could see the lights from Ocracoke and the water tower at the naval station until after midnight, when the wind and rain blew so hard that it obscured the view. They stayed up all night as the wind and rain blew horizontally. Stella slept through the night until she got up at five in the morning.

Nick and Joe put on their rain suits and walked out into the wind and rain toward the beach. The station stood close to the water between the village and the beach, overlooking Ocracoke Inlet. A small tidal creek came in from the inlet almost to the station to a dock where they tied their boats. A concrete ramp led from the boathouse to the creek. A ramp on the other side of the building led to the yard of the station. All the boats were in the boathouse, as was the Jeep. The boathouse was at the same level as the first floor of the station, about thirty-six inches from ground level.

They were not gone long before they came back. "The ocean and the waves have breached the dunes; the water is pouring in over the sand flats from the beach," Nick said, pushing hard to close the door against the blowing wind and rain. "I checked the anemometer, and the winds are almost sixty knots, almost hurricane force."

"I don't think you need to go out again until things settle down," Sam said, coming down the stairs from above. "All I can see is whitecaps and waves in the inlet. I can't see Ocracoke."

Stella started to cry. Marcia held her in her arms and sang to her. The wind howled outside, and the rain pummeled the roof, sounding like lead pellets against the wood shingles. Marcia gave Stella a bottle. Then she decided to make some breakfast for the men. Sam took over feeding Stella while Marcia got eggs and bacon out of the icebox. With the wind howling outside, she fried eggs and bacon, which the men ate hungrily.

"That really hit the spot," Nick said with a smile. "You need to move over here permanently, Marcia."

"You wish," she said, eating her own breakfast. "As soon as this storm is over, I'm going home."

The men cleaned up, and she took the baby. Stella was scared, so Marcia tried to distract her with dolls and stories.

By seven that morning, the winds were coming from the north-east at seventy-five miles per hour, driving the water from the ocean onto the island. The barometer was at 28.40 inches. The water rose quickly over the boat dock and around the perimeter of the station. Everyone went to the second floor. Victor climbed to the third-floor lookout and could see nothing but horizontal rain. Occasionally it would subside, and he could see the huge waves breaching the dunes on the beach and washing over the sand flats and into the inlet. The wind blew wave after wave through the inlet into the swelling sound. The water rose into the yard of the station and into the village. He hoped everyone in the village was safe in their homes. He saw several outbuildings blow off their foundations and tumble to the ground. One chicken house exploded when the roof blew off and the walls collapsed. He saw feathers fly into the wind and disappear. The wind whistled around the tower and through every crack in the windows, doors, and walls. He thought he felt the place shake in the wind, but the station was built well. He was not afraid; the station could withstand the wind. He was more concerned about the houses and buildings in the village. He looked out past the steeple of the Methodist church. Most of the houses were standing. The trees were not as fortunate, however; the cedars seemed to go first, while the live oaks held their ground.

At seven-thirty, the winds shifted to the northwest. The water came barreling in from the sound, and before he knew it the entire village was underwater. It seemed to happen in an instant. Victor figured all that water that had blown into the sound for those many hours was now being blown out and over the banks in its quest for the sea. Everywhere he looked there was water.

"About a foot of water on the first floor," Nick called up to Joe, who was in the tower with Victor. "And rising. I got everything off the floor onto the countertops and tables."

"You ought to see this," Joe called down the ladder. "Water is everywhere in the village; I don't see ground anywhere. Even the dunes are covered, and more is coming in." He saw one of the single-story houses float off its foundation. Then the post office and variety store began to shift on its foundation. So far the two-story houses, where most of the island's people were sheltered, were standing their ground. He saw the front door open at the Dixon-Salter house. Henry Pigott's house was under about two feet of water. More outbuildings floated off their foundations. Two one-story houses near the sound on the haul-over road disintegrated into the water. Boats floated through the village, lodging in trees and thickets of cedar. He saw a cow swim through the village seeking high ground, only its head poking above the water. Then he thought about the horses. He looked at the stable. It stood firm but was surrounded by two or three feet of water. Much higher and the horses would have to swim. He hoped the Jeep wasn't underwater. "Nick, can you get out to check on the horses?" Joe called down.

"Not on your life. There is a foot of water on the first floor, and the wind is blowing too hard to open the door."

"What about the Jeep?"

"Oh, my God, the Jeep!" Nick said, sloshing through the water to open the door to the boathouse. The water was just up to the bottom of the Jeep and rising. He located two metal ramps used to elevate the Jeep when they wanted to work on it. He put them under the front tires and drove the front of the Jeep onto the metal ramps, just enough to keep the engine out of the water. If the water rose much more, the Jeep would be in trouble.

"She's okay," Nick called up, "for now."

Marcia held Stella, who sucked her thumb while the rain pummeled the station and the wind roared outside. She sang to her daughter, lullabies and baby songs.

Joe saw the porch collapse on the Tom Gilgo house; then a porch blew off the Washington-Roberts house, shingles flying everywhere. Another roof collapsed near the water; he thought it was the Frank Gaskill house but couldn't be sure. The water continued to rise in the village as it was pummeled by the raging wind. He thought about the villagers huddled in the second floors of houses and hoped everyone was safe.

Nick climbed up to look. "I want to see," he said. "Wow, man, I had no idea." The entire island was underwater. Huge waves rolled in from the sea, and the sound seemed to have taken the village. They could not see Ocracoke. Boats were tossed in the waves like toys. Structures floated through the village, bumping into houses. A few of the houses seemed to shake and then shift, floating off their foundations, only to be stopped in their movement by trees or piles of debris.

By nine-thirty the wind began to die down. At first they thought it was the eye of the storm. But the clouds were still dark overhead. There was no eye; the hurricane was offshore. By twelve-thirty it was completely calm, and the sun was poking through the clouds. Water still covered everything.

Nick, Joe, and Sam pulled on their waders and ventured out, slogging through the water that covered the first floor. Victor stayed in the station. They had to push hard on the door with their shoulders to open it. The water parted to let them out.

The first place they checked was the stable, where they found their horses and Marcia's scared but safe. The water had apparently risen over two feet in the stable. Then they pulled a skiff out of the boathouse and made their way to the village. A group of fifteen people was in the Dixon-Salter house, a big two-story frame home; a group of ten was in the Tom Bragg house; and five people huddled in the upper floors of the Babb house near the church. A few houses floated off their foundations. There was lots of debris from outbuildings, fences, and trees, but everyone was fine. No one was dead and no one seriously injured—just some cuts and bruises from broken glass. The village was a wreck. The post office and variety store had shifted off its foundation but was in good shape otherwise. Two-thirds of the houses had sustained some damage, either from collapsed porches or from floating off their foundations.

As the water receded, the men got the people to the Coast Guard Station because they had emergency supplies there. Marcia and Helen Babb helped prepare meals for everyone to give them strength for the cleanup effort. Marcia worked through the day helping the villagers. She didn't even think about her house, which was about a mile south of the village, past the schoolhouse. Nick, Joe, Victor, and Sam were so busy they didn't have time to take her there, so she stayed a second night at the station. The next morning they got the Jeep out and took her home.

She decided to leave the horses at the stable until she had seen her house. They passed the old schoolhouse, crossed the marshland, and drove by thickets of cedar, fording a few small creeks until they reached her home.

The house was intact, but the outbuildings had been damaged. It was hard to open the front door, as the water had made it swell shut. Thankfully she had left the trapdoor open in the central hall; they could see by the watermarks on the walls that water had risen about one foot in the house. Chairs and tables were overturned, but other than that things were mostly in good shape. Marcia saw a shiny black snake slither out from under her bed, and when she opened a closet door water poured out and with it a large channel bass. She also found fish in the springs of the bed and trapped under the sink in the kitchen. Ants were everywhere, having surged into the house to escape the high water. They found not one but several snakes, which Joe and Nick took care of. The old summer kitchen had begun to shift off its foundation but was still intact; the old cast-iron stove must have helped keep it in place.

When they examined the foundation of the house, they saw that it had shifted, too, but the brick piers still held it. A few had collapsed, and more would have to be built, but the house was still relatively plumb and held firm. One of the supports for the front porch had given way, and the porch roof sagged, but the men got a board and propped it up. The workshop, which had floated off it foundation, was missing a wall, and the stable had been moved but was still in fairly good shape. The outhouse and cooling house were nowhere to be seen. Wood and debris were all over the yard. Several trees, mostly cedars, had blown over, but the old live oaks stood their ground. Marcia looked for the cow and finally found her on top of a dune, eating sea grass. She lifted the trapdoor that led to the attic and found her clothes still dry. The house needed to dry, and it would take weeks to get it cleaned up, so she opened the doors and windows and left it to air out. The boys needed her, so she decided to take Nick and Joe up on their offer to let her stay in the Coast Guard Station for a few more days until she could get back to start the cleanup at her house. She gathered some of her things from the attic, and they returned to the station.

The next day Nick and Joe took a Coast Guard skiff to Ocracoke to report the damage on Portsmouth and to see what damage had been done to Ocracoke. The first things they noticed when they entered the harbor at Ocracoke were that the water tower was gone and that few boats were in the harbor. Then they looked to shore and gasped. Boats littered the shoreline, among them the mailboat *Aleta*, which was sitting on the front lawn of the Island Inn. Big fishing boats and shrimp boats stood on shore next to houses, rested on the road, and pushed into stores and warehouses along the edge of the harbor. The 1940 Coast Guard Station had lost shingles but was otherwise in good shape. The navy section base was battered but still standing, having lost shingles and been stripped to the tarpaper in places. The water tower lay in pieces on the ground. Several stores and buildings along the shore of Silver Lake were destroyed or displaced by the high water. Six houses were completely demolished, others had lost shingles, and a few porches had collapsed. As they motored through the channel between Portsmouth and Ocracoke, which took them close to shore at Springer's Point, they could see the ruins of the Pamlico Inn. The inn's porches had collapsed, the pier had been torn up, and it looked like water had damaged the first floor. The windows and doors stood open, hanging off their hinges, and part of the roof was gone. The electric power plant was shut down, the generators flooded. Communications were down. But no one had been killed or seriously injured, and for that the people of Ocracoke considered themselves lucky. More than four feet of water had covered the village, but people had escaped to second floors and made it through the storm.

Nick and Joe reported to the commander of the section base about conditions at Portsmouth. They told him they had enough supplies for a week. He told them to do the best they could, as Ocracoke itself had similar needs. He promised to send supplies when they arrived from the mainland.

Helen Babb, Annie Salter, and Marcia Styron ran the kitchen at the Coast Guard Station and fed people lunch and dinner. Lunch was mostly soup and bread. But it was hot and good, and it was all they had until supplies came from the mainland. Since most of the cisterns had been flooded, the first thing everyone needed was fresh water.

The Coast Guard quickly sent in boats with supplies to both Portsmouth and Ocracoke.

Chapter 14

Sanger and the men from the *U-352* were kept at Fort Bragg for several months. On May 13, 1943, more than 248,000 Axis troops formerly under the command of German general Erwin Rommel surrendered to the British and Americans in Tunisia. The Allies also captured Rommel's replacement, General Jürgen von Arnim, and he and most of the Axis troops were sent to POW camps in the United States. These were some of the best combat troops in the German army. Large POW camps were built mainly in the South, in Mississippi and Texas, with smaller ones scattered around the country, usually near military bases. In the late spring of 1943, Sanger and the other U-boat men were sent via rail to a prison camp at Fort Clinton, Mississippi. In Europe, German troops were transported in slow-moving freight trains and cattle cars. In the United States, they traveled in comfortable passenger coaches manned by black porters who said "Yes, sir" and "No, sir" to the German prisoners of war. The POWs were fed well and by some accounts treated much better than as servicemen in Germany.

Sanger looked out the window as the train passed endless fields of cotton, wheat, peanuts, soybeans, and other crops. He had never seen a country as vast as this. As the miles ticked by, he began to understand why the Germans would never win this war. The Japanese had truly awakened a sleeping giant when they attacked Pearl Harbor. The Axis powers had no idea how vast and rich were America's resources. America was sleepy, slow to act, bumbling, yes, but there was no way that Germany could defeat this vast nation on its own turf. The best it could hope for was to take so much of Europe that the Americans could not take it back, and to play on the fears of the isolationists.

The POWs passed mile after mile of rich agricultural fields and pine forests for two days on their way through the South to Mississippi. The Germans were not used to such heat. The men wanted to strip down to their undershirts, but Rathke would not permit it. Discipline and dignity were his way. He wanted to demonstrate the superiority of his troops over the undisciplined and lax Americans every chance that he could. He also wanted to demonstrate the superiority of his race over the Negro porters. He treated them with disdain at every opportunity.

"Can I get you gentlemen some water?" a kindly black porter asked Rathke and one of his officers sitting in the plush seats of the passenger car.

"Yes," he answered, but when the water arrived Rathke made a point of wiping the glass where the porter had touched it. The porter did not miss this. Some of the Germans had never seen black men or women before they came to America. But in the camp at Fort Bragg, blacks cooked for the men. Blacks were clearly treated as an inferior race in the American South. The whites showed a clear disdain for them, as did the Germans, even though the Germans were POWs.

Once in Mississippi they disembarked at a small wooden railroad station and were loaded onto buses for the drive to the camp. The town of Clinton was small, with a few brick stores, tree-lined streets, a small college, and several impressive homes. Surrounding the core of the town were rows of neatly painted white houses, some modest, some grand with white columns and magnolia trees in the front yards. The state capital of Jackson was only a few miles away. Once they left the town heading south, they encountered more fields, the predominant crop being cotton. Occasionally they would see big, columned white houses cooled by groves of huge oak trees. In the rear of the houses were numerous outbuildings and rows of unpainted shanties of black sharecroppers. The black children played barefoot and in tattered clothes in dirt yards. Mothers swept the dirt in the front yards, stirring up dust. Some of the trees in front of the houses were painted white a few feet up from the ground. Ramshackle country stores and gas stations stood by the road on the way to the camp, as well as more humble farmhouses owned by white families, some painted, some unpainted and not much better than the black shanties. Most of the poor whites were also barefoot and wore shabby clothes. Poverty amid such plenty, it is the way of the world everywhere, Sanger thought.

After passing several plantations, they came to the new POW camp, constructed of freshly milled wood and crisp, shiny, new wire fencing topped with barbed wire. Towers surrounded the wire enclosure. The barracks were covered in tarpaper and were arranged neatly in rows. The camp was already full of men, the remnants of Rommel's elite Africa Corps, all excellent specimens of mankind, even in defeat. Bigger and more muscular and athletic than the smaller submariners, they were also more adapted to the summer heat of Mississippi after their experience in North Africa. Camp Clinton held about thirty-four hundred POWs.

They were led from the buses to be processed as before. They were told to strip, then they were marched to showers, where they were deloused with a spray of water and chemicals, told to dry off, and issued new prison clothes more suited for the warmer climate of Mississippi. They were allowed to keep their uniforms, if they had them, for use in ceremonial occasions such as funerals and holidays. Most of the time, they wore black or khaki shirts and pants with the letters *PW* stenciled in paint on each leg. Winter clothes were wool jackets and pants. Athletic shorts and shirts were issued for games. There were five barracks. Each held up to fifty men and had a mess hall with cooks, waiters, silverware, and good food. Most of the food was prepared by German cooks with ingredients provided by the Americans. A sample breakfast was cereal, toast, jam, coffee, milk, and sugar. Lunch typically was roast pork, potato salad, carrots, and ice water. Supper might be meat loaf, scrambled eggs, coffee, milk, and bread. Beer could be bought in the canteen. Individual barracks had their own sports teams in horseshoes, volleyball, and soccer. Sanger led the soccer team of his barracks. Contests between the barracks were highly competitive, and some of the outcomes were reported in the *Mississippi Post.*

The submariners were kept together as before and given their own barracks. They were allowed to interact with the other prisoners, too. With so many men, the Americans began to segregate them according to their politics. The men were still under the control of German officers, but the more hard-line Nazis were sent to another camp.

The camp was surrounded by double barbed wire fencing, watchtowers, floodlights, and dog patrols. The day began with reveille at 5:45 A.M., and lights were turned off at 10:00 P.M. The men were allowed to see American movies, as well as nonpolitical German movies brought by the Red Cross. The American movies were more popular than the sanitized movies from Germany. Often as many as a thousand men would watch movies at night in the open air. In 1944 the War Department issued a directive listing twenty-four acceptable movies. Cartoons were some of the favorites. A typical night would include a showing of *Tigers of the Deep; Pittsburgh, the Steel Town;* and *The Great Victor Herbert.* Another night they would see *Andy Panda Goes Fishing,* a cartoon; *Fire, the Red Poacher,* a documentary; and *The Gentleman from West Point.* They also had theatrical performances and musical concerts. They loved American music. Some of the tunes popular with the Germans were "Tuxedo Junction," "Missouri Waltz," "Home on the Range," "Whistling Cowboy," and of course "Don't Fence Me In" by Bing Crosby.

Because the men came from such a wide range of backgrounds—teachers, bankers, carpenters, watchmakers, lawyers, mechanics—the camp was a huge reservoir of talent for teaching courses. The prisoners elected a study leader, who was responsible for setting the camp's educational curriculum. By the end of 1943, most POW camps had courses in English, Spanish, German literature, shorthand, chemistry, mathematics, and commerce. At Camp Clinton prisoners took courses on the history of the American Indian, Chinese culture, and the plants of the United States. In time university-level courses were offered through local colleges. On May 19, 1944, the Reich Ministry of Education offered full high-school and university credit for courses taken by German prisoners in the United States.

German officers were not required to work under the Geneva Convention, but the enlisted men could be made to work. Most of the time, the Germans were happy to work, get out of the camp, and make some money, which they could spend at the camp PX. Fort Clinton had a high concentration of German generals and high-ranking officers. Twenty-three generals were housed there, along with several colonels, majors, and captains. They had special housing and were treated differently from the others. General Von Arnim, Rommel's replacement, lived in a house and was furnished a car and driver. It was rumored that he attended movies in Jackson because it was the only place in town that was air-conditioned. Other than the heat, the Germans found camp life, and especially the food, to be acceptable. They were fed much better than in Africa and on board the cramped submarines; they had plenty of fresh vegetables, pork, chicken, and beef.

It was the duty of every German POW to try to escape, but being in the middle of Mississippi, even if you did escape, where would you go? To New Orleans and try to catch a boat to South America? To Mexico? Canada was hundreds of miles away and perhaps more hostile than American territory. But nevertheless it was the duty of a good German to try. The Americans knew it would be difficult for Germans to make it home from the middle of Mississippi, so security was lax. One time two German soldiers from Rommel's Africa Corps decided to escape from the farm where they were working. They easily ran away and walked into the town of Clinton. Once there they had no idea what to do. The police found them wandering around town looking into store windows in their POW clothes. They had no money, could not speak English, and were obviously from the camp. The local police picked them up and brought them back. The escape was easy, but the hard part was what to do afterward.

The war had taken most of the able-bodied men in the area, and crops were rotting on the stalk and vine with no one to harvest them. Local farmers were grateful for the labor provided by the German soldiers, and they paid the government the prevailing rate of $1.50 per day per worker. Of this the prisoner was paid $.80 in canteen coupons, and the difference went to the federal treasury to pay for the POW program. Many farmers maintained warm friendships with the Germans. Most of the men worked on cotton and tree plantations. The men did not like picking cotton; it was backbreaking work that required thick, tough skin. Pickers had to stoop to pick the cotton, and their fingers were shredded and bloody from the hard husks by the end of the day. Another project the POWs from Fort Clinton worked on was the Mississippi River Basin Model, a one-square-mile model of the entire Mississippi River Basin that was used by the United States Army Corps of Engineers to assess water flow and predict floods on the Mississippi and its tributaries.

Sanger decided to work for local planters taking care of farm animals, mainly hogs, chickens, horses, mules, and cattle. Because he spoke English so well, he was in demand and could work for whomever he wanted. He worked for some of the larger planters until he settled in with one family, the Bellamys.

Mr. and Mrs. Bellamy had two sons who were in the South Pacific and two daughters in their early twenties who lived on the plantation. They lived in a large red-brick antebellum house wrapped on three sides with a two-story porch supported by white Corinthian columns. It was the seat of a thousand-acre cotton plantation. The columns needed to be painted, evidence that the Bellamys had fallen on hard times during the Depression. But they had managed to keep their plantation, and now cotton prices were good because of the war and things were looking up for the family fortunes.

They called the good-natured Nathaniel Bellamy—the head of the family, who was in his early sixties—"Captain Bellamy," though Sanger could never determine whether he had ever had any real military service. Captain Bellamy did not put the Germans in the field picking cotton; he thought that was Negro work. Captain Bellamy liked Sanger, who reminded him of one of his sons. He soon began to treat the handsome POW as a member of the family. At first Sanger and a group of the POWs took charge of slopping the hogs, then Sanger moved up to running the heavy equipment. Two other Germans started to manage the black field hands working the cotton. The black farmworkers resented being bossed by German POWs, but they had little choice, as this was Captain Bellamy's decision. The twins, Katherine and Sarah Jane, both had beaus who were away at war in the South Pacific, too, but this did not keep them from admiring the handsome young German sailor from Dresden. In fact, when he pulled off his shirt and rinsed off with the hose beside the barn, curtains in the house would part so that the ladies could take a peek. They admired the same physical attributes that had attracted Marcia Styron—his trim athletic build, close-cropped blond hair, well-defined muscles, and blue eyes that a woman could get lost in.

"I wonder what he thinks of Southern girls?" Katherine asked her sister with a wry smile.

"I don't know, but I'm willing to find out," said Sarah Jane, formulating a plan.

The next day when Sanger was working in the barn, the girls decided they would wash their father's 1936 black Packard Super Eight sedan. Katherine, barefoot and wearing a thin floral-patterned rayon sundress, had wrapped her long auburn hair up in a terry cloth. She walked out of the house with a large pail filled with soapy water and two sponges. Sarah Jane followed wearing khaki mid-calf capris and a white blouse with her shirttails tied at her midriff. She was also barefoot, and her brown hair was wrapped up in a terry cloth. Sarah Jane held a garden hose attached to a pipe beside the barn.

First Sarah Jane sprayed the car with the hose, then they each took a sponge and began to soap it up. The girls were shapely and attractive, with large breasts. Katherine made sure that Sanger was in the yard when she began to soap down the side windows, pressing her breasts against them. Sarah Jane hosed down what Katherine had just soaped, and the water sprayed Katherine, making her dress cling to her body. Katherine then wrested the hose from Sarah Jane and sprayed her sister with water. Sarah Jane picked up a sponge from the bucket and threw it at Katherine, hitting her squarely in her chest. Sanger and the other German workers dropped what they were doing to watch the show.

Sarah Jane got control of the hose and completely soaked Katherine, whose dress clung to her, revealing intimate details of her body. Sarah Jane was soaking wet, her blouse almost transparent. The girls began to laugh and giggle as they threw the soapy sponges and sprayed each other with the hose. Then Katherine got the idea of spraying the men who stood gawking at them, to cool them off. She first got Sanger, whose white T-shirt went transparent with the soaking. He stood still and let them soak him, not daring to say a word. Then they sprayed the other men, who were not as reserved as Sanger; he knew the twins and their antics.

One of the men grabbed the hose from Katherine. "Let me have that," the German soldier said good-naturedly. Sanger glanced toward the kitchen door of the house, hoping Mrs. Bellamy would rescue them.

Sure enough, Mrs. Bellamy came flying out, shouting to her daughters. "Girls, get in the house this minute; you-all are not even decent. Can't you see you are keeping the men from their work?"

Mrs. Bellamy took an arm of each of her daughters and led them into the house. Katherine and Sarah Jane looked back at the men staring at them, smiled, and waved, as if to say they would be back.

"I'm telling you, them two is trouble with a capital T," Hank, the foreman of the work crew, said. He had worked for the Bellamy family for years.

A few days later when Sanger was working alone putting hay up in the barn, Katherine came in wearing the same rayon sundress as when she washed the car.

"Bet it's been a long time since you have been with a woman," Katherine said. "Daddy told me you were a sailor on a submarine. Sailors spend a lot time at sea without ever seeing a woman. I bet you would really like to be with a woman right now, wouldn't you?"

"It has been a long time—over a year," Sanger said as he kept working.

"When was the last time you were with someone? Was she a whore?"

"No."

"Was she a girlfriend?"

"Yes."

"What was her name?"

"Marcia," Sanger said absently.

"Marcia, that sounds like an American name. Were you with an American girl while you were a POW?" Katherine said, becoming a little excited.

"No, Miss Bellamy. She was a girl I met in France. Marcia is a French name," he lied.

"She wasn't a whore?"

"No, she was a nice girl who I liked very much."

"Do you love her?"

"Yes."

"Are you going to be faithful to her, or are you going to fool around on her?" she said, moving closer to him.

"It is not like I have much opportunity to fool around while I am a POW."

"You might be surprised," she said, rubbing up against him. Then she grabbed his crotch. "Nice. Are you going to let me see it?"

"Miss Bellamy, you know that I would get into a lot of trouble if I did that," he said, her hand still on his crotch, which began to respond to her touch.

"I won't tell," she said with a wry grin. Then she pulled his head around to face her and kissed him.

"Miss Bellamy, what would your father say? What would your boyfriend say? Isn't he away in the Pacific?" Sanger said, pulling away.

"They don't have to know," she said, pulling him to her to kiss him again.

Sanger was in a dilemma. If he responded he could get into trouble and probably wouldn't be allowed to work for the Bellamys again. He enjoyed getting out of the camp and working. But he was also young, and it *had* been a long time since he had been with a woman. He had been with plenty of loose women in France; it wasn't that he was a prude. He also knew how furious a woman scorned could be.

"Do you find me attractive?" Katherine asked.

He knew the right answer to this one. "You are very attractive, Miss Bellamy."

"Don't call me Miss Bellamy; call me Kat."

"You are a beautiful woman, Miss Kat," he said. She pulled him to her and kissed him again. Then she squeezed his crotch to feel his bulging manhood. "But you must realize what a position this puts me in. I am a German POW working here by the good graces of your father. I don't want to jeopardize that. I am afraid that if he found us he would let me go and I would never be allowed to return."

"We can be discreet."

"What about your sister?"

"My sister and I share everything," Katherine said with a grin.

At that moment Hank walked into the barn. He saw how close Sanger and Katherine were and knew immediately what Katherine was up to. "Sanger, we need you outside."

"Yes, sir," Sanger said, glad to be rescued. Katherine brushed her hand across his face and blew him a kiss.

"Watch out for that one, Sanger," Hank said with a knowing look. "She's trouble. I know from experience."

Sanger was not invited back to work at the Bellamy plantation. He figured Hank must have said something to Captain Bellamy. He was relieved. He didn't know how he could hold Katherine off much longer without either doing something he shouldn't or rejecting her and making her mad. It was a no-win situation.

The next farmer he worked for was considerably poorer and more unsophisticated than Captain Bellamy. His name was Henry Williams. He raised hogs and cotton on his small farm, and he worked his Germans hard. His only son was in Europe fighting the

Germans. He hated the Germans, but they were cheap labor, and he didn't mind using them. He also had some black tenant farmers. He worked them hard and called them niggers, a word the Bellamys never used.

Sanger didn't last long there. As soon as a position came open with another farmer, he took it. Sanger was an officer, and he did not have to work on the farms, or for people who mistreated him. He was not a slave laborer; he worked because he wanted to.

The next farmer he worked for had lost his only son in the Pacific. Sam Harris and his wife, Isabel, needed the help of the Germans. They were Quakers and were opposed to the war, but their son had enlisted against their will. He died barely two years after the war began. This left them with no heirs to run their six-hundred-acre farm in the fertile Mississippi Valley. They took to Sanger immediately and treated their German laborers with respect and dignity. They insisted that Sanger and the others join them for lunch in the house. Sam Harris treated Kurt Sanger like a son, and Sanger returned the favor, treating the Harrises like a son would treat his parents. They were the same age as his own parents and reminded him of them.

"Kurt, I love you like a son. You have been so good to Isabel and me and have helped us so much on the farm. I wish I could do more for you," Sam said to Kurt at the dinner table one night just as he was to be picked up by the prison bus. "After the war I wish you would return. I would give you this farm if you would return. I have nephews who will inherit it, but they don't care about it, not like you do. I would adopt you if I could."

"Thank you, Mr. Harris. I have truly enjoyed working for you and Mrs. Harris and getting to know you. You have no idea. But my home is in Germany. I hope you understand that. I will never forget my friends here in America, however. If I can I will return after the war," Sanger said, then boarded the bus back to the camp.

The next day all the submariners were called into the mess hall for an announcement.

"Tomorrow morning at five o'clock all submariners shall report to the parade grounds with all their gear packed. We are going to relocate you to Arizona," the American officer announced. "All U-boat men will be brought together at a special camp at Papago Park near Phoenix, Arizona. This is part of our effort to segregate POWs by their branch of service."

Sanger would not have a chance to say good-bye to the Harrises. He would write them. He would miss them. They had truly become good friends. With them he felt he had a family again. According to letters from home, his father was very ill, and his mother was worried. The Allies had not bombed Dresden, but it was only a matter of time; they were bombing other German cities daily. Dresden was not a prime target, but it was an important rail link and the site of an optics plant and some other industries. He was worried about his mother and father. He was a POW, but he felt safer than his parents in the homeland. He also continued to write Marcia, but she never wrote him back. He wanted to see her again; he wanted to see Portsmouth again. He knew instinctively that there was a reason he must return.

That night he dreamt about Portsmouth again. He was running on the beach in his athletic shorts. He did not wear a shirt. He had a tan. It was summertime, hot, but a fresh breeze was blowing in from the ocean. In the distance at the horizon was a bank of dark clouds. Then he saw a jagged crack of brilliant red light peek through them. It was the sun, just after sunrise. The great red ball continued to rise and broke above the dark clouds. Its lower edge was jagged from the clouds, while the top was perfectly round. The light from the new sun and the clouds reflected on the wet beach, giving it the color and luster of mother-of-pearl. Birds stood guard on the beach, watching the water for fish. A ghost crab sidled by and scampered to a large hole in the sand, standing at the entrance until he went by. No one was on the beach. He stopped and took off his running shorts and waded into the water. It was crystal clear. He swam out toward the waves, then came back in. He walked for a while naked on the beach until he dried off. The sun, now clear of the clouds, colored the edges of the water with fire. He felt a sense of danger and turned around looking in all directions, but no one was there.

Chapter 15

Aunt Charlotte O'Neal knew that Marcia needed a break from taking care of Stella, so she offered to baby-sit. This was hardly a hardship, since Stella was the only baby on the island and Aunt Charlotte loved babies. Still, Marcia rarely took her up on her offer. On one such rare occasion, Nick and Joe were at the house and suggested they go flounder gigging and have a big seafood dinner at Marcia's. She said no at first but then agreed. They could gather some clams and oysters, too, and have a regular feast. It was November 1944; fall was always a good time for fishing. For the most part, Portsmouth had recovered from the storm, been picked up and fixed up. Marcia got her house straight, the porch fixed, and the outbuildings mostly rebuilt. Things were getting back to normal for her. It was time to relax and enjoy the season with her friends. She had a little flat-bottomed skiff that her husband had kept in the shed, so with Aunt Charlotte baby-sitting, she, Joe, and Nick decided to go flounder gigging one night.

They took a kerosene lamp, big Coast Guard flashlights, long metal gigs with wooden handles, a good bucket, and poles to push the boat through the water. They also wore high rubber boots in case they needed to go in the water to gather oysters when they found them along the edges of the tidal creeks.

"You must be very quiet," Marcia said to the two men, who had never gigged a flounder before. All bundled up, they quietly pushed the boat through the winding creek behind Marcia's house. Just enough light came from the three-quarter moon to show the way without lights. "Give me a flashlight," she said, taking one from Nick and pointing it in the water. All they could see through the clear water was sand, oyster shells, and sea grass. Then she whispered, "Stop poling and give me a gig. I see one."

Nick and Joe could see nothing but sand.

Then Marcia jabbed, and the edges of a pancake-sized flounder began to flutter in the sand around the gig. "Got it," she said, pulling up a good-sized flounder, taking it off the gig, and placing it in the pail.

"I didn't see a thing," Nick said, looking at the flounder flopping about in the pail.

"You've got to look closely; you can see the eyes. The rest of it is buried in the sand. They freeze when you shine the light on them. Here, look." She handed him the flashlight.

Nick slowly surveyed the water with the light but saw nothing.

"Let me have it," she said, taking the light. Once again she stabbed the water and came up with a twelve-inch flounder flapping on the gig.

Joe took the gig and started to scan the water. He did not see anything.

"Look very closely; look for their eyes. There's one. Do you see it?" she said, pointing.

Joe peered into the water and at first did not see it. Then he thought he saw a black eye glint in the light. "I think I see it." He jabbed at it with the gig, and sure enough he had one. A good-sized flounder, about fourteen inches, flopped around on the end of the gig. "That is neat. I think I like this flounder-gigging business," Joe said.

"Here, let me try," Nick said, taking the gig after Joe had gotten the fish off the end.

"If you look real close, you can see the outline of the fish in the sand sometimes, too," Marcia said. "There's one. Can you see it, Nick?"

"Yeah, I think I do," he said, then jabbed at the water, pulling out a flounder flopping at the end of the gig.

"One more and then we look for oysters. We don't want to get greedy here," Marcia said.

"I see one," Joe said, and jabbed at the water. But he came up with nothing. "Must have been a rock or a shell."

Marcia took the gig and after a few minutes spotted one and took it. After that the guys stepped out of the boat and gathered a few clumps of oysters along the edges of the creek.

"We are going to have a feast tonight," Joe said.

"We sure are. I hope Aunt Charlotte is ready for us when we return," Nick chimed in.

Chapter 16

Sanger was sorry that he did not have a chance to say good-bye to the Harrises, but orders were orders. He would write them from Papago Park. He had seen Arizona on a map; it was to the west. Little did he know just how far it was. It took days through the back country of Louisiana and across the plains of Texas, then into the mountains of New Mexico, across deserts, to finally reach dry and arid Arizona, only recently made a state, not long ago a Wild West territory. The landscape was like none the German submariners had ever seen—desert similar to what Rommel's men had experienced in North Africa. Monument Valley, the Petrified Forest, vast desert sands, gorges, canyons, arid mountains, extinct volcanic cones— there was nothing like it in Europe. The men were amazed at the vastness of the country, and they were still not all the way across it. California was hundreds of miles to the west of Arizona.

They were not quite sure why the U-boat men were sent to Arizona. Perhaps because they were so renowned and feared. Perhaps the Americans thought they would be more likely than others to try to escape. There were few farms to work on near Phoenix, only a few citrus groves. The camp was located in a dry area surrounded by mountains and a desert landscape on the outskirts of Phoenix.

They could work in town with merchants, on public works such as highways, and in the citrus groves, but the heat was so great that few of the German prisoners wanted to do that. So they mainly stayed at camp. Sports were their only outlet, but sports in the Arizona heat were a challenge. When they arrived they met other submariners there. Then they got the full story about how the Americans had finally organized convoys. After the summer of 1942, there had been little action along the American East Coast. The Germans shifted their focus to the mid-Atlantic and the Mediterranean. The U-boat men were still brave and had victories to brag about, but their effectiveness was diminished. With the German surface navy decimated and confined to the Baltic, British and American control of the seas was almost complete. The U-boats were relegated to little more than guerilla warfare at sea.

It was suspected that some of their comrades in the camps were feeding information to the Americans. The German commanders set out to identify the spies and eliminate them. Sanger had heard whisperings, but he was not in on the plans for handling the traitors. Because there were not as many U-boat men as other prisoners, the prison population at Papago Park was not huge—only about seventeen hundred. Under Dönitz, the Ubootwaffe was a close-knit group. The men knew each other, even though they had been captured at different times. It soon became apparent to the commanders who the spies were, and news traveled between camps.

On the night of March 12, 1944, Sanger was taking a shower with a group of about twenty men. Papago offered several large communal showers. They were close to the toilets and sinks, where the men could shave and brush their teeth. In the steamy shower room, the naked bodies of the well-formed men glistened with water and soap under the glare of the bright incandescent lights. Suddenly several of the men began to sing an old, familiar German drinking song. The man showering beside Sanger put his finger to his lips and said, "You have seen nothing tonight." Sanger watched a group of seven men, including Otto Stenger from the *U-352*, form a circle around a slender young man known as Leimi, who had just arrived from a camp in Maryland. The young man looked not much older than a teenager. He sported a goatee and had close-cropped brown hair, nervous eyes, angular features, and a prominent Adam's apple. He was in the middle row of showers. His milk-white skin and underdeveloped body contrasted with the tanned, muscular bodies of the men who had been in the Arizona desert for months.

"So you're the spy," Stenger said, roughly taking the young man by the arm and twisting it behind his back.

"I don't know what you are talking about," Leimi replied.

"Word from Maryland has it that you cooperated with the Americans and fed them information about your camp mates and the Ubootwaffe. I am here to tell you that you won't be doing that at Papago Park." Stenger then roughly threw the boy on the concrete floor and kicked him in the groin. Leimi rolled into a fetal position and cupped his genitals with his hands to protect himself. Then, one by one, the other men began to kick him as he lay on the floor, in the ribs, the side, the back, the groin, anyplace they could find. Leimi whimpered as he tried to ball himself up tighter to fend off the attacks. The song grew louder.

Then one of the men produced a rope and threw one end over a ceiling rafter. The other end was tied in a noose. While the young man was lying on the concrete floor in a fetal position, his attackers tied his hands and wrapped his legs with strips of sheets, then shoved a gag in his mouth and slipped the noose around his neck and tightened it. He struggled as hard as he could against the grip of the bigger men. Then three of them pulled the end of the rope, lifting him off the floor, and tied the rope to a water pipe. His legs kicked wildly as his body danced in the air. This struggle lasted several minutes as the other men continued to sing their beer song. Soon his struggle ended and his pale white body, naked and dripping with water, dangled limply from the noose, his head hanging to one side.

The young man was known as Petty Officer Leimi, but this was a name given to him as cover by the Americans. He was barely twenty-one years old. His real name was Werner Drechsler, and he was from Muhlberg, Germany. He was one of sixteen survivors of the *U-118*, which was sunk off the Azores, but he had agreed to cooperate with the Joint Interrogation Center of the navy and was placed in a POW camp near Fort Meade, Maryland. He was bitter against the Nazis because his father was detained in a concentration camp as a political prisoner. In the POW camp, he gathered information from other U-boat men and passed it on to the Americans. After a while, his comrades began to suspect him of spying, and he was transferred to the custody of the army. On March 12, 1944, the army transferred him to Papago Park, which was filled with other submariners despite the fact that the navy investigators stipulated that he should never be sent to a camp where other German naval POWs were being held. Also, some of the other survivors of the *U-118* who knew his real name were at Papago Park. This amounted to a death sentence for Leimi. Within six and a half hours of arriving at Papago, he was recognized by other U-boat men as a traitor, tried by his peers while he slept, and hanged by the neck.

When the shower emptied, the guards found Drechsler hanging from the rafters. They cut him down, slashed the material binding his hands and legs, and removed the gag from his mouth. They ordered Sanger and another man to carry the body to the infirmary. They laid it out with eyes still open on an examining table. Sanger closed Leimi's eyes, and the camp doctor covered his nakedness with a sheet. Later Leimi's body was packed in sawdust and shipped to Fort Bliss in El Paso, Texas, where it was buried with other German POWs. The men suspected of killing Drechsler were sent to Fort Leavenworth, Kansas, where they were tried and executed for the murder.

Of the seven men executed, one of them, Otto Stenger, was from the *U-352*. Sanger knew him well. The others were Helmut Fischer, Fritz Franke, Günther Kuelson, Heinrich Ludwig, Bernard Ryak, and Rolf Wizuy. Sanger had been with Stenger since he was put with the survivors of the *U-352*. It was a terrible business, war. Sanger was ready for it to be over.

The war dragged on. The German Sixth Army was defeated at Stalingrad on February 2, 1943, and the Allies landed in Sicily on July 9, 1943, and entered Rome on June 4, 1944. On June 6, 1944, the Allies landed at Normandy in France. They invaded southern France on August 15 and liberated Paris by August 25, 1944. The Soviets began their offensive in the east on June 22, 1944. But the battle dragged on in Europe. As the Allies prepared to invade Germany through the Low Countries, the Germans pushed back against their advance at the Battle of the Bulge in Belgium on December 16, 1944.

The British and the Americans were bombing German cities daily. Hamburg had been firebombed in 1943, when more than forty thousand civilians were killed in one raid as the firestorm melted the asphalt of the streets and temperatures rose to fifteen hundred degrees Fahrenheit. The oxygen was sucked out of the air, and people hiding in shelters suffocated. Tornado-like winds whipped up to 150 miles per hour, tossing people around the streets like leaves.

Berlin had been bombed early in the war, but an all-out blanket bombing began in late 1944 and early 1945 as the Russians advanced from the east on the German capital. Dresden, Sanger's home and the capital of Saxony, was affectionately known as "the Florence on the Elbe" because of its art, culture, and architecture. It had seen little of the war and so far had missed the bombing altogether, though it was swollen with German refugees from the east. Sanger heard from his parents on a regular basis. His father still taught math at the Technische Universität Dresden, and his mother taught in a high school, but they were sick of seeing all the boys they had loved and trained and watched grow to manhood be taken out of school and sent to war.

Cold weather swept the United States as the bad news came from Belgium a few days before Christmas 1944. Temperatures dropped to thirty-four below zero in parts of the Northeast, snow fell across the northern plains, and a cold drizzle soaked Phoenix. Hopes of an early end to the war with the invasion of Germany faded with the news of the American lines being overrun by the Germans at the Battle of the Bulge.

The prisoners of war at Papago Park cheered as they heard radio broadcasts of the German victories in Belgium. The German prisoners tended not to believe the many reports of American and Allied victories, thinking they were propaganda. A festive mood and an air of cockiness, hell-raising, and celebration prevailed at Papago in response to the German successes. On the night of December 23, submarine captain Jürgen Wattenberg encouraged the men in the adjoining compound, including Sanger, to have a rowdy celebration. The men were not told why, but it was to distract the guards so a group of German navy officers and enlisted men could escape using a tunnel they had built. Wattenberg, forty-three, was a blond, steely-eyed, determined man of medium build. Athletic and well built, he ran and worked out every day, conditioning himself for the challenge of escape.

The Papago prisoner-of-war camp was isolated in the desert, so the American guards considered escape impossible. They were certain that the rocky ground was too hard for digging tunnels. But that is exactly what the Germans did. The digging began in September 1944 after the officers had surveyed the camp for the best places for the entrance and exit of the tunnel. Since the guards did not expect tunnels, they did not look for them. The exit was located out of view of the watch towers.

The POWs asked for permission to build a volleyball court,

which required tools to level the rough desert landscape. They used these same tools to dig the tunnel by night. The tunnel ended up being 178 feet long and 3 feet tall and wide and lay about 6 to 14 feet below the surface, going under the prison fence, a drainage ditch, and a road. The exit was near a power pole in a clump of bushes about 15 feet from the Cross Cut Canal. The men stuffed the dirt in their pants pockets, which had holes in the bottoms, and they shuffled the dirt out along the ground as they walked. They also flushed a large amount of dirt down the toilets. They called it the Volleyball Tunnel. To cover up the exit, they built a square box, filled it with dirt, and planted native plants in it for a lid, making it look like undisturbed desert. Sanger knew about the tunnel and did not alert the guards, but he did not help build the tunnel either. He did not want to take part in the escape. He thought it was foolhardy and did not want to jeopardize his good standing with the American guards and their commanders.

Beginning about nine in the evening on December 23, prisoners started crawling out the tunnel in teams of two or three. Next door their buddies were singing, breaking bottles, waving flags, and generally having a big, loud, riotous party. Each of the men who escaped carried clothing, food, forged papers, cigarettes, and medical supplies, plus anything else they would need on the outside. Wattenberg had managed to procure the names and addresses of people in Mexico who might help them get back to Germany.

Using maps of the area, they planned to float down the Cross Cut Canal, then travel by way of the Salt River and the Gila River to the Colorado River, which would take them into Mexico. Three of the men built a canoe that could be taken apart and carried in three pieces. They didn't know that when a map of Arizona shows a river, it will be filled with water only part of the year. The men found that the Salt River had no water, so they decided to carry their canoe twenty miles to the Gila River, only to find it, too, had no running water but was a series of large puddles. It was then that they realized their predicament.

By two-thirty in the morning on December 24, twelve officers and thirteen enlisted men had escaped in one of the largest POW breakouts in the United States. Few of the men actually hoped to return to Germany. But at least two of them made it to Mexico, where they were almost shot as spies before they could be rescued by the Americans.

Ironically, camp officials and guards didn't know anything had happened until some of the escapees started to give themselves up on Christmas Eve. The first to return was Herbert Fuchs, who decided he had been cold, wet, and hungry long enough. Thinking about his dry, warm bed and the hot meals that the men in the prison camp were enjoying, the twenty-two-year-old U-boat crewman hitched a ride on East Van Buren Street and asked the driver to take him to the sheriff's office, where he surrendered. When the sheriff called the camp, it was a complete surprise.

Then a woman called from Tempe to say that two prisoners had knocked on her door and surrendered. Then a Tempe man called to say he had two escaped prisoners at his house who needed to be picked up.

Commander Jürgen Wattenburg who masterminded the plan, and two of his U-boat crewmen, Walter Kozur and Johann Kremer, stayed on the loose for a longer time. By two in the morning on the twenty-fourth, they found themselves in a citrus grove located northwest of the camp through the desert; they ate grapefruit for breakfast before getting some sleep in the cold drizzle. By sunrise, they found an old shack and took turns sleeping and guarding. Kremer took out his harmonica and quietly played "Stille Nacht" on Christmas Eve.

After eating some of the provisions they had brought with them, they made their way through the countryside, hiding in gullies by day and exploring the mountains by night.

Meanwhile, back at Papago Park, the guards had been called in from holiday leave to look for the escapees. They were joined by men from the Ninth Service Command, Fort Douglas, Utah; the provost marshal general's office in Washington, D.C.; the Federal Bureau of Investigation; and other governmental agencies. Several days passed before Private First Class Lawrence Jorgensen of the American army discovered the hatch concealing the tunnel and figured out how the POWs had escaped.

Near the Squaw Peak area, Wattenberg and his two companions found a cave they used for cover. They rolled several large rocks to block the entrance and covered it with brush. Kremer scooped out a firepit, and they had their first pot of coffee brewing by sunrise. They were able to fill their canteens from an irrigation pipe nearby.

At the end of the first week of January 1945, Kremer and Kozur slipped into Phoenix at night to get information about their comrades. When they returned they had newspapers but no maps. The headline in the local paper read, "TWO NAZIS APPREHENDED AT

MEXICAN BORDER," referring to the capture and near shooting of Reinhard Mark, a midshipman, and Heinrich Palmer, a petty officer, south of Sells, Arizona.

Before the escape Wattenberg had told one of the men in his barracks who stayed behind that he intended to hide in the mountains to the north until he could escape farther south. He drew a sketch and asked the crewman to leave some supplies there when he was out on a work party. By January 18 their food supplies were running low, so Wattenberg sent Kremer to the agreed-upon place, where in an abandoned, dismantled vehicle he found fruit, bread, and several packs of cigarettes. Kremer left a thank-you note. Then Kremer decided to sneak back into camp by infiltrating one of the work details. There, he could get news of the other escapees, as well as more food, before slipping away from another work detail the next day. He was partially successful. He made it back into camp. But during a surprise inspection on the afternoon of Tuesday, January 23, Kremer was caught after having been in the camp undetected for three days. The next day Walter Kozur was captured by three soldiers while foraging for supplies. That left only Wattenberg still at large.

Wattenberg decided that he would go into Phoenix and try to get a job at a restaurant as a dishwasher. He also considered hopping a freight train, hoping to arrive at some faraway place that hadn't heard of the POW escape, perhaps a farm where he might get a job. After sundown he walked into town along East Van Buren. No one noticed him as the cars moved along the busy thoroughfare. Walking into the central business district of Phoenix, Wattenberg stepped into the American Kitchen restaurant. In his best voice, with as little accent as he could manage, he ordered beef noodle soup and a cold beer.

Wattenberg then went to several small hotels looking for a room for the night; they were all full. Then he came to the Hotel Adams, where the desk clerk told him no rooms were open but that one might open up in the morning after checkout. Wattenberg sat in a big overstuffed chair in the lobby and started to read a newspaper but soon fell asleep.

When he woke, he noticed that the bellhop was watching him with more than passing interest. He wondered if his picture had appeared in the newspapers. He decided to leave. The bellhop, Ken Vance, reported later that Wattenberg left the hotel at one-thirty in the morning on Sunday, January 28. Wattenberg headed north. At

Central and Van Buren, he stopped Clarence V. Cherry, a city of Phoenix street foreman. Tired and hungry, he asked in heavily accented English for directions to the railroad station. When Wattenberg turned to walk down the street, Cherry caught the attention of Sergeant Gilbert Brady of the Phoenix Police Department. Pointing at Wattenberg, he told Brady that the man in the yellow checked shirt had just spoken to him with a heavy German accent. Brady caught up with Wattenberg at Third Avenue and Van Buren.

"Sir, could I see your Selective Service registration?" Brady asked.

"I left it at home."

"Where is home?" Brady asked.

"Glendale."

"Glendale, Arizona, or Glendale, California?" Brady asked.

"Glendale—uh, Glendale, back east," Wattenberg replied.

"You need to come with me to the police station," Brady ordered, then offered a cigarette.

At the station, the police searched Wattenberg and found he had fifty cents in coins, a blank notebook, and several newspaper clippings—some about the escape, others with restaurant job openings circled, and the Saturday directory of churches.

When Wattenberg was returned to Papago Park, he was taken to the hospital, where he received a Sunday dinner of beef broth, roasted chicken, vegetables, and ice cream. After this meal, his punishment for the escape was bread and water rations for fourteen days. Sanger chuckled when he saw Wattenberg. He admired the officer's bravado and was surprised he had been able to avoid recapture for as long as he had. Still, Sanger thought the escape attempt was foolish. Besides, all the news from Europe was bad for the Germans. It looked like the war would end soon. If that happened the Germans needed the Americans to be their friends. Better that than to be left to the Russians.

Chapter 17

As the Russians advanced from the east and German refugees poured into eastern Germany, the British and American military leadership decided to help the Russian advance by bombing Berlin and several eastern German cities to sever transportation and communication lines. They hoped to cause confusion in the evacuation from the east and hamper movement of German troops from the Western Front. The primary targets of the air campaign were oil production, submarine yards, and jet aircraft facilities. Prior to World War II, civilians had never been targeted in air attacks, but then the Germans bombed London and other British cities. So the genie was out of the bottle, and when it came their turn the British and Americans felt no remorse in attacking German civilians with their air raids.

Sir Norman Bottomley, deputy chief of the British Air Staff, asked Arthur "Bomber" Harris, commander in chief of RAF Bomber Command and a supporter of area bombing, to bomb Berlin, Dresden, Leipzig, and Chemnitz to exploit the confusion that existed in those cities as large refugee populations filled them during the Russian advance. More than two hundred thousand refugees were in Dresden alone. The prewar population of the city had been around six hundred thousand. Immediately after the Yalta Conference on February 4, 1945, between British prime minister Winston Churchill, United States president Franklin Delano Roosevelt, and Soviet premier Joseph Stalin, the bombings were ordered.

Dresden had been relatively untouched. It was well known as a cultural center, the former capital of the kingdom of Saxony. Renowned for its baroque palaces, cathedrals, museums, libraries, opera houses, theaters, and universities. Wealthy tourists had considered it one of the must-see cities during the nineteenth-century grand tour. It had little strategic value; a few factories were in the suburbs, but little of military value was made there except at an optics factory. Many wounded German soldiers convalesced in Dresden hospitals, the city was filled with refugees, and it did have a critical rail link. Still, since it had not been targeted so far, the local authorities were ill prepared for what was about to happen.

The bombing of Dresden began just after 2200 hours on the night of February 13, 1945, when the RAF dropped 1,478 pounds of high explosives and 1,182 tons of incendiary bombs. It targeted not the industrial suburbs but the center of the old city. On February 14, the United States B-17s dropped 771 tons of bombs aimed at the railway yards. The Americans continued their attack on February 15, dropping 466 tons of bombs. During these four raids, a total of 3,900 bombs were dropped.

Firebombing had become something of a science. The standard method was to drop large amounts of high-explosive bombs to blow the roofs off houses and buildings to expose the timbers within. This was followed by incendiary devices (fire sticks) to ignite the buildings, then high explosives to hinder the efforts of fire services. This method had worked so effectively in Hamburg in 1943 that more than half the city was destroyed in a single night.

It was equally effective in Dresden. The bombing created a self-sustaining firestorm, which is something like a tornado, carrying winds of up to 150 miles per hour (240 kilometers per hour) and creating temperatures of 2,700 degrees Fahrenheit (1,500 degrees centigrade). After a large area caught fire, the air above it rose quickly, then cold air rushed in at ground level to fill the void. People were sucked into the fire, which consumed all the oxygen out of the air and out of shelters, where people passed out and then were incinerated. After the two main raids in February, B-17s dropped 940 tons of high-explosive bombs and 141 tons of incendiaries on

March 2 and 1,554 tons of high explosives and 165 tons of incendiaries on April 17.

Shortly after the attacks in February, the police in Dresden reported that 12,000 dwellings had been destroyed, as well as 24 banks, 26 insurance buildings, 31 stores, 6,470 shops, 640 warehouses, 256 market halls, 31 large hotels, 26 public houses, 63 administrative buildings, 3 theaters, 18 cinemas, 11 churches, 60 chapels, 50 cultural buildings, and 19 hospitals. It was total chaos. Ideal weather conditions, the wood-frame buildings in the center of the old city, and the lack of preparation by local authorities conspired to make the attacks particularly devastating. The Propaganda Ministry under the leadership of Joseph Goebbels made the most of the destruction, publishing reports that more than two hundred thousand were killed. Later estimates ranged from twenty-five thousand to thirty-five thousand. But any way it was figured, it was a terrible disaster. What was once one of the great cultural capitals of Europe was reduced to a pile of rubble in a matter of days. Thousands of innocent civilians were incinerated in their homes, in shelters, and trying to escape. Countless cultural artifacts and works of art were destroyed, including the original manuscripts of the great musical masters of the seventeenth and eighteenth centuries. One of only four original Mayan codices that was not destroyed by the Spanish invaders of Mexico succumbed at Dresden. Baroque architectural masterpieces such as the Dresden Frauenkirche, the Saxon State Opera Building, the Saxon State Library, and the Zwinger Palace were destroyed or heavily damaged. The Germans were outraged and wanted to use the bombing as a pretext to abandon the Geneva Convention on the Western Front. The Germans pledged revenge, but in the end the only thing they did was exploit the bombings for propaganda purposes.

There was a backlash in Britain, and Churchill distanced himself from the bombings. Some said it was revenge for the pointless bombing of historic Coventry by the Germans earlier in the war. Some later charged that it was a war crime.

Details of the destruction of Dresden gradually filtered back to the camps in America. Sanger did not hear from his parents for weeks. Then he received a letter from a colleague of his father's at the university who had survived. He told Sanger that both his parents and his unmarried sister, who lived with them, had been killed in their house in the old town near the Saxon State Library. Nothing but rubble was left to mark the spot where their eighteenth-century townhouse had been. All that Sanger had known and loved in his life was gone; even his old girlfriend and her family were not heard from. He had no family, nothing to go back to now.

The war dragged on for another few weeks as the Russians continued their relentless drive through Poland and eastern Germany. After they overwhelmed the German defenders at the Vistula River, it took the Russians only two weeks to advance three hundred miles to the Oder River within forty miles of Berlin.

Roosevelt died on April 12, 1945, from a cerebral hemorrhage, and Harry S Truman, his inexperienced vice president, became president. On April 30, 1945, Adolf Hitler committed suicide in his bunker, cursing the Jews, the Bolsheviks, and the German people, who he said had let him down. Admiral Dönitz was named the new Reich president. On May 3, 1945, Dönitz tried to make a deal to surrender his remaining troops to the British and not the Russians, but British general marshal Bernard Law Montgomery insisted on an unconditional surrender. Dönitz returned to Montgomery's headquarters on May 4 to sign that surrender. Hostilities were to end May 8. On May 5 the Germans traveled to General Dwight D. Eisenhower's headquarters in Rheims, France, and Alfred Jodl, representing Admiral Dönitz, signed the unconditional surrender for all German forces, to take effect one minute past midnight on May 9, 1945. Between May 8 and 9, more than two million German soldiers crossed British and American lines to surrender, rather than fall into Soviet hands. When the deadline passed under the surrender document on May 9, some 1.25 million German soldiers became Soviet POWs.

In Moscow three million people crowded Red Square to celebrate. In New York more than a half a million people crowded Times Square. In London thousands marched in the streets as blackout restrictions were finally lifted. Paris was one big party, crowds singing and drinking wine and cognac. Little celebration took place on the front lines, as the troops worried about being transferred to the South Pacific. But finally, after the atomic bombs were dropped on Hiroshima and Nagasaki, even the war in the Pacific came to an end on August 15, 1945.

The last of the German POWs were not sent home from Papago until March 1946. In the meantime their American captors became less deferential to them. Photographs from German concentration camps and reports of millions of Jews, Poles, Gypsies, Russians, and others being incinerated at Auschwitz-Birkenau and other camps turned the American public against the Germans after the war. The Nuremberg trials began to hold the German leadership accountable for war crimes in November 1945. The POWs complained about the poor quality of food after V-E day, and mail service to Germany was almost nonexistent. But by March 1946, the last of the Papago Park POWs were sent back east to board ships for their home countries.

On June 16, 1946, Jürgen Wattenberg was reunited with his wife and two sons at Neustadt in Holstein, a German seaport village on the Baltic Sea.

Sanger did not want to return to Germany. Dresden was in the Russian sector, and it was clear that the Russians intended to install a communist government in East Germany. He had no family left in Dresden and no desire to return to a land dominated by the Soviets. He wanted to stay in the United States. He spoke perfect English, and he was university educated. He wrote Mr. Harris in Mississippi and asked if he could help. The Immigration Act of 1924 had been passed to discourage immigration from eastern and southern Europe and Asia. It gave preference to immigrants from Germany, Austria, England, and Northern Europe. This was still the law of the land. Mr. Harris knew his congressman well and applied for a work visa for Sanger. He said Sanger was not a Nazi and that he needed Sanger to work on his cotton plantation, that he was indispensable due to his extensive experience there while he was at Fort Clinton.

United States Immigration granted Sanger the visa, and Mr. Harris sent him travel money to return to Mississippi. When he was released from Papago Park in March 1946, he boarded a train headed there. He had continued to write Marcia periodically, but she did not write back. He didn't know if she was alive or dead. He also did not know if she even wanted to see him. He wrote her from Mississippi in the spring telling her he had been released from the POW camp and that, if she wanted, he would come see her. He did not hear back.

Sanger stayed through the summer with the Harrises, helping them plant and harvest their cotton crop and working around the farm. He was indebted to them for providing him with money and helping him obtain a visa. He couldn't just turn around and leave them. But he still held out hope that someday he could return to Portsmouth Island. He wrote Marcia again in late September. He was busy during the fall helping the Harrises bring in the cotton crop.

Finally, in October, she answered.

Kurt,

I am sorry that I never answered your many letters. I saved them and finally decided to open your last letter because it was from Mississippi. The war is over, and there is something I must tell you. You have a daughter. I did not tell you at first because I was mad at you. But she looks just like you, and she needs to know her father. Her name is Stella, and she is three years old. Can you come see us?

Marcia

It was a short note, but what a message! Sanger, of course, had no idea that he had a child in Portsmouth. He could not wait to see Stella and Marcia. He had not forgotten her these many years. He still dreamed of Portsmouth and of their brief time together. He told the Harrises about Stella and Marcia and said he must go to them.

"I understand," Mr. Harris said. "You must see your daughter. If you need anything, let me know. We will not need you again until the spring. Stay for the winter. Your visa should be okay. If there are any questions, I will answer them." Mr. Harris had grown so fond of Kurt that he had begun to think of him as a son. He offered to give Kurt money for the trip to North Carolina, but Sanger had saved his wages from working on the farm.

"I cannot thank you enough for all that you have done for me; I will never forget you. You created a safe haven for me during this terrible war. I will always think of your farm as home."

"Go to your family in North Carolina, Kurt. Maybe you could even bring them back with you in the spring. We have lots of room, and it would be wonderful to hear the voice of a child around here again."

"We shall see. I haven't even seen them yet. They may not want me to stay. I will let you know how it goes. But I must go to them now, and thank you for letting me." He hugged Mrs. Harris, who was short and stout, with short gray hair and bright blue eyes. Mr. Harris was tall and slightly stooped; he looked like a lanky, overgrown teenager except for his wavy gray hair and leathered skin.

At first Sanger had resisted the lure of America, but after a while he found himself falling in love with it—the beauty of its wide open spaces, its open, honest, and optimistic people. It was still raw and unformed, not like the refined beauty of his home, but in it he found a refreshing quality, a sense that anything was possible and that people were not judged by how they were born, but by what they did for themselves. He first thought of Americans as crude and bumbling, but now, since he had no home to go back to, he was determined to make this his new home. His parents and sister were gone; the Harrises treated him like an adopted son. He loved them and their generosity, their openness and lack of judgment of him, but now he had a family, a real family, that he had not even known existed. He had to go to them.

He booked passage on a train that, with connections, eventually made its way to Morehead City, North Carolina. From there he took a bus to the little fishing village of Atlantic on the Core Sound, and from there he left at noon on the mailboat *Aleta*, which would land in Ocracoke at about four-thirty in the afternoon, weather permitting. The boat arrived off Portsmouth Island around three-thirty, where a black man poled a skiff out to meet the mailboat. It was too shallow for the *Aleta* to land at the dock in Portsmouth. Henry Pigott met it every day, picking up mail, supplies, and any passengers going to Portsmouth. When the *Aleta* headed back toward Ocracoke, Henry Pigott slowly began to pole his boat to the Portsmouth dock with Kurt Sanger his only passenger. Sanger gave Mr. Pigott a few coins for his trouble.

Chapter 18

Marcia followed the progress of the war from her home on Portsmouth. After the spring of 1942, things calmed down on Portsmouth and Ocracoke. The Germans stopped sinking ships off the North Carolina coast after the Americans started using convoys and battleship escorts, and the Germans never came back in any organized way. Everyone was relieved. Now the communities along the Outer Banks went back to life as usual, except with blackouts and restrictions about use of the beach. Fishermen continued to fish in the sound, and the villagers were able to return to their lives as before. Of course the navy and the Coast Guard still maintained a presence, which added life, vitality, and new blood to the community; many navy men married local girls. Nick Galantis and Joe Guidos left Portsmouth after the war, and the old Coast Guard Station closed for good. But the Pennsylvania boys had fallen in love with the North Carolina coast. After the war they moved to Morehead City, where Nick opened a restaurant and Joe got a job at a hardware store. They met local girls, got married, and raised families. Joe was even elected a town commissioner in later years. They never forgot their connection to Portsmouth, however, and often came back to visit.

By the end of 1945, most of the personnel at the navy base

in Ocracoke had left; the base was decommissioned in early 1946. Locals scavenged the navy barracks and shops, taking building materials from the larger ones—and even moving some of the smaller buildings—until eventually all of the base structures were gone. The property was deeded to the University of North Carolina in 1948, but the deed required that the property be used for educational purposes for a period of ten years from the date of the conveyance. By 1951 the state had still not used it for educational purposes and had no such plans, so it was deeded back to the federal government and became part of the Cape Hatteras National Seashore.

By 1946 only about twenty permanent residents were left on Portsmouth, most of them elderly women. There was no school because there weren't enough children. In fact, Stella was the only child left on the island. Marcia knew she would have to move when Stella was old enough to go to school, but until then she decided to enjoy her home. She loved her solitude and the wild, unspoiled nature of the island. She had all she needed; there was no need for anything else. She thought about men, dreamed about them, but after her husband died and Kurt Sanger came and went, her heart had closed. She didn't have room for another man. She focused all of her energy and love on her daughter, who grew up like a wild child on the island. Stella went fishing and crabbing with her mother and helped her dig oysters. She helped her mother gather vegetables and herbs out of the garden. She loved the beach and would spend hours in the sun if her mother let her. She even wanted to learn how to ride a horse, but Marcia thought Stella was still a little young for that. She was born in March 1943 and by October 1946 had so much energy her mother could barely keep up with her.

As much as she fought it, every time Marcia looked into Stella's eyes she saw Sanger. Stella had his fair skin, blond hair that hung in ringlets around her ears and forehead, and eyes the color of the sky on a clear, sunny day. She even seemed to have his smile. Marcia was so mad at Sanger that she refused to open his letters or respond to them, but she did keep them. Maybe one day her daughter would want to know her father. Marcia could not deny her that. Marcia was also touched by the fact that Sanger continued to write. She thought that surely he would grow tired of it. At first she thought he must be doing it because he was lonely or bored. But the fact that he continued to write even three years after he was taken away left an impression on her.

She had truly fallen in love with Kurt Sanger. She had opened her heart to him and believed in him, and he had betrayed her. She could never forgive him for that. But as the years passed and the letters piled up in the wooden box on the mantel in the living room, her curiosity grew. Then the war ended, and the letters continued to come from Arizona. She found out that the German POWs were still being held in this country until things in Germany were sufficiently settled to send them home. She read that some of them were being sent to Britain and France to help repair war damage, while others were returned to Germany to help rebuild the country.

There was much talk about making the Germans pay for what they did during the war. United States treasury secretary Henry Morgenthau, Jr., advocated extracting huge war reparations from Germany to help rebuild the countries the war had devastated. The French wanted to control the coal areas of the Ruhr and Saar. Some advocated permanently restricting the industrial output of Germany to prewar Depression-era levels. But many saw what had happened when similar policies were imposed on Germany after World War I, and how it had led to the rise of the Nazi Party. This time people feared a communist takeover of Europe. The Truman government and the Churchill administration advocated a policy of containment to keep communism at bay. The Russians were still allies of the United States and Britain, but they had effectively taken control of Eastern Europe. Churchill gave his famous speech about the Iron Curtain in Truman's presence on March 5, 1946, at Westminster College in Fulton, Missouri: "From Stettin in the Baltic to Trieste in the Adriatic, an iron curtain has descended across the continent. Behind that line lie all the capitals of the ancient states of central and Eastern Europe. Warsaw, Berlin, Prague, Vienna, Budapest, Belgrade, Bucharest, and Sofia; all these famous cities and the populations around them lie in what I must call the Soviet sphere, and all are subject, in one form or another, not only to Soviet influence but to a very high and in some cases increasing measure of control from Moscow."

Europe was devastated after the war, much more so than after World War I. Major European cities such as Berlin and Warsaw were reduced to rubble. Others such as London and Rotterdam were severely damaged. The great German industrial heartland lay in ruins. The winters of 1945 and 1946 were particularly harsh. Many people, having no shelter or heat, froze to death. They also faced widespread starvation and malnutrition. Agricultural production was 83 percent of 1938 levels; industrial production, 88 percent;

and exports, only 59 percent. But the United States economy was strong. Wartime factories were converting to postwar production of consumer goods, and the nation was enjoying a huge housing boom. The United States needed Europe to be strong so it could be a market for goods. Also with the rise of communism in Eastern Europe and the growing strength of the communist parties in France and Italy, there was a growing consensus in the United States that Europe had to be strong for America to be strong. Talk even circulated about a New Deal–type plan that could be used to rebuild Europe. But in the summer of 1946, the occupying forces still operated under JCS 1067, a punitive occupation order that directed the United States forces of occupation in Germany to "take no steps looking toward the economic rehabilitation of Germany."

At Yalta the Allies agreed to a new structure for the United Nations, establishing permanent members of the Security Council and giving several Soviet republics their own seats in the general assembly. The Russians solidified their control over Eastern Europe, where they installed communist regimes. Marcia wondered if Sanger's family had survived the war and if he would return to Germany. When she got the second letter from Mississippi and it had not been censored and was obviously not from a POW camp, her curiosity got the best of her. She opened it.

Marcia,

I know that you are probably not reading my letters, but I write to you one more time in hope that you will read this. I left the POW camp at Papago and have gotten a visa so that I can work on the Mississippi farm of my friends the Harrises, whom I worked for when I was at Fort Clinton. They have no children and treat me like a son. They are so good to me.

My parents and my sister were killed during the bombing of Dresden. Now that the communists control eastern Germany, I have no home to return to and no desire to return. Europe is a wasteland. I want to make America my home. I wish you would write. I wish I could see you. I still think of you and dream of our wonderful time together on Portsmouth Island.

Affectionately,
Kurt Sanger

She looked at Stella. She needed to meet her father. It was time. The time for anger was over; it was time to heal. She decided to write Sanger. After making her decision, she opened the box on the mantel and read his unopened letters. Letter after letter, she read, and as she read she experienced a torrent of emotions—anger, guilt, fear, passion, compassion, and, yes, love. She felt as if her emotions had been walled up and sealed in a forgotten room for the past three years. This was the first time that light began to enter that room. She did not know where it would lead, but she was ready to ride her emotions to wherever they would take her. The truth can bring much pain, but it can also bring freedom and release from bondage.

She told him about Stella in her letter. She didn't know how he would react. Maybe the news would scare him away. Or maybe he would read about Stella and decide to come see her. If that happened, then their lives could go in a number of different directions. Marcia was tired of control; she wanted to let go and let fate take her where it would. She felt an incredible freedom with this decision.

Marcia decided to walk on the beach with Stella at about three in the afternoon. The wind blew her hair; the breeze was cool but refreshing. She felt strong and ready for what would come, though she had no idea what form it would take. High, feathery cirrus clouds looked like angel wings against the deep blue of the sky.

So far she had not heard back from Sanger. She did not know that as soon as he received her letter he made all haste to Portsmouth. He put a letter in the mail telling her when he planned to arrive. It arrived on Portsmouth when he did, in a sack of mail that Henry Pigott picked up when he loaded Kurt Sanger into his skiff from the mailboat *Aleta*.

When Marcia finished her walk and crested the dunes to head back to her house, she saw a man sitting in a rocker on the front porch. He looked to be a young man. She hadn't seen a young man on the island since the Coast Guard boys left. The closer she got, the more familiar he looked. She did not have a photograph of Sanger; she had only a memory of him. That memory was as much about his body and its movement—the way he walked, his smile, his gestures—as it was about his looks. He stood and started across the yard to greet her. The moment he stood and smiled, she knew who it was. She tried with all her might to resist the urge to run to him and throw her arms around him. Her body propelled her forward, but her mind held her back. He had no such hesitation. He first walked, then ran to greet her. He held out his arms to her, and sunshine filled his eyes as he looked at the beautiful three-year-old girl at her side.

"Kurt, I didn't know you were coming," Marcia said.

"I wrote to tell you; you didn't get my letter?" he responded, concerned.

"No."

"Well, frankly, I left as soon as I posted the letter. I must have beaten the letter here. I was so excited when you told me about Stella." He stooped and held out his arms to her. "May I hold her?" he asked Marcia.

"Of course. Stella, I want you to meet this nice man. His name is Kurt Sanger."

"Mr. Kurt," Stella said, looking him over closely.

"Yes, Mr. Kurt," he said, smiling, still holding his arms out to her.

"You can go to him; he won't hurt you," Marcia reassured her daughter. Stella then walked to Kurt, and he shook her hand. He wanted to put his arms around her and hug her, but he felt it was a bit premature. He stood and turned to Marcia. Stella held out her arms for him to hold her. He picked her up and swung her around in the air.

"I like Mr. Kurt," Stella said to her mother, smiling and laughing.

He put her down, and she held out her hands to him, indicating that she wanted to be held. He picked her up and held her as he followed Marcia onto the porch, where they sat down.

"Well, it has been a long time," Marcia started off, trying to be cool, trying to break the ice.

"It has. How have things been here? I haven't heard from you."

"Well, things are slow, as usual. There was a terrible hurricane in 1944. Many people left after that. Only a handful of families are left, mainly elderly people. When Stella is old enough to go to school, I think we will have to move to Ocracoke. There is no school here anymore."

"You still have some time before you need to do that," Sanger said, looking down at the child.

"I know," Marcia said with a sly, knowing smile.

"What?" he asked.

"What do you mean, what?"

"What just crossed your mind?" he asked with a twinkle in his eye.

"It's as if you never left," she said.

"I know what you mean. I feel at home, like nothing has transpired over the past four years, that it was all a dream and I have finally woken up." He reached out and took her hand. "I missed you."

"I missed you, too." She squeezed his hand.

"May I kiss you?" he asked.

"Yes," she answered demurely. Stella had run off in the side yard to chase the chickens.

"I love you," Sanger said, kissing her slow and hard.

"I am not ready to go there yet, but give me time," she said. "I read your letters all at once. I'd kept them, unopened, in a box on the mantel. When I figured you were out of the prison camp, I decided to sit down and read them all, from start to finish. It took me awhile. I still can't believe that you remembered me after all this time. I thought for sure you would forget me. I was so mad at you. I felt betrayed, violated, and used. But after reading your letters and knowing you didn't have to write, I thought that maybe you started out to use me, but something changed."

"I never intended to use or hurt you. I had no idea that I would fall in love with an American girl once I landed here, but then I met you. I was on a mission in a time of war. I couldn't have told you my true identity, since I was a soldier, but you stole my heart. You crept right up behind me and stole my heart before I had a chance to defend myself. I have been smitten ever since, and, no, I have not been able to forget you."

He looked off into the distance, then turned to her. "I thought that surely you had forgotten about me, or did not care, that what I felt we had was not real, but I couldn't give up. I had to keep writing. I knew you were mad. I knew you were justified in being mad; that is why I gave you time and the benefit of the doubt. But by this summer, I was really about to give up, then you wrote. I couldn't believe it. As I told you in my letter, my family is gone. My home is in the hands of the communists. Europe is in ruins. I have nothing to return to. Despite myself, this country has seduced me. I used to hate it, thinking it clumsy and crude, but I love it now. I love its wildness, its wide-open spaces, and, yes, I love its people. You Americans have no pretense; you're open and honest and full of optimism, the sense that anything is possible. It is not that way back home." He took her hand and smiled. "That is why I am here. My friends in Mississippi obtained a visa for me. I will need to return to

Mississippi in the spring. There is not as much for me to do there in the winter, so Mr. Harris let me come here for now."

Marcia returned his smile. "I thought my life had ended, that I would never love another man or let another man into my life, and then you came. And there is Stella. Every time I look at her, I see your eyes, your smile, your laugh. I hope that you will learn to love her as much as I do. It is a miracle that you are here after all these years. I have to let go and believe. That is all I know. I don't know what the future will bring, but for now it is you and me again. I have you back, and I want to enjoy every minute of it." She looked around the corner of the house and saw Stella still chasing the chickens, trying to catch one. "Stella, come here. I want us to walk with Mr. Kurt on the beach."

"Does Mr. Kurt like to build sandcastles?" Stella asked as she ran up to her mother, excited.

"He sure does," Kurt answered. "First let me put my things in the house and pull on a bathing suit and a T-shirt, and I will be right out." Marcia followed him into the house. "Where do you want me to put my things?"

"In my bedroom," she said, helping him with his bags. He had a teddy bear for Stella. He didn't know what she would like but figured every little girl would enjoy a stuffed animal. When he pulled it out of his bag and gave it to her, she wrapped her arms around it and hugged it.

"For me?" she asked.

"For you."

He started to change into a dark blue bathing suit and a white T-shirt, clothes he had bought in Morehead City. Stella ran into her room to play with the teddy bear and introduce it to her other toys and change into her bathing suit. Marcia pulled the door shut and stayed in the bedroom with Sanger, watching him dress. He was more tanned than before from the sun in Mississippi. He was more filled out, too; he had been eating well. But he was also in much better shape, if that were possible. She could not take her eyes off his firm, flat chest and well-formed shoulders and back as he changed shirts.

"Looks like it has been awhile since you have seen a man," he said, noticing her gaze.

"It has been a long time, since you were here." She placed her hand on his chest before he had a chance to pull his T-shirt on. "How about you? Have you had lots of women?"

"In a POW camp? Are you kidding? I have seen too many men and not nearly enough women. I have not been with another woman since I was with you."

"Just checking," she said, running her hands over his hard, rippled abs and firm chest, feeling his knotted biceps and helmet-shaped triceps, all nicely bronzed by the sun.

"I believe the last time I was here I was as red as a beet. Spending months in the hot sun in Mississippi and Arizona has given me a tan," he said, not taking his eyes off her.

"You better believe it. It becomes you," she said admiringly. She had also filled out in the right places. She was very active, and she ate well. The pregnancy had not affected her shape; if anything she was more shapely and appealing than before. He wrapped his arm around her, still without his shirt on, and pulled her to kiss him. Then they heard someone pulling at the door.

"Mommy, when are we going to the beach?" they heard Stella say as she turned the doorknob. Kurt quickly pulled his T-shirt on, and Marcia opened the door and let Stella in. Dressed in her bathing suit, Stella was ready to go to the beach.

"Kurt, could you take Stella while I change into my bathing suit?"

Stella took Kurt's hand and led him into her bedroom. She showed him where she had put the teddy bear he brought her. "See, Teddy is at home between my other dolls and animals," Stella said, still holding his hand and pointing to the bed, where she had arranged two Raggedy Ann dolls, a stuffed puppy, and her new teddy bear. "This is Ann and Andy, and my puppy dog, Ruff. How do you like them?"

"I like them very much," he said. Stella then showed him around her room, pointing out everything, its name and its meaning to her.

Marcia stood in the doorway in her bathing suit. "Let's go; I'm ready," she said. "I'll get some towels."

They then walked onto the beach. It was late, about four-thirty, and the sun was not nearly as strong as earlier in the day. That was the time Marcia liked to take Stella on the beach. She didn't want her to get too much sun. But this was a special day for Stella. She had never seen a young man before, except for Nick and Joe, when they came to visit. So this was a real treat, especially having a man who paid her so much attention and was so much fun to be with. He even liked to build sandcastles.

They stayed on the beach until about six-thirty, building sand-castles and jumping the waves. Sanger and Marcia stood on either side of Stella and held her hands as she jumped the waves.

"More, more—one more time," Stella cried in glee. Marcia and Kurt were ready to stop, but not Stella; she couldn't get enough of it.

Kurt taught her how to make a drip castle, running wet sand through his fingers, letting the sand dribble out, forming tall, lacy spires that looked like gothic cathedrals. She loved it. Even when he tired of it, she wanted him to build more. She was insatiable. She had been starved for the attention of a man for so long, and now she had the complete attention of one. She didn't want a minute to be wasted.

Chapter 19

At six-thirty they came in, and Marcia fixed a supper of chicken breasts, fresh green beans from the garden, and boiled potatoes. After supper they sat on the back porch and watched the sun set over the marsh. It was just as beautiful as Sanger remembered. He thought he had died and gone to heaven.

Soon it was time for Stella to turn in. She did not want to go to bed.

"Mr. Kurt, tell me a story," she said as she lay in bed hugging her teddy bear. He thought for a while, then told her the story of Goldilocks and the Three Bears. She loved it and wanted to hear more stories. It had been a busy day for her, and she was tired, even though she fought it.

"It is time for you to go to bed. Mr. Kurt can tell you more stories another night. Tonight you need to go to bed," Marcia said. Stella cried and fought sleep. Marcia told Kurt he needed to leave, since he made Stella want to stay up, so he went outside and sat on the porch. About an hour passed while Marcia and Stella struggled with each other, Stella crying, fighting sleep, Marcia rubbing her back and singing to her. Eventually Stella drifted off, and Marcia joined Kurt on the porch.

"Finally," Marcia said, relaxing in the rocker. "I thought she would never go to sleep. She is so excited about having you here—a new person, someone new to play with, *a man!*" She turned to look at him and pinched his thigh between her thumb and index finger. "And she doesn't even know you're her father. We need to find the right time to tell her."

"I know. I just do something to women," he teased.

"In your dreams," Marcia said, turning her nose up in the air, trying to put him in his place.

They chatted for a while, and soon Marcia was yawning. Kurt was also tired after such a day full of travel, new faces, emotions, excitement, meeting his daughter for the first time, and finally seeing Marcia after three years' absence. He followed her into the bedroom.

It had been three long years for both of them. Electricity was in the air. He pulled her to him, and they kissed. They were barely even conscious of what happened next. Their desires drove them on; they were unable to control themselves. They quickly undressed each other, smothering each other with kisses as each body part was revealed. She got hung up with her bra, and he helped her unhook it. They fell onto the bed. His hands were all over her as he kissed her from her neck down to her breasts and below. She ran her fingers over his back, digging in at times, throwing her head back and moaning, not too loud because she didn't want to wake Stella.

He was on top of her, and she dug her nails into his firm butt cheeks; he tensed up. He kissed her breasts, her neck, her cheeks, her lips. He had to be careful not to climax too quickly; it was such a long time since he had felt the folds of a woman's tender parts. Finally he could hold it no longer; she seemed to reach climax at the same time. His head collapsed on her shoulder. She ran her hands through his short hair and kissed him on the neck. They made love through the night; they were both so hungry for love, so starved for it.

When he woke at sunrise, Kurt moved her arm from his chest and gently laid it to the side, then got up, pulled on some shorts, and jogged out to the beach. He wanted to run. No one would be out there; he had the whole beach to himself. The air was perfect, about seventy degrees. The great red ball of the sun hung low in the sky just above where the beach met the ocean to the east, lighting the undersides of the dark gray clouds with a fire opal red. He understood what Homer meant by the rosy-fingered dawn, because that was a perfect description of the sunrise over the beach this day.

He ran southwest down the hard beach with the sun at his back. The tide was low, and the beach was wide. The ocean was calm and curled into shore with perfectly symmetrical emerald green waves, moving in slowly and peacefully, then crashing on the beach in a rush of white foam. After about a mile, he decided to strip down and walk into the waves. He felt the cool water swirl around his body. Then he dove in and began to swim parallel to the shore for a short distance. When he grew tired, he rode a wave into shore with ease.

He found a shallow pool and lay on his back, letting the waves wash over him. He looked down at his nakedness and remembered the night before with Marcia. He walked out of the water, picked up his shorts, and decided to walk naked on the beach for a while. His only companions were the birds—sanderlings that scampered up and down the beach, following the water as it washed the sand, brown willets with their long legs and long beaks, black-and-white terns, big, solitary gulls that stood on the upper beach watching the ocean. Then a line of pelicans appeared in perfect formation over the waves, dipping one by one until they were just inches from the water, skimming the surface, looking for fish. Out beyond the waves, he saw a black shiny fin, then another and another; they rose out of the water, revealing shiny black arched backs. It was a pod of porpoises swimming parallel to the beach, arching and diving.

Above the beach were the dunes, topped by sea grass and oats, broken by openings created by overwash. The beach was filled with shells: oyster shells, cockleshells, clams, scallops, conks, murex, and the occasional Scotch bonnet, prized because they were so delicate and rarely survived the trip through the waves to the beach. After a mile or so of walking naked, he slipped on his shorts and ran back to Marcia's house, where he found her cooking a stack of pancakes and bacon.

"Have a nice run on the beach?" she asked.

"Yes, it was beautiful. The temperature was just right, not too much wind, a gentle ocean breeze—just as I remembered it." His arm snaked around her waist, and he kissed her on the neck. Then Stella walked into the room still in her pajamas, holding her teddy bear.

"Mr. Kurt," she began, "are you going to stay with us for a while? Can we play on the beach again today?"

He looked at Marcia, then at Stella. "If your mother will let me, I will stay."

"Momma, please let Mr. Kurt stay," Stella pleaded.

"We'll see," Marcia said, not wanting to commit. She had been disappointed before and did not want to create an expectation with Stella that she could not meet.

Later, while Marcia went into town to the post office to check her mail and pick up some groceries, Kurt stayed with Stella.

"Where is your cute little girl? You always bring her with you when you come to the store," said nosy Annie Salter, the post-mistress.

"I have a guest at the house who is watching her."

"I heard from Henry Pigott that he picked up a young man from the mailboat yesterday who said he was coming to see you." Miss Annie remembered the "British" sailor who left Stella and never returned. She and the other townspeople had seen the sailor only briefly three years ago, not long enough to remember what he looked like, other than that he was blond, handsome, and well built. Marcia told everyone that he had died at sea.

"He's an old friend who has come to see me. He just returned from the war."

"Oh."

"I need to find some work for him this winter. Do you know of anything?"

"Not much goes on around here this time of year except guided duck-hunting trips. Ed Willis said he is looking for some help at his hunting camp on Bird Island. Can he shoot?" Miss Annie asked.

"I think so; he was in the war."

"I'll tell Ed to stop by your place next time he's on the island and talk to your friend." Then she sorted through the mail and found a letter for Marcia. "This came over on the same boat as your friend." Miss Annie handed her the letter postmarked Mississippi.

Sanger couldn't get enough of Stella, and she of him. They played cards and romped on the beach. He jumped the waves and built sandcastles. He went crabbing. She squealed when a crab approached the chicken neck on a string but loved it when Sanger scooped up the blue crab in the net and put it in a pail.

One night Sanger tossed and turned. Marcia woke up. It looked like he was having a nightmare.

Sanger was back at the POW camp at Papago Park. He walked into the camp medical center. Lying on a shiny metal table under glaring lights was the pale white body of the young man who had been hanged in the shower. Nothing covered his nakedness. Kurt stood over the body on the table. Then something moved in the body's mouth. He didn't know what it was; was the boy still alive? A blue claw emerged from the mouth, then another, and out crawled a large blue crab. It was followed by another crab, and then another. He ran from the room.

Next he found himself walking down the familiar streets where he had grown up in Dresden. He tipped his hat as neighbors passed on the cobblestone streets near the center of the lovely baroque city. He was trying to find his parents' house. He passed under an ornate stone bridge that crossed the street overhead, connecting two buildings. Then he heard sirens and saw planes and heard the sickening sound of bombs being dropped. Suddenly the buildings all around him exploded in flames, and the charming bridge between the buildings collapsed. He started to run. People panicked, scrambling through the streets, trying to find shelter. He heard fire engines and more sirens. A blast of hot air hit him in the face, and then the air began to swirl like a tornado. He saw people being lifted into the air, sucked into the fires around him. Suddenly he could not breathe. The fire had sucked the oxygen out of the air. He saw his mother, father, and sister in the distance, running from their burning home. They turned and looked at him. Then a blast of hot air hit them, and they froze. He watched in horror as the wind swept them up and blew them into the fire, where they disappeared.

He woke screaming. "Momma, Pappa!" It was the first time he had dreamed of what had happened at Dresden. He had heard the firestorms described in news reports, but this was the first time he actually felt it and experienced it.

"Kurt, are you all right?" Marcia asked, wrapping her arms around him. He was covered with sweat and was burning up.

"I saw my parents in Dresden during the bombing. I could not save them. I was helpless. All I could do was watch them die. It was horrible," Sanger said, shaking.

"It wasn't right what they did at Dresden. The war was almost over," Marcia said, holding him tight.

"War is a terrible thing," Sanger said. "What does it bring but death and destruction? The cycle must end."

"I know," Marcia said.

Sanger stayed in bed for three days. He had a high fever and ate nothing but broth and water. But eventually the illness ran its course.

About a week after Marcia talked to Miss Annie in the post office, Ed Willis dropped by to see Sanger. He asked if Sanger knew how to handle a rifle, which he did. Sanger had hunted with his father in Germany before the war and knew about hunting birds.

"I can sure use you, then," Willis said.

Before long Kurt was accompanying Willis on hunting trips. The hunters were from all over the East Coast, as far away as Washington, D.C., and New York. At first Sanger was reluctant to tell Willis about his background, but Willis did not mind. He liked Sanger, the war was over, and the Germans were defeated. The enemy now was communism, not the Germans.

"My home was in Dresden; my family is gone, the city is in ruins, and now the communists control eastern Germany."

"Don't worry. You know the old coots we take out hunting. Several of them are congressmen and senators, lawyers, judges, and a general or two. If you need help with immigration, let me know," Willis said, smiling and patting him on the back. Sanger was relieved to hear this.

Marcia and Kurt didn't know how to tell Stella that he was her father. But they didn't want to wait too long. Marcia had told Stella that her father had gone off to war and did not return, that he had been killed at sea when his ship sank. They tried to figure out the best way to tell her. Finally Marcia figured it out—tell her the truth but not the whole truth, at least not yet.

"Stella, Mr. Kurt and I have something to tell you. You remember I told you that your father went away to war and never came back, and that I thought he died at sea. Well, I have a surprise for you. I was wrong. Your father did not die at sea. He has returned; Mr. Kurt is your father," Marcia said, sitting with Kurt in Stella's room one night before bed.

"Daddy!" Stella said, hugging Kurt around the neck so tightly he thought he was going to choke.

"We didn't tell you right away because we didn't want to upset you," Marcia said.

"Upset me? I'm so happy I could bust. I love you, Mr. Kurt, um, Daddy. Does this mean that you can stay?"

"Yes, this means that I can stay." Kurt smiled.

They put Stella to bed, hugging her teddy bear. She looked so happy.

Kurt and Marcia walked out on the porch to sit in the rockers and talk.

I guess the next thing to do is get married, Kurt thought. He had been preparing for this moment and had asked Ed Willis to buy him a ring with some of the money he had earned on the hunting trips. It was a simple gold band.

"Marcia Styron, will you marry me?" he asked on bent knee.

"I guess it is the right thing to do, to give Stella a real father and real parents," Marcia said. "Yes, Mr. Sanger, I will marry you."

They retired to the bedroom for another night of lovemaking.

The wedding was held the first Saturday in December at the Portsmouth Methodist Church, the minister from Ocracoke presiding. The church was a simple white frame structure with arched windows and opaque glass. The roof was made of cedar shingles. The steeple over the front door was shingled, with louvered vents. The steeple was the tallest structure on the island, the next tallest being the Coast Guard Station. The entire island turned out for the ceremony. Marcia asked Nick to give her away and Joe to act as best man. Miss Annie Salter was the maid of honor. Stella was the flower girl. The reception was held at the Babb house near the church. It was a potluck, and everyone brought something, mostly covered dishes. By the time of the wedding, everyone knew the true identity of Sanger, that he was German and was Stella's father. There was no use keeping it a secret anymore. Besides, everybody liked Sanger, the war was over, and the world was on to other things. Now that Sanger had married an American citizen, he could apply for permanent residency and, eventually, citizenship.

Jessie Babb kept Stella on the wedding night. After the reception the people followed the newlyweds as they rode horses out to Marcia's house. A group of musicians from Ocracoke, who had been invited by Ed Willis, played music on the porch into the wee hours. Ed also provided beer and whiskey. Alcohol was not easy to come by on the island. About one in the morning, the group left the couple alone as they retired to their bedroom with one final violin serenade from James Howard. There was no honeymoon, but Ed Willis gave Sanger a nice gift of money, which he saved for the future.

The winter of 1946–47 was terrible in Europe. Many people without shelter or heat died in Germany and throughout Europe. There was not enough food to feed the hungry; food riots broke out. The communists were making inroads in France and Italy. Europe was in tatters. Punishing the Germans was not working; such a philosophy arguably had led to World War II in the first place. A new approach was needed. On June 5, 1947, Secretary of State George

Marshall gave a speech at Harvard College that was intentionally not covered widely by the United States press but was widely reported in Europe. On the steps of Memorial Church in Harvard Yard, he said, "It is logical that the United States should do whatever it is able to do to assist in the return of normal economic health to the world, without which there can be no political stability and no assured peace. Our policy is not directed against any country, but against hunger, poverty, desperation, and chaos. Any government that is willing to assist in recovery will find full cooperation on the part of the U.S.A."

Then he outlined a broad plan of economic support through grants and loans to the European countries affected by the war, including Germany. In July 1947, staff directive 1067 was rescinded, and a new emphasis was placed on building up Germany's economy, not tearing it down. The same deal was offered to the Russians and the Eastern European countries, but Russian foreign minister Vyacheslav Molotov refused. It was too much like capitalism, he thought, and the United States banks would have oversight, which the Russians did not want. The Europeans were charged with coming up with a plan to spend the money. From 1947 to 1951, more than $13 billion was invested in European recovery. This was the foundation of renewal in Europe, and soon the countries of Western Europe were more prosperous than ever before. Eastern Europe would have a longer wait.

In April 1947 Kurt took Stella and Marcia with him to Mississippi, where they stayed until October. That winter back in Portsmouth, he worked again for Ed Willis at the hunting camp. He traveled with his family to Mississippi in April 1948 and returned to Portsmouth that fall. In 1948 Congress passed the Displaced Persons Act, which allowed Kurt to apply for permanent immigrant status, due to the fact that he could not be forced to return home to Dresden and live under a system of government he did not agree with. A lot of paperwork was involved, but he had plenty of sponsors and friends of friends in government to help him.

When the family returned to Mississippi for the summer of 1948, the heat was stifling and Marcia was miserable. The first summer it had been something of an adventure. Marcia had never been outside North Carolina, and she liked the train trip west. The Harrises were nice to Marcia and Stella and did everything they could to make them feel welcome and comfortable. But after the second summer, Marcia knew she did not want to ever return to Mississippi. The Harrises gave the young family pleasant living quarters in a little house on the plantation, and Mrs. Harris doted on Stella, but Marcia still missed Portsmouth, the wonderful sea breezes, and the freedom of her island home.

"I hate it here," Marcia told Kurt one night in bed. She was in tears. "I want to go home. I want to go clamming and fishing and oystering. I want to ride horses at night and walk on the beach just after a storm and collect seashells."

"The Harrises have been very good to us. They want me to stay and run the farm. I think they would give it to me if I stayed," Kurt said, looking up at the ceiling in the dark room.

"Yes, they have been wonderful, but this will never be home for me," she said.

Stella hated it, too. One day when she was feeding the chickens with Mrs. Harris, Stella turned to her and declared, "I want to go to the beach today."

"We don't have a beach here, honey. It is miles away on the Gulf Coast," Mrs. Harris said.

"I don't care. I want to go to the beach, and I don't understand why I can't go. I can always go to the beach when I want to back home. I hate Mississippi." She then began to cry.

Marcia walked up about that time and asked Stella what was wrong.

"I want to go home. I hate this place. It's hot, and there's no breeze. And worse, there's no beach," Stella said, wrapping her arms around Marcia.

Marcia was embarrassed. "I'm sorry, Mrs. Harris. I'll take her back to the house. I think she's just tired and grumpy." But Marcia understood how Stella felt. She felt the same way. She could not wait to get back to Portsmouth and her home by the sea.

Chapter 20

"Kurt, Stella will be six in February, and she will need to start school in September," Marcia said, rocking in her favorite chair on the front porch after Christmas 1948.

"I know."

"I'm concerned that if we go to Mississippi again, we will come back in late fall, and she will miss school. I need to find a house in Ocracoke so that she can start school there."

"We could stay in Mississippi," Kurt said, looking for Marcia's reaction.

"Kurt, I love the Harrises. They are wonderful people, and they've been good to all of us, but this is home, and this is where Stella and I want to stay," Marcia said.

"Of the two places, I love the North Carolina coast better than Mississippi. But you know that if we stayed there, the Harrises would probably give us the farm," Kurt said, wanting to fully explore the ramifications of their decision. "If I stay here, I will have to find a full-time job in Ocracoke. Jobs are not easy to come by out here, you know. The work with Ed Willis is seasonal. The immigration authorities require that I have a job and not be a burden on the state."

"After New Year's, let's go to Ocracoke and look for a house and a job. Who knows? We may get lucky," Marcia said, putting her hand on his arm and looking into his eyes. He looked distant and distracted.

It was a big decision. If they stayed in Portsmouth or Ocracoke, he would be giving up the opportunity to eventually own the Harrises' prosperous farm. He did not like Mississippi, but he truly appreciated the opportunity the Harrises had offered him and was grateful for their kindness and help. He, like Marcia, loved the North Carolina coast and the Outer Banks. But how could he find work? He may have no choice but to return to Mississippi.

The first week in January 1949, they arranged for a boat to take them to Ocracoke so they could look around for housing and jobs. Now that the navy base was closed and the navy families had left, lots of housing was available. There was also some rental housing for the summer tourist season, in addition to the few inns and boardinghouses. So housing was plentiful and fairly inexpensive. Marcia quickly found a small house on Howard Street, a dirt road shaded by ancient live oaks and bordered by picket fences and old houses with cisterns and outbuildings. At one end of the street was a large group of family cemeteries. The street ended at School Road, which ended at the Ocracoke School and the Methodist church. It was not on Silver Lake but was one street over from it. It was a perfect neighborhood of small, old homes and friendly people. The home Marcia selected was the old Midgett house, which used to be occupied by the matriarch of the family, Madge Midgett, who had died in her late eighties. Her large family had scattered all over the North Carolina and Virginia coasts, but they didn't want to sell their mother's house, so they offered it for rent, furnished. Stella could walk to school and come home for lunch. Marcia would always know where she was.

"This house is perfect!" Marcia said, walking around the quaint two-story home with a screened porch in front and a small kitchen porch in the rear. They entered the front door into a living room with a fireplace and a narrow stairway that went up one side of the room. Beside the living room was a small bedroom. Behind it were the dining room and the kitchen. Upstairs were two bedrooms divided by a narrow hallway. The walls were all painted bead board. The outside was shingled with cedar shakes and had two dormers in front. The house boasted quaint island furniture. The Midgetts mainly wanted a nice family to live there who would take care of their mother's house, so they did not charge much rent.

"That is all well and good, but what about the other part of the equation—a job?" Kurt said. He also liked the charming house, the picket fences, and the tree-lined street that respectfully wound around centuries-old live oak trees. Ocracoke was larger than Portsmouth, with a little over five hundred permanent residents, but in many ways the two were similar. It was a close community; most people were related to each other. The men went barefoot and wore long khaki pants and white T-shirts, while the women wore gingham sundresses and no makeup. Life was simple and good. It didn't take much money to live there, as long as you liked seafood, of which there was plenty. So if you had a job and you liked the pace of life on the Outer Banks, you had it made. It was said that a person could live well on Ocracoke for a hundred dollars a month. The best jobs on the island were with the Coast Guard. But Sanger knew that, being a foreigner, he could never get a government job. There were also the stores and shops, the inns and boardinghouses, but if you didn't own one, the work was very seasonal. Men could also fish, shrimp, and work as hunting guides. He decided to go to the post office and community store, where he heard job openings were posted.

He examined the corkboard at the post office, which had public announcements; notices of sales of personal property such as boats, motors, nets, crab pots, Jeeps, etc.; and a few job notices, mainly for men to crew on shrimp and fishing boats.

Kurt also talked to the clerk in the store.

"Do you know of any jobs available?" Kurt asked the clerk, a large woman with short salt-and-pepper hair.

"Nope, not right now. You may want to go down to the docks and see if any of the fishing and shrimp boats need help or not."

A tall, lanky man with graying hair, wire glasses, and a mustache who looked to be about fifty quietly worked his way down the aisles, gathering groceries in a basket. He overheard Kurt ask the clerk about a job. He sized Kurt up and saw that he looked to be an intelligent, attractive man and noticed that he spoke with a slight accent. He could swear it sounded German.

"You're not from around here, are you?" the man asked Kurt at the checkout counter.

"No," Kurt answered. He noticed the man did not have the local brogue that was so prominent in Ocracoke. It was obvious from his speech and demeanor that he was well educated.

"My name is Theodore Rondthaler. I am the new principal at the Ocracoke School." Mr. Rondthaler offered his hand, which Kurt shook.

"My name is Kurt Sanger. My wife and I came over from Portsmouth today looking for housing and work. Our daughter is going to be six years old this spring, and we need to enroll her in school in the fall. There is no school on Portsmouth."

Mr. Rondthaler noted the man's good looks and his clear blue eyes, which met his when he talked, but he was especially impressed by how well Sanger spoke. "Where are you from?" Rondthaler asked.

Sanger hesitated. "I am originally from Dresden, Germany, sir."

"When I was a young man after I finished graduate school in New Jersey in 1922, I saved my money and took a steamer to Athens, Greece. I bought a motorcycle and rode through Eastern Europe. I met some university students in Dresden and stayed with them for several days. They were most hospitable. What a beautiful city Dresden was. What a terrible shame that it was so devastated during the war."

"Is Rondthaler a German name?"

"No, it is Moravian. My people moved here in the eighteenth century and founded a colony of Moravians near Winston-Salem, North Carolina. My family were ministers and educators by profession." Rondthaler was a modest man; on his father's side were six generations of Moravian teachers, preachers, missionaries, and bishops. His father, Dr. Howard E. Rondthaler, was the president of Salem College in Winston-Salem, and his grandfather was a bishop of the Moravian Church from 1891 to 1931. Rondthaler was educated at the University of North Carolina at Chapel Hill and got his master's degree from Princeton University. He had studied German at the University of Munich the year he spent in Europe.

"You mentioned a university in Dresden. Which one?" Kurt asked.

"The Technical University of Dresden. I stayed there for several weeks with some students who took me in. It was a lovely old school."

"My father was a professor of English literature there for most of his life. I grew up surrounded by students and professors from the school. I graduated from the university in mathematics."

"Would you like to teach at my school?" Rondthaler asked.

Sanger was overwhelmed. Without even thinking he said, "Yes. Teaching is in my blood. If I were able to return home, I would have sought a job teaching, probably high school. My father taught at the university, and my mother taught in the high school. I would like nothing better than to teach at your school."

"The children at the school are island kids who have known nothing but the Coast Guard, boats, and fishing. I am trying to locate teachers for the school right now. It is not easy to find teachers who are willing to come out here and live. Once they come they love it, but getting them here is the hard part. You are already here and apparently have put down roots with your family. I am curious, what brought you here?" Rondthaler asked.

"It is a long story. But I must tell you that I am here on a work visa and have applied for refugee status under the new immigration law passed this year, because I do not want to return to East Germany, which is under Soviet control. I need a job to be able to stay in this country. Otherwise I may be forced to return to Germany. I do not know if I will ever be able to return to Dresden. I lost my entire family in the firebombing, so I have nothing to return to. I fell in love with my wife, Marcia, an American citizen who lived in Portsmouth after her husband died at sea. We have one daughter, Stella. This is my home now, where I want to stay and raise my family."

"This is not like a big-city school or a high school in Dresden. There are a total of ninety children at the Ocracoke School, first grade through the end of high school. A teacher here has to be prepared to teach an array of subjects—math, science, history, and English—to all ages. Do you think you are up to it, young man?" Rondthaler asked with enthusiasm.

"Yes, sir. I can't wait to tell my wife."

And at that moment, Marcia walked in the door. She had lingered to talk to the Midgetts about details of the rental house, then decided to find Kurt.

"Mr. Rondthaler, this is my wife, Marcia," Kurt said.

"Pleased to meet you, ma'am. I am most impressed by your husband. He has agreed to start work at the Ocracoke School immediately."

Marcia was taken by surprise. She literally jumped for joy. "How wonderful! We just found a house not far from the school that suits us perfectly. Our only worry was finding a job for Kurt. Thank you, Mr. Rondthaler. This is great!" she said, beaming.

"You never told me how you got here and how you met your

wife," Mr. Rondthaler said.

Marcia and Kurt looked at each other.

"Can we continue our conversation outside?" Kurt noticed the store clerk was listening to every word they said.

"Certainly," Mr. Rondthaler said, and they stepped out to the front porch and sat on a long bench. A big, fluffy collie lay on the porch beside the bench. Mr. Rondthaler began to rub the dog's golden hair. "This is Jake, our dog," Mr. Rondthaler said. "Jake, meet Kurt and Marcia Sanger." Jake held out a paw and let Kurt shake it.

Then Sanger and Marcia told Mr. Rondthaler their story. He was fascinated. "What a story! I can't believe it. What richness you will bring to this community and to my children, Kurt. I feel honored to be in your presence. I am even more excited than before that you will be teaching at the Ocracoke School," Mr. Rondthaler said.

Sanger was relieved. Rondthaler could just as easily have told him to leave because of his service on a German U-boat. Many Americans were still bitter against Germany. But Rondthaler was much too worldly for that.

Mr. Rondthaler said, "This is our first full year on Ocracoke. We first came here in 1935, staying at the Pamlico Inn. We bought a house on Ocracoke that summer and have spent our summers here ever since. For the past three years, I have taught at Black Mountain College in the North Carolina mountains, where a lot of German refugees also teach, but finally this year I was offered a position at the Ocracoke School, and we were able to move here permanently. Both of our children live in Oregon. My family is in Winston-Salem, and my wife's family is in Somers, Connecticut."

Chapter 21

Marcia and Kurt put a deposit down on the Midgett house and returned to Portsmouth to pack their things.

"I don't want to leave," Stella said when they told her they were moving to Ocracoke. "Do they have a beach at Ocracoke?" She was remembering Mississippi.

"Yes," Marcia said, running her hands through Stella's curly blond hair. "Ocracoke is a lot like Portsmouth, only bigger, with more people and more children your age. You will really like it. We found a house on a quiet street lined with big oak trees and picket fences."

"Can we take the horses, the cow, and the chickens?" she asked.

"Of course we can," Marcia said.

"I want to say good-bye to the beach," Stella said, and took her mother's hand and walked with her and Kurt to the beach.

When they walked out onto the flat sand, a cool breeze lifted Stella's hair. "I love this place and don't ever want to leave," Stella sighed.

"I love it, too, Stella," Marcia said, looking at Kurt. It was where she had found refuge after her husband died and where she met

Kurt. It was where she had raised Stella. It would be sad for her to leave, too, leaving behind Miss Annie Salter, the memories of the boys at the Coast Guard Station, the Babbs, and Henry Pigott, but Stella needed to go to school and Kurt needed to work. They would learn to love their new home on Ocracoke.

It took several trips with the animals: two horses, a cow, and several chickens. They left most of the furniture in the house; Marcia took only what was hers, leaving behind what had come with the house. When they finally left, Marcia closed the storm shutters and bolted the front door. She had so many wonderful memories there. Perhaps they could return in the summers when Kurt was not working at the school, she thought. She hoped the Styrons would let her continue to use the house.

Mr. Rondthaler gave Kurt a week to get settled into the Midgett house and to go over his study plans and prepare for class, then he put him straight to work at the school, throwing him into the midst of a new environment and a new profession. At first Kurt struggled, but he soon caught on. Teaching was in his blood. The children loved him and his exotic accent. He loved them as well, with their island brogue and stories of the sea. Mr. and Mrs. Rondthaler took the young couple under their wing, introducing them to people and getting them involved with the Methodist church and Ocracoke civic and social life.

The house on Ocracoke was not as close to the beach as theirs had been on Portsmouth. The beach was about a mile southeast of the village, across a wide swath of hot, deep sand. Sanger was able to locate a surplus army Jeep that had been left on the island; he rebuilt the engine and adapted the Jeep for the deep sand. He used it to drive out to the beach in the mornings, where he took his run and a dip in the ocean while the water was warm.

He wrote Mr. and Mrs. Harris and told them that he would not be returning to Mississippi. They were not happy, having hoped he would return, but they understood that his family came first and released him from his obligation to them.

It was a warm and sunny day in February 1949 when Stella turned six. She said she wanted to go to the beach. It had just rained, and the ocean was a little rough, with whitecaps and large waves rolling in. Clouds were in the sky, but the sun was out. They drove across the sand flats east of the village in Kurt's Jeep with a big picnic basket and a bucket of cold Coca-Colas. Once on the beach, they looked back toward the village and saw a beautiful rainbow.

"Daddy, can we build a sandcastle?" Stella asked.

"Honey, it's your birthday. We will do whatever you want to do," Kurt said, rolling up his sleeves and proceeding to dig a hole in the sand to create the central mound of a sandcastle. They built a moat and a wall around the castle, then dribbled wet sand between their fingers, making tall, lacy towers and spires.

Marcia spread a blanket on the sand and pulled out sandwiches, potato salad, and drinks.

"When y'all get hungry, lunch is ready."

Stella ran to her mother and grabbed a peanut butter and jelly sandwich, which she quickly devoured. Kurt chose a ham and cheese sandwich, and Marcia ate a pimento cheese sandwich.

"Ocracoke is not Portsmouth," Marcia said, looking out over the water. "But I love our house here and the people and the school."

"More is going on here, too," Kurt said. "I have never seen such a busy bunch of people, working on civic improvements like getting paved roads and regular ferry service. And then there is the church, Sunday school, Wednesday-night choir practice, pageants, and church socials. I almost miss the solitude of Portsmouth. But I like it here. If you want to be alone, you can be. If you want to be surrounded by people, conversation, and activity, you can find that, too."

"I like peanut butter and jelly sandwiches and ice-cold Coca-Colas," Stella said. On Portsmouth such delicacies were hard to come by.

"If it hadn't been for Stella, we probably wouldn't have moved here. We might have even had to return to Mississippi," Kurt said.

"Yuck!" Stella said. "I would much rather be in Ocracoke than Mississippi."

"Me, too," Marcia said, grabbing Stella and tickling her tummy.

Kurt looked out at the ocean, where whitecaps rolled in as if from a storm. He remembered his days on the submarine, the war, and the years in the POW camps. How things had changed in just a few years! Before the war he could never have imagined that he would end up in 1949 sitting on a beach on Ocracoke Island, North Carolina, with his young family. How strange fate is, he thought.

That night after they put Stella to bed, Kurt was working on his lesson plan for the coming week while Marcia sat in her chair sewing the hem on a sundress she had made for Stella.

"Do you ever regret coming back to North Carolina for me?" she asked Kurt.

"What do you mean?" Kurt said, looking up from his work.

"I mean, you grew up in Dresden surrounded by art, history, universities, music, opera, and culture, and now you are living in an isolated fishing village on the North Carolina coast, where people talk funny and walk around barefoot all day. Do you think you'll ever get bored and want a life that is more exciting than this?"

"I don't know."

"Well, I certainly hope not. I love you."

"I love you, too," he said. But he did wonder if one day he would become bored and want to move to a more exciting, urban setting. If he ever wanted a change, he would have to face that then. But for now he was happy and content. These Outer Banks were like a refuge from the madness of the world. Yes, Dresden had been a center of culture, learning, art, architecture, history, and music. But look at it now; it lay in ruins. Is that what the old ways led to? He didn't know the answer. All he knew was that he had found happiness in a simple place with simple people who cared passionately about their lives, their families, and their world. Was there more? Would he become bored and want to move on? He didn't know, but for now he could rest easy and find peace in his quiet refuge.

"I know that you love me. But sometimes I wonder what you will end up doing with your life. Sometimes I wonder why you stay with me, with all that you know and all that you have seen. I am who I am. I can't offer more than that. I hope it is enough for you," Marcia worried.

"It is more than enough, my dear," he said, rising from his chair and kissing her.

She smiled and kissed him back, but she had her doubts.

A few weeks later in early May, following a now-daily routine, Kurt drove out to the beach in his Jeep and ran a couple of miles in his cotton shorts and white T-shirt. The air was warm, and the sun hung low over the beach to the east, a big red ball emerging from the distant dark clouds over the horizon. At that point the island almost ran east to west, so the sun rose just where the beach met the ocean. The wash from the waves shellacked the sand, which glowed with iridescent hues, reflecting the sun and clouds overhead.

He looked up and down the beach. A bank of white haze was in the distance, spray from the waves kicking up into the air. Thick pieces of ancient shells smoothed by the ocean littered the beach like precious stones or pirate's booty. No one was in sight. It was spring, and the weather was warm, so he decided to take off his T-shirt and shorts and wade into the ocean almost to his waist. The water was cool but refreshing. He splashed himself with the salt water, then walked out of the ocean and sat on the hard sand. He loved his freedom on this island. He also valued his solitude and loved Marcia for respecting it as well. He looked down at his naked body. He was still in great shape; he would turn twenty-nine in August. He had been thinking since they settled down in Ocracoke that he wanted to have at least one more child, perhaps a son. He thought certainly that was still in him, after all he had been through. God was forgiving; even after the horrors of war, life went on. Children grew into adults; adults grew older and wiser, perhaps. After he was good and dry, he put on his T-shirt and shorts and sprinted back to the Jeep, which waited for him in the sand, perched over the ocean.

That night lying in bed with Marcia, Kurt turned to her and said, "Marcia, there's something I want to talk to you about."

"What is it?" Marcia wondered what he could be thinking; he looked so serious.

"I want to have another child."

"Isn't Stella enough?" she asked.

"I love Stella. She is the light of my life, but I think we should have at least one more child. Perhaps it could even be a son," he said.

"What if we don't have a son?" she asked. This could go on forever, trying to have a son. "What if we have another daughter? Would you want to keep trying 'til we had a son, sort of like the kings of England did?"

"I promise not to push for another child after our second one, even if we do not have a son, unless you want to. It will be completely your decision. I will consider it God's will and be content. But I would like to at least try for another child. I think Stella needs a playmate anyway. It is not good to be an only child."

"Okay," Marcia said. "We'll try. You're almost twenty-nine; I'm twenty-seven. It's not too late. But if we wait much longer, it will be." She paused. "There will be a big age difference between the child and Stella."

"I know, but this way she will always be in charge. The new child will be like a baby doll to her. I think she will love it," he said.

"I think we ought to talk to her about it."

"I agree," he said, but he did not want to wait. He wanted to make love that night. He began to run his fingers around her nipples then kissed her breasts. She did not resist. She arched her back and threw her hair back. Actually she had been thinking the same thing—that they should have another child—but hadn't told him. Stella needed a playmate, and now was the time. They did not have a lot of time to wait. But by not telling him her desire, she had more control over him, and she could exact promises from him, letting him think it was his idea. Then he wouldn't insist on trying again if the second child was a girl.

He ran his fingers along her belly, moving slowly downward. He kissed her, then nibbled at her neck and ears. Finally his fingers found the secret folds of her sex. They continued to kiss, and he rolled on top of her. They made love passionately through the night.

When he woke the next morning, he lay face down beside her, naked, his arm around her naked breast. He looked at her. She had a smile on her face. He got up for his morning run. Her habit was to stay in bed until he left. Then she would get up, tidy the kitchen, and fix breakfast when he came in.

Toward the end of January 1950, Marcia gave birth to another child. They named him William, after Kurt's father, Wilhelm Frederick Sanger. William was their last child.

Chapter 22

Kurt became an American citizen in 1954. He continued to teach at the school for the next twenty-six years, when he retired. Mr. Rondthaler remained at the school until the early 1960s. He died in 1966, but his widow stayed on Ocracoke into the late 1970s, and it is where she died.

With the exception of about 775 privately owned acres in Ocracoke village, the entire island became part of the Cape Hatteras National Seashore, a wild and natural area reserved for recreation and wildlife habitat. The acquisition of land for the seashore began August 11, 1937, with an act of Congress. The land was to be purchased by the state, then given to the federal government. A minimum of 10,000 acres had to be acquired by the state, using public and private funds, before the park could be established. By 1952 the minimum was met, and the state conveyed 12,414 acres into the federal government's control. By January 12, 1953, the Cape Hatteras National Seashore was formally established. Over the years the park grew to some 30,000 acres. There were some hard feelings among local landowners when the land was purchased for the park, but all in all the people approved of it.

In the 1930s the Civilian Conservation Corps under the Works

Project Administration had begun to build up the dunes on the island, using sand fences and sea grass. But work had stopped during World War II. After the war the effort was renewed, and a strong line of tall dunes stretched the entire length of the island by the early 1950s, providing protection from overwash and protection for a road. The dune stabilization in the Cape Hatteras National Seashore never occurred on Portsmouth Island. What were once broad, sandy flats on Ocracoke overwashed by ocean water during storms now grew up with wax myrtle, cedar, marsh grass, and sea grass.

After the war the only paved road on the island was the one built by the navy, which ran between the naval station and the ammunition bunkers on the north side of the village in the upper Trent area, near the sound. By 1950 another 2 miles of road were paved in the village through the efforts of a committee of local residents. The village was not incorporated, and no local government existed. During this time, there were approximately forty cars on the island. The number increased after the road was finished in September 1950. But bicycles far outnumbered cars, as children found bikes could ride easily on the newly paved road that led to the school. Eventually a 6.8-mile section of highway was built from the present-day National Park Service campground to within 2.5 miles of the northeast end of the island at the Hatteras ferry landing.

An organization named the All Seashore Highway Association was formed to promote the construction of a highway from Manteo to Hatteras and Ocracoke through the Cape Hatteras National Seashore. By the end of 1963, the highway was completed. The Herbert C. Bonner Bridge, named for a local congressman, was built over Oregon Inlet in 1964, connecting Hatteras Island with Nags Head, Kitty Hawk, and the beaches to the north. For years people had been forced to drive on the beach on Ocracoke to get to the Hatteras ferry. The road was completed from the village to the north end of the island, and the state began to provide regular ferry service from Hatteras to Ocracoke Island in 1963.

In 1960 regular ferry service began between Ocracoke and Cedar Island. At first the ferry was privately operated, but within six months it was taken over by the state at the request of the owners. A good paved highway stretched between Cedar Island and Morehead City and Beaufort, bypassing Atlantic. So by 1963 Ocracoke was connected to the outside world.

The state also bought up land along the Core and Shackleford banks, including Cape Lookout, up to Portsmouth village with a four-hundred-thousand-dollar legislative appropriation to preserve the land from erosion and deterioration. In November 1963 Governor Terry Sanford and the counsel of state authorized the transfer of twenty thousand acres of Outer Banks land to the federal government for use as a national park. The United States Congress authorized the creation of the park in 1966, and Portsmouth became part of the new Cape Lookout National Seashore. The population of Portsmouth had dwindled until, in the late 1960s, there were only three residents: Elma Dixon, her niece Marian Gray Babb, and Henry Pigott. Henry Pigott died in 1971, and the government decided it was not worth the money and effort to continue providing postal service to the island. On June 30, 1972, postal service ceased, and the two remaining residents were moved to the mainland. The houses, church, post office, and Coast Guard Station remained, becoming part of the national seashore. People were able to rent the houses for a nominal fee if they took charge of their upkeep. An annual homecoming is held every year at the Methodist church, where former residents and their descendants return.

Kurt and Marcia went back to the Styron house on Portsmouth during the summers in the 1950s and stayed for several weeks at a time. But as Stella and William got older and more involved with their friends, boyfriends, and girlfriends, the family spent less and less time on Portsmouth. Kurt nevertheless arranged a long-term lease from the National Park Service for the house after it was bought by the government from the Styron family.

Mr. Harris died in 1955 and Mrs. Harris soon thereafter in 1956. A nephew inherited the farm, but the Harrises left fifty thousand dollars to Kurt and Marcia Sanger. Kurt went to Mississippi to help settle the estate. He was now comfortable financially and continued to teach at the Ocracoke School. He and Marcia were able to finally talk the Midgetts into selling their mother's home to them. Kurt also bought up other island real estate, both commercial and residential rental properties, which eventually made him a wealthy man.

Stella was a momma's girl who wanted to stay close to home. The Rondthalers tried to talk her into going to Salem College in Winston-Salem, but she instead went to East Carolina University in Greenville and got her teacher's certificate. In 1965 she returned from school and married Will Styron, a relation of Marcia's first husband and a fisherman whose family owned a lot of property on the island. They had two girls—Marcia Styron, born in 1967, and Mary Alice Styron (named for Will's mother), born in 1969—and finally a boy, Kurt Styron, born in 1971. They lived in an old Styron family home near the lighthouse. Stella started teaching in the elementary grades at the Ocracoke School in 1966.

William was a bit more restless. He was a smart boy and just as attractive as his father had been as a young man. He became a good surfer and worked as a lifeguard for the National Park Service during the summers after he turned eighteen. He went to the University of North Carolina at Chapel Hill, where he studied German. He took a year off after graduation and traveled to Europe with some friends. Then he decided to do his postgraduate work in German at the University of Munich. He studied and taught in Germany for several years before returning to the United States, where he got his Ph.D. at UNC in German and comparative literature. He then landed a job teaching German at the University of North Carolina at Wilmington in 1979. In Wilmington he continued to surf with friends at Wrightsville Beach. He met Jennifer Johanson, who taught comparative literature at Wilmington, and they married in 1981. They had two sons: John (named for Jennifer's father) in 1983 and Kurt in 1987.

The Berlin Wall fell in November 1989. Germany was formally reunited on October 3, 1990. The following year Kurt and Marcia traveled with William and Jennifer to Germany, where they visited Dresden and laid a wreath in memory of Kurt's parents at the monument to the victims of the firebombing of 1945. His parents' bodies were never found or identified. They stayed in Germany for several weeks, William catching up with old friends and Kurt visiting what little of his family remained. Kurt discovered that Günther Krech and Helmut Rathke were still living in Germany, as were several commanders of the old Ubootwaffe. Krech, commander of the *U-558*, died in June 2000 at the age of eighty-five, while Rathke, of the *U-352*, died in July 2001 at the age of ninety-one.

Commander Jürgen Wattenberg, who had escaped from Papago Park in 1944, died in 1995; he was ninety-five. On January 5, 1985, the Papago Park Prisoner of War Camp Commission held a commemorative observance at the site of the old camp, which had been turned into a city park in Phoenix. The event was attended by the mayors of Phoenix, Tempe, and Scottsdale. The eighty-five-year-old Wattenberg returned as a special guest of honor and remarked how much he had enjoyed the Spam dinners. Kurt was invited to the commemoration but after much thought decided not to attend. Later he received a booklet about the reunion and found the names and addresses of many of his old comrades, most of whom had returned to Germany but some of whom had moved to the United States and other countries.

Admiral Karl Dönitz, commander of the Ubootwaffe and later commander in chief of the German navy despite never becoming a member of the Nazi Party, served as president of the Third Reich for twenty-three days after Adolph Hitler committed suicide. He died of a heart attack on Christmas Eve 1980 at the age of eighty-nine.

Aycock Brown, who married Esther Styron Brown of Ocracoke, became the editor of the *Ocracoke Island Beacon* newspaper and later a tireless promoter of Outer Banks tourism, serving as the first director of the Dare County Tourism Board. He was a well-known Outer Banks historian, photographer, and writer. After he died in 1984, the North Carolina Legislature passed a resolution in his memory and called him "Mr. Outer Banks."

The graves of the men who washed ashore from the wreck of the *Bedfordshire* are maintained on Ocracoke by the Coast Guard. In 1976 the state of North Carolina purchased the cemetery from the Williams family and leased it in perpetuity to the British Commonwealth War Graves Commission. The "British Cemetery" is now a popular tourist destination on the island.

On July 3, 2001, Roger Hunting and a group who had been diving the wreck of the *U-85* for years found in its radio room the four-rotor naval Enigma machine, Type M4, serial number M2946, and its printer and stacks of log sheets. Two days later they found the second machine, the M3131 Enigma. In 2002, the four-rotor machine and printer were given to The Graveyard of the Atlantic Museum in Hatteras village by Roger Hunting, his dive team, and the German government. They are on display there today.

In 2002, sixty years after Kurt Sanger first came ashore on Portsmouth in 1942, he still took his early-morning walks on the beach. Though in their early eighties, both he and Marcia were in good health, having eaten local seafood and fresh vegetables most of their lives. They had five grandchildren and six great-grandchildren. Stella and her husband had three children, and William and his wife had two. Stella's two daughters and one son married in their early twenties, and each had two children. In 2002 William's two sons were ages nineteen and fifteen. Kurt and Marcia never left

Ocracoke except for vacations, business trips, and family visits.

In 2002 Ocracoke had about eight hundred full-time residents. During the summer tourist season, the population swelled to about five thousand. The Ocracoke School served about ninety students from kindergarten through twelfth grade. The island was a popular tourist destination, with many vacation rental cottages, some small hotels and inns, several good restaurants, and many shops. Tourism was the main industry on the island, but there were still those who made their living fishing or working on the ferries or for the Coast Guard, the National Park Service, or the school. Ocracoke was the main source of property-tax income for Hyde County, a poor coastal county of about five thousand residents. The village was still not incorporated in 2002, nor were any towns in Hyde County. But Ocracoke did have some zoning because of the North Carolina Coastal Area Management Act. The only way to get to Ocracoke was still by ferry or boat. The beaches were magnificent; the village, now listed on the National Register of Historic Places, was still quaint, with century-old houses, picket fences, and streets lines with live oak trees. The ponies were penned in a fenced enclosure of more than one hundred acres with barns and pastures, and they were looked after by volunteers and National Park Service employees. Newcomers—artists, retired people, writers, expatriates—were on the island, but the old families remained.

Portsmouth was a ghost town, manned by National Park Service employees and volunteers. Some of the houses had been restored by people leasing them, but there was no water, electricity, or phone service.

Epilogue

Kurt Sanger took his morning walk a little later than usual on Saturday, June 8, 2002. William and his family were visiting from Wilmington, and he couldn't quite get away as easily as he usually could. He parked his Jeep Cherokee in the parking lot at the life-guard beach on Highway 12 a little after nine. As he headed toward the boardwalk that crossed the dunes, he saw his friend Edward Nelson park his dark blue Buick Roadmaster station wagon and get out.

"Edward, want to join me?" he asked, waving.

"Sure, Kurt." Edward, born in 1916, and Kurt, born in 1920, were both in their eighties. Edward and his wife had retired to their island home, a modern house designed by their daughter, on Silver Lake at the entrance to the harbor at the ditch. Edward was retired from the State Department, having served as the United States am-bassador to Hungry during the 1960s. He was a learned and schol-arly man. Since his retirement he had become active in local affairs, serving on the Ocracoke Planning Board and several committees of the Ocracoke Preservation Society. His son had recently been elected the mayor of Greensboro, North Carolina.

"Marcia is working at the Ocracoke Preservation Society booth at the Ocrafolk Festival this morning. Stella will be there, too, at the booth for the Volunteer Fire Department." Stella and her husband, Will Styron, worked tirelessly for the fire department, raising money, selling raffle tickets, and working bingo night. "Did you know that my grandson Kurt Styron is now a volunteer fireman? William and his family are visiting from Wilmington," Kurt said to Edward. "We have a houseful, between William, his wife, and the two boys."

The Ocrafolk Festival was put on by the large arts and music community of Ocracoke to celebrate their craft. Favorite performers were Molasses Creek, Noah Paley, Martin Garish, Coyote, Fiddler Dave, Cheryl Roberts, and Roy Parsons, who like Edward and Kurt was in his eighties.

"I love family when they come to visit, but I love them even more when they leave," Edward said, stripping off his shirt. He had a dark tan and wore only shorts and sandals.

"I don't see how you do it, Edward. I worry about getting skin cancer. That's why I wear a shirt and shorts and a big floppy hat. Marcia insists that I wear sunscreen. I had a few precancerous spots removed a year ago, so I try to be careful," Kurt said. He was still trim, but his hair was pure white and his hairline had receded considerably. Though his skin was fair, he had a good tan, and his eyes were just as blue and their luster just as bright as when Marcia first met him.

"I should be more careful. I do wear sunscreen, but I love the sun so much. I will keep taking my shirt off 'til a doctor tells me different," Edward said.

They walked over the wooden walkway to the beach and quickly made their way through the deep, hot sand until they got to the cool, dark sand near the water. The lifeguard stand was empty. The guards, who worked for the National Park Service, would come out about nine-thirty and be set up for business by ten.

It was a bright, sunny day. The water, stirred up by the wind, had whitecaps and was pretty rough. A stiff breeze was coming from the sound; when the waves broke, the wind chopped off their tops and reduced them to spray. It was dry; there had not been any rain in weeks.

"Edward, I don't know if you knew this or not, but it was sixty years ago this May when I first came ashore on Portsmouth Island to gather intelligence for the Ubootwaffe," Kurt said, looking at Edward for a reaction.

"I did not know it was this May, but I know your story. We were all certain that the coast was teeming with spies back then. But few actually came ashore," Edward said. "A few were captured in Florida and a few in New York. At least that is all we know about."

"There was little reason to send German spies ashore. We were well supplied by the milch cows in the mid-Atlantic, and the United States Navy offered little resistance, at least in the first half of 1942. So we had little reason to come ashore for intelligence. But I was sent specifically to discover the fate of the *U-85* and her Enigma machines. I understand that divers recently dove the wreck and found them. If divers had done that in 1942, the war in the Atlantic would have been very different. You Americans were so new to war; you blew it when it came to the *U-85*," he said.

"Well, you can't get everything right," Edward said with a wry smile.

"When I came ashore in May 1942, I had no idea that I would end up staying in this country and raising a family, no idea that I would not return to Germany for four decades, and then only as a tourist," Kurt said, looking out to sea wistfully.

"I guess your commanders didn't warn you about our American women," Edward teased.

"No, not a word." Kurt smiled. "We would have been well advised if they did, though."

"Frankly, Kurt, I am surprised you stayed on Ocracoke for as long as you have," Edward said.

"I am, too, Edward," he said. "When I first started teaching at the Ocracoke School, I needed a job. But honestly, I thought once I became established in this country Marcia and I would move around. But you know, like old Ted Mutro once said, 'Don't take your shoes off on Ocracoke or let the sand get between your toes or eat the seafood. If you do, you'll never leave.' I know that Ocracoke isn't for everybody, but it sure does have a way of worming its way into your soul. For years I maintained the illusion that we would move to a larger city. But you know, we just never got around to it. Now the world has come to us. There is no need to leave."

"You have that right," Edward said. "I have lived in or visited most of the great cities of the world, but I keep coming back here. There's something about it, the simplicity of the place, the great natural beauty, the fact that a man like me in his mid-eighties can walk on the beach half-naked and not get a second glance. I love it, and, yes, I can understand why you stayed here. It's hard to get away from it."

"Then there is all this confounded community spirit. You Americans are such do-gooders. Volunteering at the museum, at the fire department, for the Ocrafolk Festival—I was on the school board, for Pete's sake. You're on the planning board. Isn't it time for us to retire?"

"When you retire you stop living. I'm not ready for that yet," Edward said.

"We can at least slow down a little, can't we? Let the young people do the work so we can relax."

"Yes, but as long as I can, I will contribute. I think it is something about being American. We can never be still; we've always got to be doing something," Edward said, smiling.

After walking down the beach for a couple of miles toward the campground, they turned around and headed back, facing a stiff headwind. They both wore sunglasses in the bright sun.

"You know, Edward, this is a healthy place to live. Marcia and I have had very few health problems. I mean, she has her arthritis, and I have had a few patches of skin removed but nothing cancerous. We have rarely been sick and have had nothing chronic. There must be something to what Roy Parsons says about growing up here eating fish for breakfast, fish for lunch, and fish for dinner, and living to a ripe old age," Kurt said.

"You're right. We know where the seafood comes from, right offshore. We know where the vegetables come from, either here or from farmers on the mainland who bring them over on the ferry. There is no fast food or packaged food here. What we have is fresh and healthy. And something else—when you live here, you face very little stress. Stress is a killer, let me tell you."

"I know that," Kurt said.

When they got to the lifeguard stand, two lifeguards were setting up, handsome young men with dark tans, sun-streaked hair, and bright red bathing suits. They were displaying their umbrellas for rental, where they made most of their money. They waved at the two octogenarians they saw walking every day on the beach.

"Oh, to be young again," Edward said, looking at the tall, slim, handsome young men with hard bodies moving so lithely on the beach.

"To have the body of a twenty-year-old, yes, but not the hormones and the worries and uncertainties. They can keep that," Kurt said.

The two friends climbed the steps of the boardwalk and crested the dune, looking toward the village. A strong wind blew across the marsh from the sound to the west, carrying with it a black plume of smoke.

"What's that?" Edward asked.

"It looks like a fire in the marsh. With this wind, fire could sweep through the village in no time. We need to get home," Kurt said, then started to run to his car.

When he drove by School Road, which was blocked off and filled with artists' booths and platforms for the performers, the street was almost empty. There were also few cars. Ordinarily the street would have been full of people, with no place to park along the road. It looked like it had cleared out.

When he got home to Howard Street, he found a note pinned to the screen door."Kurt, we are at the fire; go by the fire station and pick up water bottles. I will see you there. Love, Marcia."

Kurt jumped into the Jeep. His job was to pass out water to the men and help with crowd control. He knew the drill. So he stopped by the fire department to pick up crates of bottled water, then followed the smoke to the fire.

The fire was located in a marsh facing the sound near Oyster Creek. It was huge; the entire marsh looked to be involved. The high winds were blowing sparks across the road that separated the marsh from several houses. Kurt found Marcia and started handing out water bottles to the young firefighters when they came in from the fire.

"William is out there with his two boys, John and Kurt. I couldn't stop them. Will Styron is out there as well with his Kurt," Marcia said, concerned for their safety but knowing she could do nothing to keep them away from the fire.

William's wife, Jennifer, helped Marcia. She was not as cool and collected as Marcia, however. "I can't understand why William has to go out there. He said he did it in the past, but how long has that been? And taking the boys with him? If something happens to either of my boys, there will be hell to pay," Jennifer Sanger said, handing water to a thirsty young man dressed in bright yellow fire pants and suspenders but wearing no shirt, a bright-red star tattooed on his bicep.

"I told him to stay behind, but he wouldn't listen to me," Marcia said. Then she looked at Kurt for help. She could see Jennifer was upset.

"William will be fine. He has had good fire training. I am sure that if he gets in over his head, he will get out. I know he will watch the boys and not let them get into trouble," Kurt said. He could see that answer was not what Jennifer wanted to hear, but he also knew there was nothing any of them could do to keep William and the boys from fighting the fire. He knew William well enough to know that he would not have missed this for anything.

The two fire trucks were on the road pumping water into the long black hoses, which were connected to fire hydrants. The black rubber hoses puffed up with water, looking like huge anacondas snaking their way over the blacktop. Kurt looked out into the smoke and fire and watched the men haul hoses across the deep, swampy marsh, wearing rubber boots and fire equipment. He had taught most of the men fighting the fire, or their parents, at the Ocracoke School. The wind picked up and carried sparks everywhere.

He saw Stella working with Will Styron in the distance, directing traffic and helping the men suit up. Will was an assistant fire chief.

On the other side of the road was a row of houses. If the fire spread to the houses, it would be all over; half the island would be lost. A group of Hispanic men drove up and quickly jumped into the fray. Ocracoke had a lot of Hispanic workers, who cleaned houses, worked in the kitchens of restaurants, and worked construction. He recognized several young men who were working the Ocrafolk Festival, including some of the musicians. He recognized every able-bodied bartender, waiter, ship captain, electrician, ship's mate, and shop owner in town, slogging through the muddy marsh in black knee boots and carrying hoses to fight the fire. Sparks flew everywhere as the wind picked up again. There were others, too—the summer help who worked as waiters, bartenders, and busboys, who crewed the charter fishing boats, who bagged or stocked groceries in the variety store, shirtless, blackened by soot and smoke, wearing the ubiquitous black rubber boots. Several of the better-trained volunteer firemen wore heavy bright yellow firefighting equipment.

Frightened but curious tourists also gathered. The residents tried to keep the tourists out of the way so they would not interfere with the firefighters. But the tourists wanted to see and help if they could. Kurt, Marcia, Jennifer, Stella, and the other women and older men from the village scurried around the road helping the men suit up or giving them water. It seemed the entire village was there.

The word went out that if they couldn't get the fire under control, the National Forest Service stood ready to fly in airplanes that would scoop water out of the sound and dump it on the fire. But those planes were an hour away. They didn't have that much time, with the wind driving the fire and the sparks flying.

Kurt noticed a young couple who had ridden up on bikes. He didn't recognize them. The young man held his wife, who was visibly shaking and sobbing.

He walked over to them. "Are you all right?" he asked the young woman.

"We just bought our house this spring. It is only two blocks away. I smelled smoke and looked outside and thought the whole island was on fire," the woman said. "We've been coming here for ten years and finally saved enough money to be able to afford a house. We're working on it now. It needs a lot of work, but we love it. I'm afraid that if the fire jumps the road we'll lose everything." She started to cry and held her husband.

"Is there anything we can do?" the young man asked.

"You can help us give the firefighters water. With the heavy equipment and the heat, they dehydrate pretty quickly. And you look strong enough to help us move these hoses," Kurt said.

The young couple then picked up bottles of water and helped pass them out. The young man helped move the hoses as the firefighters changed position in the marsh.

"Is there enough water to fight the fire?" Kurt asked one of the firemen, a native Ocracoker.

"Yes, thank goodness. If the hydrants weren't nearby, we would have to rely on the water truck. We have a new fire engine, too; that's helping out a lot."

Kurt and Marcia watched as the valiant young men and women of the village fought the fire. Marcia took Kurt's arm and squeezed it. She knew what was at risk if the fire got out of control. "I hope and pray they can contain it. I don't want to imagine what would happen if it crossed the road and got into the village, with this wind," Marcia said.

"If anyone can stop this fire, it is this community. I have great faith in these people. Don't even let yourself think about not beating it. We will beat it," Kurt said. "We must."

Finally the firefighters seemed to get the upper hand. The wind died a little, and they got the flames under control.

"How did the fire start?" Kurt asked one of the firemen.

"Firecrackers. Some kids were shooting off bottle rockets, and they caught the marsh grass on fire. We haven't had any rain in weeks." He was not happy with those kids. "They must have been tourists."

With time, the firefighters gained control, and the flames did not cross the road or catch the houses on fire. The homeowners across the road used their garden hoses to spray their roofs and sides of their houses to keep the sparks from igniting the wood shingles, and it worked.

Kurt walked over to the young couple who had just bought a house and said, "It looks like the fire is contained. I think your home is safe."

"Thank you, Mr. . . . ," the young woman said.

"Sanger, Kurt Sanger."

"Thank you for your kindness," the man said, taking his hand.

The firefighters stayed for a few more hours as hot spots continued to flare up, but eventually the fire was extinguished. The marsh grass and a line of trees were blackened, but Kurt knew that they would quickly be green again.

Kurt knew that this village was resilient. It had survived hurricanes, nor'easters, fires, droughts, and famines. It had survived an invasion by Spanish marauders in the early 1700s, British invaders during the Revolution, Yankees during the Civil War, and, yes, German U-boats. It would survive this fire and go on to live and thrive. He knew how strong this community was; that strength was part of what made him love it so, and why he made it his home.

William appeared with his two boys blackened by soot. The boys were shirtless; William wore a white T-shirt that was now black and clung to his body, soaking wet. All three of them had huge grins on their faces.

"That was fun," John said.

"Yeah, Dad. I could do that again," Kurt Junior said with a grin.

Kurt knew William and the boys had a great time fighting the fire.

Jennifer ran to William and hugged him, getting filthy with soot and soaking wet. "Why did you go out there? You could have been killed," she said.

"When there is a fire in Ocracoke, everyone responds. I don't care how many years I have been gone. I wouldn't have missed this for anything," he said, his teeth shining white through his blackened face.

"What about the boys?" she asked. "Did you think about them?" They were both teenagers.

"What about it, boys?" William asked.

"I wouldn't have missed that for the world," John, the older one, said.

"That was really cool," Kurt said, a big, toothy grin shining through his sooty face.

Then Stella and Will Styron came up with their son, Kurt, who was thirty-one. Kurt wore a heavy yellow suit and a firefighter's hat. He looked tired and sweaty and was blackened with soot.

"I just wanted to thank you-all, especially William and the boys, for helping out. I think it took every one of us to beat this fire. I don't think we could have done it with one less person," Will Styron said, shaking William's hand and the hands of the boys.

Kurt Styron then ruffled young John's and Kurt's hair. "Yeah, you guys were great; I was really proud of you. I told everyone, 'Look there, those boys are my cousins. Look how hard they are working that hose.' You did me proud."

Kurt Senior put his arm around Marcia. She looked up at him with a smile. They were both proud of their family.

"Let's get washed up, and all you men and your families plan on coming over for dinner. It will be potluck—Ocracoke potluck. I want to celebrate beating the fire and, most of all, having my whole family together on the island," Marcia said. Then she and Kurt got into the Jeep and drove home. William's boys rode with them. Jennifer and William drove back in their car.

After everyone got cleaned up, Jennifer and Marcia went to work making salads. Kurt and William went to the fish house to buy several pounds of shrimp and got the big aluminum pot with the propane burner ready to cook them outside. Then Stella and Will showed up with their children and grandchildren, all carrying green bean and squash casseroles, hotdogs for the children, freshly baked bread, deviled eggs, apple strudel, carrot cake, banana pudding, and other goodies. Marcia and Kurt had prepared a cooler beside the kitchen table with ice and soft drinks and beer. The kitchen table soon filled with all the food the family had brought. It brought to mind the term *groaning board*, it was so crowded. William heated up the water in the pot, emptied a few beers into it, poured spices into the water, then dropped the shrimp in.

After everyone had eaten, one of the grandchildren said, "Grandpa Kurt, tell us about being on the U-boat when you came on shore and met Grandma Marcia for the first time." They had all heard the story but never tired of hearing it time and time again.

All the grandchildren and great-grandchildren gathered round. Kurt sat in his favorite chair, and the kids sat on the floor around him.

"It was a cold, dark night," Kurt began. "We had been cruising on the surface for some time looking for a target. The Cape Hatteras Light shone in the distance. It was just before midnight when we saw the ship. Soon we had the *Bedfordshire* in our sights, and Kapitänleutnant Günther Krech ordered two torpedoes to be fired. . . ."

Sources

Barnes, Jay. *North Carolina's Hurricane History.* 3rd ed. Chapel Hill: University of North Carolina Press, 2001.

Bunch, Jim W. *Germany's U-85: A Shadow in the Sea.* Nags Head, NC: Deep Sea Press, 2003.

Cheatham, James T. *The Atlantic Turkey Shoot: U-Boats off the Outer Banks in World War II.* Columbia, SC: Wentworth Printing Corp., 1990.

Dudley, Jack. *Ocracoke Album.* Morehead City, NC: Coastal Heritage Series, 2005.

Eubanks, Frances A., and Lynn S. Salsi. *Portsmouth Island: Outer Banks Treasure.* Columbia, SC: Monville Press, 2004.

Gannon, Michael. *Operation Drumbeat.* New York: Harper Perennial, 1991.

Gentiles, Gary. *Shipwrecks of North Carolina from Hatteras Inlet South.*

Philadelphia, PA: Gary Gentile Productions, 1992.

Goerch, Carl. *Ocracoke.* Winston-Salem, NC: John F. Blair Publisher, 1956.

Hickam, Homer H., Jr. *Torpedo Junction.* Annapolis, MD: Naval Institute Press, 1989.

Impact Assessment, Inc. *Final Technical Report for the Study Entitled an Ethnohistorical Description of the Eight Villages Adjoining Cape Hatteras National Seashore and Interpreting Their History and Heritage.* Vols. 1 and 2. U.S. Department of the Interior, National Park Service, Cape Hatteras National Seashore, November 2005.

Naisawald, L. VanLoan. *In Some Foreign Field.* Raleigh, NC: North Carolina Division of Archives and History, 1997.

O'Neal, Calvin J., Alice K. Ronthaler, and Anita Fletcher, compilers. *The Story of Ocracoke Island.* Herb Eaton, Inc., and Walsworth Publishing Co., 1976.

O'Neal, Earl W., Jr. *Ocracoke Island: Its People, the U.S. Coast Guard and Navy Base during World War II.*

Scarborough, Jenny. *Ocracoke Walking Tour and Guidebook.* 3rd ed. Manteo, NC: Michael McOwen, Publisher, 2003.

Westwood, David. *The U-Boat War.* Philadephia, PA: Casemate, 2005.

Online sources:

www.wikipedia.org

http://en.wikipedia.org/wiki/Main_Page

http://ktb.ubootwaffe.net/

www.uboatarchive.net

http://uboat.net

http://ncmuseumofhistory.org

http://diodon349.com/War/CG%20sinks%20U352.htm

www.uscg.mil/HQ/G-CP/HISTORY/IcarusThetis.html

http://uboat.net/men/

http://www.phoenix.gov/

http://home.arcor.de/kriegsgefangene/usa/camps_usa/papago_park.
html

http://www.epcc.edu/nwlibrary/borderlands/12_one_german_
pow's_story.htm

http://www.historyplace.com/speeches/ironcurtain.htm

http://scholar.lib.vt.edu/VA-news/VA-Pilot/issues/